TRACE ELEMENTS

of RANDOM TEA PARTIES

TRACE ELEMENTS
Of RANDOM TEA PARTIES

FELICIA LUNA LEMUS

Seal Press

Published by Seal Press
An Imprint of Avalon Publishing Group, Incorporated
1400 65th Street, Suite 250
Emeryville, CA 94608

A portion of this book appeared as the short story "Random Tea Parties" in ZYZZYVA, Fall 2001.

Cataloging-in-Publication data has been applied for.

ISBN 1-58005-126-X

9 8 7 6 5 4 3 2 1

Interior design by Justin Marler
Cover design by Gia Giasullo, Studio eg
Printed in the United States of America by Worzalla

TRACE ELEMENTS

of RANDOM TEA PARTIES

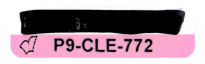

1

I tripped over a seam in the trailer's chrome floor. Real quick, before I could do any serious damage, I introduced myself, sat down in the kitchen nook, and did my best to mumble out socially appropriate words between no-blink stares. Fireworks, I watched her lick maple frosting off her fork, all flat-tongue sticking out the way Nana used to slap me upside the head for doing. I was beyond smitten. Story's name was Edith and she got to Amy's trailer half an hour after Nolan and I showed up for the Fourth of July tea party.

I might as well tell you right now that this is really about my girl Weeping Woman, Nana, and me. My best boy, Nolan, she says listening to me is like letting a drunk drive you to a gala event—no indicators given at turns and the windshield wipers are always on. Buckle up, doll. I promise I'll try not to tangle your quinceañera dress. We'll get to the ballroom soon enough.

My girl Edith: smarty-pants Mission District glamour homegrrrl moved down to Los Angeles on her leopard-print motorcycle. Edith and her amazing sex-radical dancer

3

thighs, she had a homemade guitar string tattoo on her bony wrist and there was usually a healthy touch of orange-red lipstick near the gap between her top front teeth. When she entered a room, sweet thick crisp green lilac perfume sharpened the air.

That Independence Day, only a few weeks after I'd moved to Los Angeles, Edith dug into my chest, took my sucker heart in her teeth, dared me to trust her, and promised to walk away. Two days later I got up the nerve to ask Amy for Edith's phone number. I called Edith. We made a coffee date. And when I showed up at the café, she laughed a rather icy laugh and pulled a cigarette from her monogrammed silver case. Taking time like starlight in slow motion, she placed her cigarette in this crazy sleek sterling holder and stared at me, demanding I take her lighter from the table. I wondered if she had one of those cigarette finger rings that Gloria Swanson used to perch to her lips, all talon hands. Sitting across from me was one of the few women in the world who could look fabulous perfect with such an insane gadget. My stalling, my thinking, it was annoying Edie. Once my fumbling finally brought her flame to life, she tilted her head back slightly, still inspecting me, and took a drag. Exhaling blue smoke in my direction, she announced that over the phone she had thought I was the other girl.

"Do remind me her name . . ."

I stuttered, "Oh, Nolan. She's out of town with her boyfriend." A total and complete lie, but I wasn't about to play nice and share my newfound bliss. "I can have her call you when she gets back if you want."

She bit down on the holder's dark brown Bakelite mouthpiece and smiled toothy sly.

"That won't be necessary."

And so began an affair as confused as its first date.

By our third date, I knew what made my girl Edith

pleased. Saran Wrap. She loved the stuff. Edith would bind my entire body in Saran Wrap before even licking my elbow. Let me tell you, clear microwaveable stretch 'n' cling wrap is not sexy. Especially not when it's the generic purple kind she'd watertight me in. But for Edith I gladly let myself be polyurethane girl from chin to toe. Still, I felt like a desperate and misguided mamasita, all gussied up in kitchen paraphernalia to greet her hunka-hunka at the door and try to cook up some loving. I've read about stuff like that in *Good Housekeeping* at the dentist's. You know, the path to your sexual happiness is through his digestive tract, that sort of thing. It's strange for two chicana dykes to live *Good Housekeeping* lust, but the way Edith's eyes shimmered when she'd airtight me with the Saran, I was willing to do anything to see that wild glow.

After bouts of all-night hygienic sex and pints of the dairy-free sherbet Edie seemed to have with her at all times, we'd break up and get back together again and then break up but still meet to go to a movie and get our sex on again and then get back together again but be exclusive sexually but not monogamous dating-wise. The entire time my tiny twin mattress was smack-dab next to my apartment's front door. See, Edith was always cold and I got scared by how lemon-lime Otter Pop her toes could get, so I dragged my bed to the wall furnace right next to the triple bolts and doorknob and it stayed there the whole messy six months we tortured each other.

Every time when we were near pass-out exhausted, Edith began to talk. My pupils tired, trying to make contact in the pitch-black dark, my body twitching with a need for sleep, she told me her existentialist rationale of why the "we" of she and me could not be. Each night my response was the same, "Yes, Bird." Edith had eyes as endless brown as an orchard oriole's. "Yes, Bird."

5

She was right. It was nearly impossible to "be" when we were just this side of falling asleep. The brink of dreams was the only time she ever talked and she didn't really want answers, so all I had to do was give her my one easy-to-remember-even-when-about-to-fall-asleep line and let her continue to get the tension out of her mouth. Soon we'd sleep all tangled up in each other's limbs on my bed barely wide enough for one of us.

That girl, she was dreamy. A dreamsicle. Creamy. Dreamy.

We only talked when I was asleep. Our relationship existed as I slept beside her. My eyes closed. Calm breathing. She'd talk. We'd wake.

Come morning, she'd still be cold but it was usually me doing the sniffling, my left knee bruised though no physical mark was visible. See, I was down on my knee, begging for my Edie. Me, a young gent without a ring to offer her because she already wore it. Edith took the ring but never said yes, so there I knelt, with only myself to offer and what I had to offer was not enough.

Night again. My hand cupped the curve of her waist as she once again articulately delineated the impossibility of us, her right side in the thick cushion of my feather bed. "Yes, Bird." Quills jabbing at my shoulder through the pink sheets, I shifted to reach for her.

Body in my hands. Inside. Nipple hard against my lips.

May I eat you alive?

I was spinning pleasant dizzy and then Edith broke up with me "for real this time," she said. She started leaving home-baked goods, muffins and sweet bread and stuff that tended to be undercooked in its middle at my front door, once with instructions written on a schmaltzy Hallmark card to meet her at the dressing rooms at Macy's for a slice of heaven. A week after Macy's, I found a "secret admirer" note drenched in flowery tobacco perfume on my doorstep inviting me to meet at Crystal's bar. An hour after closing time, three in the morning, an entire roll of Saran Wrap and some wax paper too, Edith explained yet again why we couldn't ever be together.

I woke the next morning with my Bird by my side and she asked me how I slept. Maybe it was the way the wall heater turned up to high made the air sandy, but for whatever reason, right then my nose started to bleed. No, I take that back, my nose was gushing as furiously as a fire hydrant does when kids break it open with a wrench. I was a sudden mess. I bled onto Edith's wrist as she reached out to touch me. My blood was on her wrist and the Saran Girl, she didn't even flinch. I answered her question.

"I slept wonderfully. Thank you very much. And you?" I ran to the bathroom.

Returning with a bundle of toilet paper at my left nostril, I smiled under the rough wad turning crimson. She stared at the blood on her right forearm and smiled slow. She slept well also, thanks for asking.

I went back to the bathroom and tilted my head over the sink. The marbled cream counter splashed bright red. Letting blood. Purification rite. Drip. Splash. Drip. Splash. Bubbles of oxygen surrounded the drops as they joined the expanding dark puddle. Blood thickening in the sink but fluidly leaving my left nostril. My face lacking its glow, all pasty olive green pale. Drip. Splash. Drip. Splash.

I returned to bed and my Bird Edith had flown away. She was like that, Edith was. A wisp of wind would blow in through the window, Edith would disappear, leaving the scent of lilacs to haunt in her wake.

Tiring of our game, there came a point when I threatened to move far far away and bail on Edith for good. My Betty Crocker Bird started crying real cruel like people do when they want you to take all their pain and then some. She said quietly and between her teeth, "You simply do not up and move without discussing your plans with your girl-friend first."

Her eyes glittered mean like I'd seen them do once when she was dancing in her majorette getup and a guy sitting at the catwalk licked his palm and reached out to touch her. The only thing he made contact with was the baton when Edith knocked him out clean cold. I knew to proceed with caution. The plain truth seemed safe enough.

"Ex-girlfriend, Edith. Ex-girlfriend. You broke up with me last week, remember?"

She stared at me and clenched her jaw until her ears turned chalk white.

Lord, I knew to watch my back with that woman then. The topper was how she wanted to hug me and then handed me a fresh loaf of prune nut bread when we said goodbye. Now, look, I know about the poison apple. It isn't just Dis-ney Snow White or Adam and Eve with the little snake in the garden. Forget for a moment that it's probably more his-torically accurate to say it was a pomegranate, not a Red Delicious, staining Eve's hands a mess. Keep things simple, we're talking Poison Apples. No doubt in my mind that food can be tainted with intent. This is old-school simple truth. I'd learned it from Nana and she learned it from Mamá Es-trella, who probably learned it from her mamá. Scared for what poison it might leak onto me, I took the loaf of bread from Edith because I figured if I didn't she'd throw it at me, hard. That and because, though I hate to admit it, I still wanted to get back together with her again, just a little bit. I mean, that gap between her teeth and those sharp minxy eyes and the way we tangled up so sweet when we slept. But I didn't let myself eat the bread. That would have signed the pact in blood. On my kitchen's faux wood counter is where the bread sat until I lost enough fear to throw it moldy and uneaten in the trash.

That Tuesday trash day I found Edith in the street going through my apartment's garbage bin. Crumpled-up foil balls were piled at her side. She was looking for the bread. Seeing her with her orange lipstick and her obsessed hunt, I forgot that I'd promised myself never to talk to her again.

"Hello, my sweet chocolate pie."

Edith dropped the torn-open black garbage bag held in her yellow dish-glove hands and leaned against the bin poised and scolding as if I'd interrupted the rising sun.

"Chocolate pie, Leticia? Why pie? And chocolate pie at that? Tell me, just what the hell is chocolate pie supposed to signify, Leticia Marisol Estrella Torrez?"

Nobody but family scolding when I was a kid ever pulled such a sneaky trick as throwing down my full name. The game was in motion.

"You rather lemon meringue or minced meat? Eh, Ms. Inmaculada Edith Contreras? Maybe key lime, or caramelo? Not apple, I can tell you that much. No, I couldn't call you apple pie even if you begged like a good little pie should."

Edith tore off her rubber duck yellow gloves and threw them to the ground. She wiped angry tears from her high Dolores del Rio cheekbones, smoothed spit curls at her temples into place, and stomped her vinyl go-go boots self up to the apartment I had rented in what I was beginning to realize was a futile attempt to outrun my Weeping Woman and Nana.

2

Not even a week after our Dumpster date, Edith Bird showed up with Nolan at Crystal's before the band came marching on. Hand in hand, Edie and Nol walked in through the bar's front door like they'd been a couple forever. Nol tried to play like she wasn't waiting for my reaction.

It wasn't like I had any right to throw a fit, I mean, Edith and I were officially broken up again, had been on and off for months, and damn if I was going to turn on Nolan just because she suddenly found her ticker going a-pitter-patter with Edith nearby. If I understood anything, it was that Edie was tempting like baker's chocolate on the top shelf when you're a kid and you don't know any better and the chocolate is luscious and it must taste good, right? I hadn't managed to detach myself from Edie's snapdragon tickle, but that was no cause for conflict. Besides, I had other more pressing complications to deal with. See, it was Weeping Woman, not Edith, who had me running scared that night.

For Edith I set out the gold paper doilies and my only

matching teacups. For Edith I looked forward to lipstick on my collar. For Edith I left my nights open just in case she might decide to pay me a visit. All that pomp and circumstance, that was just baby play compared to how Weeping Woman demanded I behave. Both of them ladies, Edie and Weeping, they could make my nose bleed with their parched hello kisses. But unlike Edith's come-and-go attention, Weeping's special something ruled my everything.

Twenty-some-odd years had passed since Nana first introduced me to my old lady Weeping. It started out that Weeping only stopped by for visits when the Santa Ana desert winds moaned sharp dry hot, but over the years our affair developed to the point where I felt my girl Weeping with each breath. Her presence settled into the crevices of my body. The joints between the segments of my toes swelled and needed to be cracked. My ears hummed a high-pitched moan. My throat burned.

Having la Weeping nearby was like singing so hard it hurt.

It was Weeping I had left behind at my apartment when I fled to Crystal's. The Crystal Room to be precise, the sign the same glowing throb it had been for centuries or decades at least, the sidewalk pulsing hot in its red-blink glow.

Crystal, now there's a mighty fine piece of work. Crystal lived in Detroit and trucked hazardous materials across the states before she saved up enough money to open her bar. When I asked her where her family was from originally, the furthest back her answer reached was "Minnesota." Crystal was way exotic intriguing to me. Crystal behind the bar with her intense shark eyes and Andy Warhol marshmallow skin and platinum wig, her flat-tone voice, a cigarette stuck to the corner of her lips when she answered the phone. I learned her messy baby of a bar like it was a tree house built just for me.

Originally, the tree house was a diner. Duke's Diner. Breakfast, Lunch, and Shakes. Steak-and-eggs, pass-the-ketchup kind of place. Crystal didn't do much to change the place when she bought it. She slapped up her delicious neon sign outside and took her position behind the high-gloss brown counter punctuated with bolted-down cracked vinyl and rusted chrome stools. Sprinkled in the center of the room's sticky-stain concrete floor were six Formica tables circled by blue high-backed unstable tin chairs. Honey brown and burnt mustard country floral print wallpaper peeled away from cobweb corners. A small makeshift stage propped itself up against the wall far opposite the bar counter. All in all, the place was nearly enough to convince me that Duke must have been the god of interior decorating. Only divinity has such nerve.

When Nol and Edie showed up, I took the minute Nol's lip biting and jumping eyes allowed me, drew in a deep breath, and then smiled as if seeing her with Edie was just the way I'd planned it. Nolan's broad shoulders relaxed down from the tense spot around her ears where they'd been waiting for my signal. Smiles and kisses and hugs hello, the three of us were going to be fine.

Edith told Nol she wanted her gin and tonic. As usual on Saturday nights, it was too hectic loud at Crystal's to have a real conversation. Our voices all false violent, jugular veins pushed up against skin, Nolan screamed she was going to buy me a beer. We huddled close to the bar, trying to hear each other. It was pointless screaming that led nowhere. We surrendered to the band.

Up onstage, the lead growled into her microphone, but she was glorious loud enough all on her own without the added benefit of sound. Shirt and pants off, tall motorcycle boots still buckled up, her thigh-length men's underwear displayed in the cigarette air, peeking out of the underwear's front flap, her harnessed penis hung rather loose in its place. A placid shade of white, like condensed milk exposed to warm air too long.

After three songs, Edith started grinding into the bit of her cigarette holder each time she inhaled. Soon she was rubbing her temples and whispering to Nol. The noise was giving Bird a headache. Strange how screaming girl Edie was so sensitive and tender that way. Nolan decided to take Ms. Edith home early. When they left, I breathed for the first time since they'd walked in. It burned, breathing did, but that was more Weeping's fault than Edie's.

I was alone, surrounded by girls, Weeping's insistent coarse whisper tease just behind the top layer of the bar's loud. I didn't want meaningless chat, and flirting was more than I could manage. I just needed to be around voices and racket to dilute some of Weeping's scratching at my ear. I got a beer from the bar and stood next to the stage.

Just as I'd settled into the cigarette-stained wallpaper, the band's assistant yelled at me polite to scoot so she could stand next to the spare equipment piled up at the wall. She rocked her head slow and calm and almost not at all to the music. A sharp ridge halfway between her pointed chin and angled collarbone bobbed slightly. Her shoulders were beyond broad. Hips vertical hard lines. I stared at her all night and bought myself a celebratory beer once I decided that at one point she might have been a he.

But not anymore. Rice-paper skin with no sign of a beard. Ageless face holding the hand of her boy turned girl. Polished postal uniform shoes, pressed vintage brown slacks, black turtleneck, and a poised stance kept wide. Weeping blew me a sudden gust of hot air and the little hairs on the back of my neck stood at attention. The band's assistant was regal. Truth be told, she was the most delightful prince I had ever seen.

The lights came on around a quarter to two. I pushed my body away from the wall and made my way outside to lean against a lamppost. I wasn't ready to walk home just quite yet. The damp not-night not-morning air wrapped its arms tight around me.

See, for me, it's the air Weeping sends that gets me tangled up in memory's confusing formal-wear dance. You know, don't scuff the shoes, this dance is fucking impossible to do without tripping up, your shoes are scuffed and you are falling on top of your date's corsage before you even pin it to her lapel. Weeping insists I take her dancing more than I care to. That lady cannot be denied what she demands.

When I was a kid, she'd tap her knotted hair on the window next to where I slept. She was a super drama queen back in those days, just like me now, though I'm only a princess if she's a queen. I learned how to please my girl Weeping and she became subtler in her greetings. Or maybe it's just that my awareness of her presence grew more acute. Regardless, I listen to the air and obey her courting commands.

The color of the air. The thick of the air. The hot or cold of the air. Subatomic particle by particle, the air funnels into my pores, and once it fills me whole, there I am wherever that same air had found me before.

And so, right then outside Crystal's in the cool crisp air, right then Weeping teased needles into the skin up the back of my neck in zigzag patterns. When inserted expertly, the needles caused no bloodshed. And my girl Weeping, she knew her tricks something good. Insisting I stand tall and quit my slouch, Weeping clamped my neck in her teeth and told me to draw a drop of my own blood.

One to never disobey Weeping, I let the early morning chill smart me deep down past goose-bumped skin. So there I stood, at the elementary school bus stop with Nana.

Nana. My nana, people outside our neighborhood often mistook her to be my mother. She was far too old for that. Silver no-time-for-fuss short hair and deep wrinkles from the

14

sun, but she was the person I was with the most, so they assumed they knew. They assumed they knew so much.

My hair was always braided intricate in the style that Nana claimed was fashionable for young girls. Satin ribbon-laced weavings pinned into a loop on either side of my head. The design that the girls with bob haircuts at school tormented me for. Skin pale like theirs, but more yellow-green in the winter than their pink cream.

I was a wiggle child, always doing a dance in my seat when told to be still. Nana held my hand at the bus stop; told me to stay away from the curb. And when I asked for the fifteenth time in two minutes if the bus was coming yet, she taught me a song to keep me from clowning too hard. I stood at the bus stop with my grandma singing, "ABC, where's the bus, DEF, where's the bus, GHI, where's the bus."

The mornings I didn't go to school, I walked to the old town circle with Nana, walked in the hot sun or the cool rain. The rain I loved the best because then I could hold my dark blue umbrella open on my left shoulder while I walked. The umbrella with its red apple design and green handle, it made me love rainy days the most. Or maybe I loved the warm, dry days because on those days I pushed my pale blue Holly Hobbie bouncy baby carriage with its "Love is sharing fun with someone special" decal on the side, its big open-cup mouth full with twelve meticulously arranged and tucked-in baby dolls.

On our way to town, Nana and I walked past the boys. The boys, specifically the grown-up gangster boys, from the last generation that was polite. Some of them my cousins, they were extra honey sweet when they saw us coming. They'd elbow their buddies to switch into "a lady is present" mode as they rolled down their dark plaid button-down shirtsleeves, the sleeves their mamás ironed smooth and creased for them each morning to wear. They rolled down those sleeves to

15

cover their tattoos and they used the proper manners with my grandma like they were one of her own. "Usted," and "doña" or "señora" when talking with my grandma. Those boys would tease me gentle about my family of a dozen.

"Where *did* such a young little lady get so many pretty babies?"

"Ay, but look, the mommy is so pretty too," the leader with his two top front teeth covered in gold would say.

I would look to the other side of the street and ignore the boys, who took Nana's attention away from me. I watched the gray pigeons on the telephone wire while she scolded those smooth talkers for being bad, for acting like proud roosters up on a fence waking the whole neighborhood up with their need to show off. She told them they should be working to help pay rent and to bring home the food they gulped down without thanks. The full plates of soupy rice with tomatoes and meaty tamales, the overflowing plates their mamás cooked for them, the food that made them so much taller than their cousins back home in Michoacán. They should be ashamed of themselves, such big strong boys standing around, feet glued to the corner, not even looking for honest work, she said. I sneaked looks and smiled smug high horse at the boys as they said "Yes ma'am" to each thing my grandma said. But mostly I watched the pigeons on the telephone wire until Nana was ready to begin our walk again.

Down the rest of Walnut Street and across the tracks and through the other side of town to the bank, the library where the librarian lady in tweed skirt suits let me feed the blotchy white and black and brown and stinky guinea pigs living cramped in cages at the children's section, the ice cream shop with pointy cones, the antique stores with the gold shine and velvet bric-a-brac fuzz, the town circle with its little sitting park and fountain in the middle. Each detail all the way was memorized. And for good reason. I had to know the way home. I told my grandma where to turn, where to go straight ahead, and when to stop. Nana Lupe said she couldn't remember the way, but I took comfort in knowing that she did.

Back home, my legs warm tired from the walk and belly full of sopa I knew to say thanks for, back home at my grandma's I fell asleep. Each night to the sounds of the trains across the street. Either the trains never traveled the tracks during the day or I just never noticed because there was too much else going on when the sun was still up. Come eight at night, I lay in the living room on the foldout sofa that was my bed. Then I heard each and every train that went by. The whistle horn of the trains filled my dreams. The plastic factory across the street made my head dizzy and my eyes burn. I slept through so much back then, but the air, it soaked into me anyway.

And the Weeping Woman, that powerhouse, from the first time she cried at my window during my childhood sleeps, scratching my name upon the windowpane, she was the center of all that I became. She knew I was something different. She told me I was her favorite child to visit. She came late, late, late when Nana was sound asleep.

Weeping Woman knew me. She knew where to come for visits each night of the week. In my family's living room, asleep on the creaking couch of a bed right under the window, that's where she'd find me.

"Weeping Lady, please leave me be," my mouth silently breathing the rhymes Nana taught me, "Now I lay me down to sleep. I pray the Lord my soul to keep. If I die before I wake, pretty please God don't let me die, I pray the Lord my soul to take . . ."

Weeping Woman's breathing audible. My own breath constricted by what I thought was fear. Electricity ran through me as she watched me careful from the window. I pulled my blankets up tight around my shoulders to hide the pale skin of my arms. I shifted so my brushed-out waist-long brown hair covered the hazel gold glimmer of my eyes. Look, Weeping Lady, I'm nothing special. I'm just like all the other children in the neighborhood.

We both knew it wasn't true.

Well, at first maybe it was. I mean, I did meet Weeping Woman no different than did all the other kids on my block. Nana told me about the Weeping Woman just like my cousins' mamás told them. Weeping Lady, she came riding into town on the cuentitos Nana handed me to teach life without spoon-feeding it. Nana's voice even deeper and more serious than usual when she would tell me. Weeping Woman was more or less like a bogeyman, but not silly Halloween make-believe.

"Don't you doubt it, girl, the Weeping Woman, she is real."

And if I was misbehaving, wasn't nobody going to stop her from taking me, not even my grandma, tucking me in careful each night, "Who wants a goat girl so troublemaking? Not me, that's for sure."

Weeping Woman traveled by wind in the night, stopping at windows and howling deep and mournful wails because she was bad and wanted to take bad children to be her own. She was the Weeping because she birthed a little girl whose father was a Spaniard. She cried because she had a mixed baby, one her Indian family and neighborhood despised. That is why she threw her little girl into the river that storming night, the night when the lightning's gleam on her baby's hazel eyes finally drove her mad. The Weeping Woman, she cried because she was la Malinche reborn.

You don't know that story either? Didn't you ever spend *any* time with your nana?

La Malinche. Everyone was taught to despise la Malinche because she loved a conquistador. Or so he said. As did his buddies. And the entire empire they set up. La Malinche. Yes, that woman, the archetype of the Wrong Kind of Woman. Not surrounded by cherubs and pink roses like the Virgen de Guadalupe, our blessed patron mother saint. Not pasted on candles in textured tall glasses that we lit for thanks. No, the Weeping Woman and her cousin Malinche, they were bad, bad, bad girls, those two were.

Those two girls, their fierce rebel lasting power made people remember them long after they had died. They were everything I wanted to be.

Crystal's sign flickered off. A pathetic two-beer anxiety-produced drunkenness sloshed acid deep in my gut. Dry winds pushed the early morning damp air away and Weeping kissed me gently. Green as a tomato not ready to be picked, I promised myself that never again would I go on an empty stomach to where Edith might show up. Weeping told me to stop mumbling at shadows, to focus my step so my toes would quit finding the cracks in the sidewalk. Weeping's hand under my elbow propping me up, I walked the couple of miles home to my apartment slow and uncomfortable tipsy.

I got to the front security door of my apartment building and had to lean my body against the metal doorframe to remember the entry combination for the security keypad. After three wrong tries, the lock buzzed and I walked in. Past the mailboxes, up the common stairs, down the carpet hall, and into my dollhouse apartment. The bed found me.

The cold was dank and I would have been even more cardboard than I was when I woke up if I hadn't worn my clothes to sleep. Denim bunched and twisted and tangled me, all night I flopped in shallow dreams.

Early in the morning, almost late at night actually, the phone rang and ripped my light sleep apart. I picked up and heard a voice force through, loud and full of boss.

"Leticia, you get over here. Now."

I pushed the receiver into my pillow, cleared my throat, and tried to respond with a melted-butter voice.

3

M orning," I crackled into the cold telephone, "I don't
think I can make it down today."

"You went out last night, didn't you?"

"I just went to say hello to some friends."

"Who? Edita and that Nolana?" Click click click of her
tongue.

"Her name is Nolan. It's her last name, remember?"

"Nolanita sounds better. That Nolan, she should go by
her first name. Like she's a soldier or something being called
by her family name . . . Leticia, you know I'm just calling to
say hello."

"I know."

Just calling to say hello. Only seven days had passed since
I'd last visited the pink square she raised me in. Our pink
house with Christmas lights up all year long on its windowsills, the house that forced me to remind myself each
day when I was growing up that I did *not* like pink. I knew I
had to hate pink because I played grown-up from the start
and pink was a thumb sucker's color. I always said I liked

red the best. Red was for low-riders waxed real good each Saturday and for the ladies in their dancing cowgirl dresses with ruffled layers and off-the-shoulder wink and flirt and carnations behind their ears.

The pink house at the corner, the blue house, then the white house next to the green house and then the purple house at the other corner. The pink house at the one corner was our house with our store attached to its front, the store's street-side wall done up with murals. It had been almost a year since I'd moved away from Walnut Street. And add some salt to the cut, as Nana would say, it was already the second time I'd moved away. Twice I declared that I didn't want to stay. The first time I went to college. The second time was a handful of months after I came home to help close down the store.

I couldn't laugh away Nana's telling me that I needed to come down to visit, that I'd been away for too long. Learned guilt filled my stomach. I rubbed the shaved-velvet hairline under my razor-sharp pageboy to ground myself. It got extra bright outside right then, the sun came in through the blinds, jabbed my eyes dry, and I was sure that Mamá Estrella was watching over the entire conversation, rattling her bony finger at me as she had each day in the store.

Mamá was in her store nearly every second it was open, from seven in the morning, when she pushed open the store's heavy red wood slab doors, until ten at night, when she bolted the thick security screen door shut. During the day, the bright red doors rested flat against the outside front wall, against a stucco canvas of Gothic script names big and bold and murals of no-name women with serious stares and widow-peaked hairlines.

The women in those painted love-letter murals, their brows were shaved and penciled-on thin black arcs above their eyes. Eyes so dark brown made darker yet by drugstore mascara, thick from pink tube wand to lashes. Azteca deities with turquoise sparkle eye shadow and round pointed cupid lips deep plum or Chevy red. I saw some of Weeping in those mural girls. I could barely handle it when the city would come out and hide the murals with rectangles of off-white paint that never quite matched any of the muting painted squares already existent. New patches of white barely dried, the boys would fix up their murals again.

Black burlap shoes with gum soles on their quick-step feet, the boys walked silent alley cat to the store's stucco wall and covered it wet with spray paint as I slept. The murals were always signed, the christened names of Jesús and Xavier exchanged for Casper and Tiny. Boys' pride, in the morning my grown-up cousins stood all tough smiles on the corner in front of the store for the world of our street to see.

The murals on our store appeared overnight. Me, I appeared in random piecemeal bits. I wasn't anything glamorous like the women honored on our store's front wall. My eyebrows were thick and met butterfly in the middle, my cheeks were round as the moon in its full, and my skinny girl bird legs forced jeans super quick to become high-waters and then shorts hemmed tidy just below my bony knees.

All gangly beside the lush painted mural girls, one day I stood in the doorway of the store, looking out to the street, singing to myself a song I learned at school. Second grade had just begun and I could barely wrap my brain around what was meant by "waves of grain." "Brotherhood" made a little more sense, but not really because my teacher assured me the song wasn't about the kind of brotherhood the grown-up gangster boys had on the street. And as for the song's shining sea, when I looked out onto the street singing my song, only stretches of concrete glimmered up in the sun.

As hot as it was under the desert summer sun outside, it was even hotter in the store. We didn't have air-conditioning, not even a stand-up plug-in fan. The comfort of cooled air was too much to ask from the cigarettes, gum, candies, avocados, fruit paletas, salted prune treats, canned goods, tortillas, chips, pan dulce, and sodas that Mamá Estrella sold at bargain prices.

My great-grandmother, she was so old nobody ever took her to be my mother. Mamá Estrella was old from the old country. The 1900s were barely born when she and Papá Estrella took off on foot to get away from the abuse their farmer families received at the hands of sour church-state politics. Long years had passed since she made the States her home, but Mamá Estrella still had rural México good girl in her blood. So we didn't sell any alcohol in the store. Don't get me wrong, it's not that Mamá was prissy. She never gave a single floppy dead-fish handshake in her life; my great-grandmother was something fierce strong.

At first she and Papá farmed here like they did back in México. German farmers were the only other people in town when they crossed the border into the pocket of scrub-covered flats just south of what would later be movie land. Our neighborhood was always just a few steps away from where movie fantasies were made to sell, but our neighborhood didn't have a fancy Hollywood name. Orange, our town was named simply for what my great-grandparents picked into heavy canvas bags slung on their shoulders and backs during long days. Our side of the railroad that sent the oranges across the country was always Mexican. But the other side was German back then. The only church was on the other side of the spikes. Protestant. So that's what my family became. And that's why Mamá Estrella knew how to say *danke* and liked to listen to band music with hints of polka beats.

Fifty years after Mamá Estrella first opened the store, I was eight years old and I leaned against one of the heavy red doors and watched the solteros across the street. Solos, all alone, come to the States looking for work. Alone, but on our street they had each other for makeshift family, ten men sharing tiny one-bedroom houses all along the block. Smoking red box tough man tough lung cigarettes in the shade of tree block sun. Creasing the bills of their baseball hats. Or tilting cowboy hats, if they had them, low to block midday glare. Threadbare button-down shirts tucked neat into heavy-buckle belted pants. Smoking cigarettes.

Way before my time, the solteros hung out all day inside the store, flirting with Mamá, joking with each other, talking about work available in the fields. Put simple, they hung out in the store looking for the México they held in their hearts, where their families were, where all their money earned went to, where their skin was common and their tongue understood—the solteros stood around in the store smoking cigarettes to try to find home. But that was a long time ago. Mamá Estrella was my age then. Like me, she was twenty-five years old back then.

Even Weeping Woman was jealous of Mamá because, cross my heart, what a stunning beauty Mamá was in her heyday. Smooth auburn hair set-curled and daring short. Strawberry kiss red lips. Simple avocado green with yellow marigolds housedress snug tied at her waist. Slender strong bones. Arms toned from years of tending fields and home and shop and family and neighborhood. Shoulders back and chin high.

For those cigarette cowboys she was something precious good. They'd smoke whole packs as an excuse to stay in the store. They would smile to hear her stories, to be "tsk tsk tsk'd" by her, to remember, for just a moment, the grace of the ladies they'd left at home when they crossed up the border to find work. Giddy sweet, they'd tap well-polished beaten-up work boots one up against another. Their pants permanently stained with mud, but pressed by hand more expertly each

Sunday they were away from their families' homes. Sugar water starch a little sticky on the backs of hot summer sweaty knees, those boys barely yet men loved Mamá Estrella and her winding stories as much as they did their Indian-eyed mothers, the blessed Virgen and that beyond hypnotic tejana guitara singer Lydia Mendoza. Some serious cowboy tears would have been shed if that generation of solteros had stayed in town long enough to learn that eventually their habits stomped out Mamá Estrella's storytelling voice.

See, when I was eight, Mamá Estrella had her voice box taken out and in its place was left a hole, a clean round nickel-size opening centered on the front of her neck. Secondhand smoke caused the cancer, the doctors said.

The doña who lived in the green house across the street from the store crocheted delicate three-by-three squares with satin laces for Mamá. Miniature blue and yellow and pastel orange couture bibs. Colors for a lady. Or a baby. A lady with no voice, Mamá wore bibs to cover the gaping spot on her neck where air went in and down to her lungs, where she would hold up a salmon-colored device that looked like an electric beard razor. She'd push a small button for the machine to buzz and her moving mouth would rattle out robotic jarring metallic words.

I was eight, standing at the store's front door, singing a song to myself, when Mamá Estrella got real bothered. She slapped the counter hard with her hand while straightening the candy. She didn't look up from the Wrigley's boxes she razor-cut open and emptied into the display case. Didn't use her voice machine. Just slap, slap, slap three times firm on the counter and I knew what she was telling me.

"Get away from the doorway. Now."

She simply was not to be questioned. I turned around, stopped my singing, didn't sass anything, and went inside. I edged past her slim body to where the old-fashioned black register sat on the counter, opened the screen door with the Coca-Cola tin diagonal across its middle, and stepped up into the hall that led to the pink house. Walked down the short narrow tunnel and my barely lifted hands touched the paneled walls on either side. Past empty chip and soda cardboard flats, twenty steps forward in a straight line. The thick black linoleum creaked dry and tired, its sparkles of color dull and worn by the influence of fifty years' tread. Through the skinny passageway to the Pine-Sol clean smell kitchen where my grandma sat at the oilcloth-covered table doing paperwork with my great-grandfather.

We were three generations in one room and right then I was the only one who wanted to talk. Papá Estrella and Nana with their sturdy sienna frames and no-nonsense thick silver hair, they didn't seem to hear my steps stop at their side. I wondered if I was too light to be seen. My small wrists and thin tangly long auburn strands and skin so rose-tinted yellow pale that the veins showed on the sides of my nose, I got that from Mamá Estrella, the only one in the family missing Indian blood. Mamá Estrella, everyone always said it was spooky how similar we were. Us with our different pale and our rambling and winding super talk-talky way. Our reputation was that we told more stories than the rest of the family combined; wasn't always true, but usually it was. Papá Estrella and Nana sat quiet at the kitchen table, pushing paper clips and pens on and off carbon-layered paper. Taxes or sales receipts or doctor's bills, I didn't know and I didn't really care, because their silence bothered me to the point of feeling that bother in my limbs wiggling all of a sudden. I creaked my foot on the floor.

"Mamá Estrella made me come inside, but I was just standing in the doorway, singing, real small-voiced, though.

I want to go back outside now. Please?"

Nana pushed down so hard on her pencil that it broke. Papá passed her the sharpener and they continued their work. They didn't look at me or say a single thing.

Years later, once I'd made my way to a university, that silent moment returned to me. In a Latin American feminist history class, surrounded by privileged women with poor Spanish ability, I sat on a hard plastic chair that made my back hurt. Lecture took me to old México where prostitutes would stand in the doorway of their home to advertise their wares.

"Commercial sex workers," the spectacled teaching assistant with imported sandals and jeans torn at the knees said. I raised my hand to correct her. At best I figured her family had taught her to be polite with her words. But really, she didn't seem to know the world she had so many facts memorized about. The words she spoke, they had no meaning where I came from.

"Nasty whore," my neighborhood liked to spit out, filled with mean intent and serious consequence.

Maybe being protective of me is why Mamá made me go inside that one day when I was eight. Or maybe it was her lost voice listening to my singing that pushed her too far. Whatever Mamá's reason was, I never did learn how to sing very well. But that doesn't stop me. I like my voice and its radio static crackle from one station to another and steady buzz in between like Mamá's jarring metallic hum. The tiny old woman who would splash holy water on my forehead when Weeping's visits in the dry summer heat would cause my nose to bleed. My voice, it crackles like Mamá's did.

And so when my throat got tight right as I talked with Nana on the telephone, I knew for sure that Mamá Estrella was hovering above, drinking tea in the good china with Weeping, both them ladies ready to slap if I showed the slightest lack of respect.

I managed to get my message out simple smooth. I told Nana again that I missed her. And that she was right, I had no excuse, not even the drive, for not coming down to visit.

But what I didn't say, what I knew better than to rattle out with no control, was that the forty minutes driving down to Walnut Street wasn't just time spent on the road. It was a countdown to her reflex cringe greeting. Nana's scowl materialized the second she opened the pink house's back porch door and saw me standing there with my bleached rust-blond bobbed hair, my motorcycle boots and thrift store ratty getups—either forties-style baubles and house-dresses or my baggy jeans, and little boys' tee-shirts, bright with ads for auto garages and tow companies, sleeves tight and high on my arm.

The shirts Nana especially disliked. "You crazy girl, they have such pretty, nice things at the Willy's. Why do you always get the rags even a little boy wouldn't want to wear?"

"The Willy's" to Nana. Goodwill to most people. Where we'd bought my clothes since I was a baby. Where twenty years ago she'd found the four cherished almost-new Bloomingdale's polyester pants suits that she wore in a predictable rotated schedule throughout her week. Purple, blue, green, and brown, purple, blue, green, brown.

If I wanted, I could go to the Willy's and snag never-been-worn name brands. That's how good Nana and Mamá had trained my clothes-rack sorting. But I wanted the undersized tee-shirts she said even little boys wouldn't make mud pies in. The shirts worn to display my Weeping Woman tattoo, my beautiful lady perfectly bronze-skinned, gold-robed and surrounded by a barbed wreath of cadmium red carnations, her shining glow warm on the upper half of my right arm permanently muscled from years of stocking the store's shelves. Around Nana, I slipped on a cardigan out of respect to hide the ink job a girlfriend needled into my skin during college.

29

Right at the pink house's back door, Nana always insisted I give her my sweater, "to be more comfortable," a demand I had to follow out of respect for the welcome into my childhood home. Each time, my sweater folded neat in her arms, the same conversation jumped me down.

"Leticianita, look at you. My baby, a ridiculous can of Campbell's soup with all that bright ink marked on her."

This from the only living person I loved more than myself.

She'd hand me my sweater and walk to the kitchen, busying herself with the copper kettle on the stove. Not looking for an answer, her back to me, she'd say, "Your cousins, they stay close to home. Sure, some of them are trouble, but look at your girl cousin Ernesta, she became a nurse and she didn't leave just because she's grown up. You tell me, do all your friends want to live far from their families like you do?"

She'd serve fresh mint tea and butter cookies from the tin engraved with countryside scenes of Holland.

My face burning from the endless scolding, the phone remained cold against my cheek. That much was appreciated. I pushed my face under the covers to block the sun. In the flowing Spanish I never used anymore except with her, Nana told me again to come get her to the afternoon Sunday service on time. I closed my eyes to drink up the accent marks and neighborhood talk and conjugations I'd near forgotten how to do proper. And to think that when I was little, English coming out of my mouth would get me sent to the living room corner.

Sometimes when I was in the corner, Papá would let me cheat and watch boxing on the black-and-white with him. Flickering grown men quiet and staring in their ring corners,

I'd do push-ups between rounds, knees never touching the ground, sleeves rolled up to show off the little rabbit in my arm that would jump when I flexed. Papá was impressed. I told him I was going to be a fighter and he said, "That's my girl." But I'd seen *Rocky* on the channel 13 Sunday night movie special and I knew boxers had to jump a lot of rope, forward and tricky style. I could only jump rope backwards. I knew I wouldn't be a boxer, but I'd practice for it just the same. There was one fight Papá and I shared that wasn't so sweet as our boxing dates.

It started out as strange cute to him, when I carried my kindergarten cartoon character lunchbox as a handbag to the first day of junior high. Soon I was going to school in black draping clothes, hair slicked with Papá's forest-scented pomade to emphasize my Draculina widow's peak, my face powdered undead white and always looking gloomy at the ground. By the time I dug my little kid umbrella out of the coat closet and took it with me everywhere to keep the sun from turning me gold, he'd had enough.

"Leticia Marisol Estrella Torrez, a broom and your costume is complete," he shoved the kitchen broom at me and told me to ride it to school, or "Go change out of that mess. Now."

I thought about arguing that it wasn't fair, that he wouldn't yell at the Vietnamese grandma who had moved into the green house to leave her parasol at home when she went for walks in the sunny afternoon. But I knew that our fight wasn't about shade. Well, actually, in some ways it was. Not shade as in the cooling shade a parasol could provide, but shade as in shades of cream pink and pale olive yellow and deep earth brown. Papá was upset because he looked at my vampire getup and what he saw was simple whiteface full of disrespect.

I returned the broom to its closet, washed my skin clean

of makeup, put on an ironed dress, and braided my hair up into a bun, tons of bobby pins jabbing my scalp like I knew Papá would approve. Breathing hard and stubborn, I ate my morning oatmeal with milk. Papá said I'd better watch my step, that he'd gladly put a ring through my nose like a fighting bull's if I kept up my crazy outfits and dared to stab holes in my earlobes like he'd seen other kids do. I did him the favor of not piercing my ears at the mall booth until after he passed away. Piercings, not to mention girls with bull-hoop piercings, never fail to remind me of Papá.

Nana continued talking.

It was a blessing Mamá and Papá passed away before I moved from our street. Same, it was good they never had to see the store's hours shrink and shrink again and eventually stop altogether after the Quicki-Mart with its wine coolers and malt liquor opened a couple of streets down. Nana missed being in the store, tending to business, saying hello to neighbors when they came in for their groceries. She missed the powerful scent of orange blossoms now that, right past her backyard, row after row of tan-colored copycat houses crouched where the groves used to be. Most of all, Nana said, she missed me. Didn't I remember where my home was?

Working to become a beautiful boy baritone, my radio static voice all crackle remained silent. I took the fluctuations of Nana's voice, added some years of getting wrinkled and a touch of metal crackle, and listened to the conversation I preferred as Mamá told me my favorite bedtime tuck-in story.

You see, there was a girl with hair as blue as the sun is bright. Ay, you don't even know how she was teased for her beautiful sunshine. But this young girl, she was special. Only her family and she knew it, but want to believe it or not, the little girl, she was a goddess princess from ancient Aztec times reborn into a little girl human body.

The little girl's great-grandmamá, her job was to stay

close to the girl and do all she could to watch over her. One day, as it often happened, the girl was sad. Her great-grandma told her not to worry, that come evening time things would be better.

The sun left and warm winds whipped through the evening sky. The young girl's great-grandma made two cups of fresh boiled wild mint tea with thick spoonfuls of honey, set them on a television tray at the foot of the back door's steps, and called for the girl to put on a sweater, come outside, and join her.

The girl put on her favorite red sweater, the one that was too thick for the whisper warm wind outside and scratched but that she loved for its gold buttons all shine from her breath and buff on the cuff of her sleeve. She put on her red sweater, carefully closed the screen door behind her, and sat down beside her great-grandma on the concrete steps.

"You see," her great-grandma wrapped one end of her shawl around the little girl and drew her close in a hug while pointing up to the cloudless night sky, "Do you see that dark blue, lighter green around the moon?"

The girl nodded, and looked from the sky to her great-grandma to the sky again.

"Before you were born, the sky, it had no color. It was blank, completely blank. The stars, they didn't twinkle. How could they without any color around them to make them shine?"

Her great-grandma paused and the girl looked down and began to pick at the steps' peeling red paint with her bitten fingernails.

"The night you were born, I knew what had to be done."

There was another pause. The girl's hands stopped their nervousness.

"I invited the rest of the family to meet you. Your grandmother, Tlazoltéotl, the one in charge of love, she cried

33

when she saw you. Cried and cried, she's always making such a fuss, that one. But who could blame her? Your blue hair. So beautiful. She borrowed a few strands of your fine baby feather hair, and she wove a quilt above the earth with it to keep you warm in your cradle. Child, it is because of you that the sky is so blue."

Even back then, when Mamá would seal the story with a good-night kiss on my forehead, I knew. I was royalty beyond the stories Mamá had tucked me in with.

In college, I told my boy that if she couldn't get me my tiara, pearls would do. Three wired rows of a pearl choker kept my princess neck long and my princess head held high. What I had really wanted were bright sprinkle diamonds about my neck. Diamonds couldn't be afforded.

4

Pearls. Close together. Wired precisely in triplet lines. Weeping, Nana, and me. Pearls. Close together. Wired precisely in triplet lines.

At seventeen, I baby-stepped toward my princess pearls. Away from the store and pink house on Walnut Street, and through three towns, I actually landed only twenty minutes away from Nana. Strange combination, I went to the closest university I could to study glamour and magic. Having lived my entire life not too far south of smoggy Hollywood dream factories, I had some serious stars in my eyes. Nothing was more fabulous than sitting around all day reading about and watching old movies. I waved my princess wand and had me a four-year carpet ride in film studies lined with scholarships and grants earned by growing up convinced that books and solitude were better friends than the kids at school. Those scholarships bought my books, paid my fees, provided me with four dorm-room walls, and gave Nana plenty of reason to scold and nag.

"You should be living at home if you're going to school so close. What, you don't love me anymore?"

Right, I was such a bad girl.

My dorm was in a campus house for honors students, basically a building full of complete dweebs. At the orientation Nana and I went to, I realized I'd be leaving home to join a building of asocial types soft with library lighting and nerd habits. Our residential adviser introduced all the roommates to each other, two people to each room in the house. My roommate wasn't there that day.

When I did meet my roommate, lord, I thought she was pulling a prank the way she carried herself. It was moving-in day and I walked into our room with Nana at my side, carrying in my boxes of things and my bedroll. There stood my roommate wearing a rhinestone-studded cat collar necklace.

"I didn't know you were allowed to keep pets in the dorms," Nana said, sniffing toward my roommate.

My roommate, she just smiled polite and offered her hand to introduce herself to Nana.

"Mucho gusto, señora. Your purple suit is fantastic."

Coming from anybody else, the words would have fallen flat with slick slime. But Joey, she had a way of holding conversation that was so real. That girl, she smoothed Nana out perfect with the charm and respect her mamá taught her same as my familia taught me. From that point on, Nana always asked how "my Josefina" was doing when I'd call home.

But the Joey I fell head over heels for, ay, she wasn't nobody's mamá's girl. My Joey, she was the toughest of bookworms and I loved being her best girl. Before I met her, I was happy without anyone to call a friend. I'd spent most of my school years learning a game. Right at the very start, even grade one had so many rules I had to figure out quick.

I had been Nana's sweet little doll in my high-glow black

leather Mary Janes, white lace anklet socks, canary yellow taffeta ruffled dress, and fuzzy green yarn woven in the two braids looped into rope circles above my ears.

"Kind of like Princess Leia's hair," I'd offer explanations to the other first-grade girls at school.

"Dumbie, your name is Leteesha, not Leia."

My name stomped upon even when I told them real patient that it kind of rhymed with "see ya."

"Yeah, see ya, Leteesha. Wouldn't want to be ya."

I was bused to their fancy elementary school on the other side of the tracks just past the town circle for being some standardized test's definition of smart. Sent to a place where the people who were supposed to be my peers thought I was from outer space, "Which planet are you from, Leteesha? My mom says you and your family are aliens."

Giggling mean as they adjusted fancy headbands, their wispy bangs caught on translucent eyelashes. That was the only time you could tell they had any lashes at all. Not like mine, dark and thick, always managing to find their way into my eyes.

Papá Estrella would meet me at the bus stop nearest Walnut Street after school and walk me home. I'd do my homework at the store counter. When it was time to close shop for the day, I'd set myself up in my barber chair with my books. The barber chair in the store's side room storage area wasn't mine exactly. It was officially Papá's, but the chair might as well have been mine. Each Saturday and Sunday when he was done clipping and fading and shaving for the afternoon, I'd Windex-clean the chair's white vinyl seat and prop myself up in my throne with books. The magic best-friend books the librarian in the children's section set aside for me, "Leticia, I think you'll like this one that just came in. Not a lot of pictures, but that doesn't bother you does it?"

The librarian worked her lips to say my name right.

I liked pictures, especially photos of people and places, like the ones in the photo albums Mamá kept up on the shelf in the living room. Yes, I liked pictures, the more the better, but the librarian always smiled big at me so I said "Thank you" in as perfect English as I could and carefully put the books on top of my babies in the Holly Hobbie buggy. When I checked out the books with the library card that had my name on it, I held my chin high and dignified like I figured Mamá Estrella would do. Like a wave from the city beauty queen on her float, I handed the laminated identification back to Nana Lupe for safekeeping in her wallet. Bounced home. Arranged the books by cover color and due date on the shelf next to the barber chair.

Evenings were spent in the barber chair with my books. And when it was hot like it was those first pop dry autumn days of school, ants came to read with me. Their arrival at my throne was always quick and without apology. I blew each one off my leg and got angry and tired and then exhausted and revved with energy at the new game.

"Nana," I yelled full of lungs like the kids at school, hollering my words toward the inside of the pink house in the English I was learning in kindergarten, "Nana, your aunt's *ants* are bugging me."

My attempt at humor was lost on her.

The answer always came in Spanish, "Do not bark loud at me like that. And you watch it, no English. You'll learn enough of it at school."

She came from the pink house with a newspaper in her hand, "Understand?"

"Yes ma'am," my Spanish low volume.

"And listen, just so you know, an 'ant' crawls around with six legs, an 'aunt' is family. Family doesn't have six legs."

The way she said the words distinguished them one from the other. "Ant" and "aunt," the *t* said real hard in both. I followed lead when I went to school. "Kitten" had four consonants and I pronounced each one. The word "mul-ti-ply" consisted of three distinct syllables. And the "ci-tee" I lived in was "Or-anj." My vowels overannunciated, my statements in English generally too precise, some words still said just plain wrong as they took their time getting cozy in my mouth.

My English didn't go unnoticed. Classmates pinched their noses and echoed my whispered voice to make me pay for being the only one with an eagerly raised hand. Mamá Estrella had told me that school existed for students to answer the teacher's questions and to obediently complete all assigned work. So each time Miss Teacher asked the class a question, I raised my hand up high in the air, my arm tense and stiff. She'd often ask me to repeat my answers because "I couldn't quite hear you with your little voice, Leticia."

If I tried big voices like the other kids, everything came out with a singsong attached so I wouldn't get bruises from the sharp and pointy sounds. But I spoke as often as I was allowed to let the teacher know how much I had listened to her. I was the one who knew color after color of the wood blocks Miss Teacher held up. The fancy sneaker girl across from me at our group desk kicked me under the table a lot that year. My neck would turn red each time. Miss Teacher saw my blush but didn't get it. She told me I didn't have to worry, that I was doing just fine. I said "Yes ma'am" and the freckled kids whispered "Jess mom" in my ears come recess time.

I had learned quick, better to stay quiet and keep the books and ideas as best friends.

But then I found myself in my university bedroom as far away as I'd ever been from Walnut Street. And there was Joey standing in front of me, seeming in her cocoa brown color and her Filipina smooth speak like she could have been some girl cousin I'd never met, but she was even more incredibly perfect because she wasn't actually family and I could afford to have a crush on her.

Joey. Joey with the deep laugh and straight-lashed almond eyes. Joey and her prized thrift store pair of Italian leather zippered knee boots and a street slicked style. Joey with two surgical steel hoops so s/m thick-gauged in each earlobe that I used to laugh out loud sometimes just trying to figure what Papá would have said. Joey who I adored for the confidence she had. Joey. We were each other's girls. We walked in sync. We lent each other our highlighted texts. A bit of her laugh became mine. A morsel of my smile could be found in hers.

Our first semester together we stole Tang from the campus store and sold it mixed with water in Dixie cups outside the student union to raise money. The drink's room-temperature tap water blah didn't live up to the dollar we charged per cup. But people gave us money once we gave them our song and dance. You see, the money was going for a worthy cause.

We handed the raised funds over to one of Joey's friends up in Los Angeles just north of downtown where her family lived. Her friend had a tattoo shop there. Joey and I wanted to remember each other "forever," we said.

Joey got a tin-man steel heart done on her right arm. She said it had my name in invisible ink at its center. And I got my arm done up with the only woman I could think of who had more divine self-assurance than Joey.

I gave Joey a dozen red carnations to match the wreath that laced Weeping Woman into my arm. Joey hung the flowers upside down and kept their dried bodies in a cleaned soda bottle on the nightstand between our beds.

When we weren't in our room reviewing each other's lives or fulfilling the honors class schedules we set up in unison, we were at the university coffee bar studying or at least pretending to study.

Each morning we got our change together and purchased one small cup of coffee each, extra sugar, topped by a stirring stick neither of us used but that helped the Styrofoam drink that had to last hours seem special. We placed our cups next to piles of books on the heavy wrought iron table we claimed as our personal property. Perched upon wobbly chairs, we would wait for Traver.

Eleven in the morning Mondays, Wednesdays, and Fridays. Sometimes later on Tuesdays and Thursdays. Traver always got a half-decaffeinated wet-foam latte. She didn't add sugar or use a stirrer. If we were lucky, she'd sit near our table, but with her back slightly to us so we could watch her while she graded papers. Traver was sexy, hot damn, pick-a-bale-of-cotton, s-e-x-y. She was a humanities teaching assistant, a gold star graduate student who taught some of our introductory classes. Beyond our reach as defined by protocol, but completely within the limits of intense admiration.

We'd plant our feet firm on the ground and act real tough in our unstable chairs when she sat near us. Alluring attitudes copped as best we could in our then limited ways. Imagine James Dean with a touch of Grace Jones. In reality, I probably looked cranky and disturbed with my pouting lips and jaw clamped shut. Joey, she had the rebellious sexy look nailed down. But even Joey's chic mask would fizzle and she'd fan her face for strength when Traver would swagger away. We'd crumble into nervous giggles, look around, paranoid of listening walls, and stitch together threads about Traver.

The summer before our senior year at school, I let Joey weave my waist-long hair into a final braid and snip it off at the baby fuzz of my neck. Sweat glued stabbing little hairs onto my back as I buzzed my head with clippers we borrowed from Joey's on-leave navy brother. Joey wrapped my braid in fancy tissue paper and kept it beneath her pillow. Only once did I make the mistake of visiting Nana with my head shaved.

"Dear precious Mother of God . . . my sweet little baby." Tears welled up in her crinkle-bordered eyes as she looked at my hair. "Did you use the medicine already?"

My tongue tangled up. I couldn't get my lies arranged fast enough. But it didn't matter. Nana kept talking to keep from crying.

"How did you go and get a headful of piojos, Leticia? It's that 'dorm' place you live at, isn't it? Too many girls in one house. I told you to never share any hats with anyone. Not pillows either. Ay, don't tell me that our Josefina got them from one of the girls there too."

Right then there was no explaining to be done. It made no difference that I'd always helped Papá sweep up around the barber chair. Made no difference that he'd let me take peppermints he saved for the little boy customers. Made no difference that before he passed away, he had sometimes given me the honor of cutting a regular customer's hair. Made no difference that after all the years I had watched him working on the weekends, I could cut hair sleek smooth and close to the skull around the neck and ocean wave beautiful at the widow's peak. Made no difference that the barber chair had been my throne, my fingerprints melted-in permanent on the chrome lever at the white vinyl seat's side.

All that mattered was that Nana knew only a single itchy reason that a woman would shave her head like I had done. I didn't have the nerve or heart to tell her different. And it never entered her thoughts that I did it because I *wanted to*, pure and simple. She wouldn't appreciate knowing that in two minutes I had shaved off the shining cascade she spent

42

my childhood priming. I crossed my fingers behind my back and soothed Nana by telling her that I promised I'd grow my hair long again and, no, Josefina hadn't gotten the lice.

It was part true. Joey hadn't cut her long hair short, but she did tumble hard for my new style. She said my new look meant I needed to wear her Italian zippered boots. It was with those boots that my life stepped in yet another new direction.

Traver. Traver liked my new-claim Italian boots. And I liked the sailor uniform she kept tucked away in a foot-locker in her bedroom. If I told how I found out about that uniform, I'd be in trouble. Let's just say that Traver liked to anchor the Italian shore when she was a sailor. I never shared that detail with Joey or anyone else. That was mine. Mine to keep and cherish selfishly. If things with Traver could only have been as flawless as I felt in those boots. Traver literally never spoke to me again after our short-fused sparkler burned out. We stopped seeing each other before I was even sure we had been seeing each other, and she left her girlfriend, Rob, a quick week later.

The next beat, at the coffee bar, Joey dared me to get a coffee when Rob showed up for hers. I did. I stood in line behind Rob. I tried to be subtle but I couldn't help look at her smooth flat boy bottom, it was something special charming. Rob got her coffee. I leaned against the bar and watched her pour cream in and stir it counterclockwise. She bit the stirring stick as she turned around in a single grounded move to face me, her thick muscle body graceful beyond what I would have expected. She had been aware of each second of my stare. To say she was arrogant and overly dramatic would only begin to explain. Likewise for "hot." She looked at me looking at her, smirked a little, and complimented me on the boots stomping out from under the hem of my raggedy housedress.

Rob was a graduate student, but she didn't teach any classes. I made logic of my new rules. Stood there, and let Rob admire my boots, "I might let you polish them sometime if you buy me a latte." I couldn't believe my own nerve. Even crazier was that she didn't laugh at me. She smiled. The wicked "I'm a big bad wolf" glimmer in her eyes brightened.

I've looked up at clouds before and wanted to take a bite out of them. Not out of some nauseating cute appreciation for their soft purity, but to consume their thick bitter dense smog into my body before it evaporates into something that will disappear from my sight. The latte Rob bought me that day tasted like a cloud.

From that day on, Rob and I were together most of the time for a long time, but in retrospect I'm not sure what that means. Joey said she didn't like how I was to her with Rob around. I bit back by calling her "Josefina" like I knew her mamá had when she was in trouble and I got a combination lock for my desk in our room. Things turned super bitchy between us after that. I offered to give back her boots. She said they were nothing to her anymore. What stung most was when she gave me her brother's hair clippers and said direct with no nice around the edges of her words that she wouldn't be cutting my hair anymore, so maybe Rob would want to help keep me tidy 'cause someone sure as hell had to. I told "Josefina" if she needed me, I could be found at Rob's apartment in graduate housing.

My final academic year went through the cycles Joey and I had learned together, but not once did she come looking for me at Rob's. And even if she had, chances are we wouldn't have answered the door. We were always busy doing something or other, usually half-naked in the process. Rob especially liked playing teacher, and since I was a good little film studies nerd, she loved extra much to screen mini film festivals for me. Leather girl with a touch of crunch, she'd make big bowls of popcorn with nutritional yeast and paprika sprinkled on top and we'd settle in for the night in front of her television. One of the most memorable nights was a triple screening of *Cleopatra*, *The Bad Seed*, and *I'm No Angel*.

Bulldagger extraordinaire, Rob cocked her eyebrows and said, "Mae West is a fucking hot drag queen."

I'm No Angel had just ended, and there we were, necking and wrestling on the couch and then Rob pinned me down and said what she said. Static started to play on the tube. I was just beginning to understand. Everything.

Rob was a teacher I shouldn't have been playing doctor with, but that, of course, made it all the more exciting. My shaved head and stomping boots, my adolescent dyke dick hard all the time, Rob took vacations swimming in my newness.

Mae West was a drag queen. I was quick and easy convinced. The way Mae held her cigarette, that stiff broad shoulder, her wide flat hips striding across the movie set. Constant growl under endless layers of eyelashes applied. She was a divine construction-site worker in a sequined gown. Oh, Mae, please wink at me, tousle my hair, me, your doting schoolboy, may I please come up and see you sometime? Crush, hot damn, what a crush a girl could have on a girl in girl drag.

I pushed Rob off me and crossed my legs fast to stay cool, to jut my jaw and think quiet. You see, with Rob I didn't talk much. She thought I was serious and grounded and all that kind of mature, but really it was more that I couldn't keep up with all the baiting she dangled in front of me. I just didn't know quite what to do around her most of the time, so I usually stayed quiet and nodded and listened. Rob liked that I took note of her everything. When I did speak, it was to make high and mighty demands that she had no choice but to satisfy.

When she wasn't busy worshipping me in her apartment, sometimes Rob would drive us up past the county line to Los Angeles in her rusty truck to go to the city's only old-school "ladies'" bar. Big blond hair, aerobics class bodies, fitted jeans worn high up above belly buttons, the West Side ladies at the Norm made Rob's militant San Francisco hairy legs in their leather motorcycle boots stomp hard and superior through what she loved to label "bleached lesbian fluff."

"They aren't dykes, Leti, they are 'lesbians.' They might even be 'homosexual' or 'gay women' for all I know," she'd say with a sneer. "Don't ever call me a 'lesbian,' got it?"

The drinks at the bar kept me satisfied, and my snooty angry dyke would buy me as many as I wanted so I didn't really care where we were or what she felt I should call the women around us. Sometimes, if we knew we were going back up to the city again the next day, we'd pit-stop on the East Side before going to the bar. Hop by the video store Rob claimed was the only one outside the Castro that had the skin flicks she liked. Exhausted mornings after our visits to the bar, she'd bring me espresso in bed and we'd watch the smooth hairless lanky boys she adored masturbate and fuck each other good morning.

But we were *not* dating. We told each other that on a regular basis. The rules were clear. Rob was nasty daddy to my princess. She claimed if her back didn't have a tendency to give out on her from all the gardening she did, she'd give it to me something good. She was full of talk. Wanting to take me to bed all the time but never letting herself do it, instead dressing me in her best pin-striped brushed cotton pajamas at night and tucking me in tight under the blankets with her at my side. Pulling me onto her lap to kiss my widow's peak and run her earth-under-short-fingernails heavy calloused hands over my shoulders and whisper secrets only princesses can hear.

That is, when she wasn't lecturing me.

"Don't try to pretend it won't happen someday," she preached. We sat on the hard steel chairs in her living room and drank coffee laced with tequila. Mine with sugar on top of that.

"Some little miss cutie pants is going to come along and you'll need her so bad that it will make you cry if you don't give in to it," she conjured up Traver as she followed me into the kitchen. Careful to not let her know how familiar her ex's voice was in my head, I yawned and took the cleaned and delabeled mayonnaise jar filled with bleached sugar from her kitchen cabinet as she continued, "And then, I know it sounds so damned Danielle Steel, so leave me alone, she's going to make you cry because it'll be time for her to leave you."

I poured three tablespoons into my cup and I smiled the coy smile that got her hard every time.

"You sure you don't want some sugar in your cup?"

We returned to the chairs and she pulled me onto her lap.

The tequila was her idea, as were most of our Tuesday morning routines. Our we-are-not-shackled-by-monogamy Monday "time off from each other" barely done, I'd leave the stiff unwelcome of my room with Joey and walk over to Rob's place each Tuesday before the sun came up. Meeting later in the day would have been fine by me, but the coffee was set to brew at 5:55 so I'd make my way to her chairs when the sky was still dark.

Coffee in hand, we'd push our chairs close to each other and make huge plans about life. Rather, she'd make huge plans for our separate lives and I'd listen, arching my eyebrows until she'd merge the two stories with room for romance between us. She only did it to amuse me so I wouldn't whine in my early morning raspy voice. Romance, she told me, only exists with a capital R in pretentious literature. It took too much energy to argue with her.

She looked at me and chose to see herself. Insecure little boy. She accused me of the things she needed to hear for herself. Like most mornings, the morning I'm thinking of she threw some sour at me to balance things out.

"You're too fucking complacent, Leticia. And when you're angry you get so passive and sassy. You are going to explode one of these days if you don't let someone have it sometime."

I watched her as she growled her words and scowled as punctuation. It was only six in the morning and she already had fire in her talk. Full of contradictions. The pinkie of her right hand always extended when she drank from her cup. She had a thing for antique china teacups with rosettes painted at the lip. I wondered if anyone had ever pointed out to her that she was a prissy little dandy underneath her stubble and snarl. I never did.

Hours walked by. Each squared angle in her arms rippled as she pushed her solid frame up from her chair to get more coffee. She took my teacup, the one with the pale blue rosettes. That morning she came back with two cups of sober black coffee in pink rosettes, a nectarine tucked under her chin, and a pearl choker looped on her thick wrist. I refused her even a moment of surprised excitement. She took out the gutting knife she kept under the mattress and sliced the fruit, fed it to me, licked dripped juice off my chin with her rough tongue, and put the choker on my neck.

When the choker still shone untarnished upon my neck, Rob brought me sunflowers from her garden nearly every day. Overloaded metaphor. Wake up and open my dorm room door, there were flowers at the threshold.

One weekend, Rob and I left town and had our only official date. Before we left on separate flights headed for San Francisco, she drew a zoom-in detail map of the Castro, pointed to a street that intersected with Market, and told me to meet her in front of a camera store I'd find there. On the night of our rendezvous, I took my sweet time walking up Market to get to Rob. The black vinyl cat suit she'd told me to wear for the occasion earned me plenty of stares. Tempting, tempted stares. I was plenty ready for Rob once I found her. Dutiful worshipper, she crowned my waist with the electrical repairman's belt I had told her to pack for me. I was only a princess, but, honey, my sashay put the loveliest of queens to shame. Small bruises from the belt's weight dug into the tops of my hips as we walked through the neighborhood, my hand dainty and decorating her offered arm. I fussed that I was catching a chill in the evening fog. She took off her leather jacket, the one with the silver thick snaps at the wrists, and placed it over my shoulders. My outfit was complete.

We joined up with the friends she knew from when she lived in San Francisco before graduate school. I petted their motorcycles and outlined their biceps with my hot pink polished nails and purred when Rob's buddy Mercedes wrapped her burly arm around me and lifted me by the waist to sit me sidesaddle on her bike. Only one other pretty girl got a bitchy look from me as I sat on my throne, the rest were simply ignored.

Rob and I got as close to sleeping with each other that night as we ever did. We tussled in a trailer turned into security office parked at the end of a blocked-off littered festival street. This chickadee Rob knew from her dungeon days was working security for pride and she let us hang out after-hours in the trailer. What we did that night was painful, full of marking bites and bruises borne up out of the annoyance I had for my tease daddy. At one point she decided she didn't like her baby teething on her neck as much as I was, so she pinned me down and pinched my nose with her right hand, her mouth over mine and her left hand pushing down hard pressure on my neck. The girl was strong. I really couldn't have moved if I had wanted to. But I didn't want to anyway. The only breath I got was the one she would occasionally lend into my mouth. I came fast and hard but we never called it sex.

That night we ended up at some random friend's house. The friend said there was only enough space in her bed for one other person, otherwise, of course, she'd have us both share the bed with her, and since she knew Rob better she'd sleep more comfortably if I didn't mind the cushy couch in the living room. On the way to brush my teeth in the bathroom, I peeked into Random's bedroom. There were more hooks and levers rigged to the walls and ceiling than I'd ever seen in any Frankenstein flick.

I tucked myself into the cigarette stink blankets Random had thrown on the couch for me. Wrapping myself up tight to keep the damp air out, I kicked the armrest hard and had myself a little tantrum. Daddy was already neglecting her duties and that was just the beginning of a very long night. Random's place was an old walk-up townhouse with echoing wood floors. Their bed didn't squeak, but chains scratched the floor and the whips slapped steady. The sleep I didn't get made me itch with hives for hearing them together and knowing I was to stay in my place on the couch. When I walked into the bedroom in the morning to tell them I was leaving to catch my plane back home, I saw an open container of Crisco at the foot of the bed. It wasn't as if they had been baking cookies in the middle of the night. They could have done me the favor of tidying up a little before falling asleep. As it was, they had kept me up past the sun rising with their annoying loud. Rob was even still chained to the bedposts. I didn't wake them before I left, but I did steal the key that kept Rob locked in her place.

Eventually, enough time passed that Rob didn't, wham zap ta-da, materialize with flowers at my door if I thought of her. Around the same time I learned the aerodynamic equation used for determining the coefficient, the constant, of drag.

Drag on a Body Moving Through Air:(Velocity)(Surface Area of the Body).

Once calculated, the resulting ratio proved that the pearl choker had grown too heavy for the slender surface area of my neck. I up and plucked my pretty princess fairy wings off. My tiara was wrapped in tissue paper and boxed away, my shaved hair grew out to a pageboy, and Rob was officially, but not yet completely, erased from my life.

My four years were up and I graduated from film studies with top honors. That much was easy. I could watch flicks with the best of them. Pass the popcorn, please. As for the tomes of theory and mounds of essay writing I had waded through, after a lifetime of practice in school, rote memorization and reformulation in the first person came easier than snapping my fingers. Joey got a fancy pants honors tassel from comparative literature and we walked together at the honors and graduation ceremonies. After the ceremonies, Joey and I gave our tassels to each other and we started talking. When she went to stay with second cousins and study in the Philippines courtesy of a Fulbright, I drove her to the airport. She gave me a goldfish-quick kiss goodbye on the lips and walked away toward the terminal. I got in my car and told off the monotone voice that droned on about how I was in a "temporary zone for immediate loading and unloading of passengers." I cried the long drive home. Once I could breathe again, I placed a call to Luzon and told Joey I was sorry for not being better to her.

"Leti, you'll always be something special to me. I've got your name on my arm, you know."

"You'll tell that to each girl in your life, won't you?"

"No, just you."

I promised her that I would send her a dozen red carnations each year on her birthday from that point on. We hung up.

I never sent any carnations her way. She knew I wouldn't and maybe she didn't really want me to anyway.

Two skips later I was back on the pink house's foldout couch and Joey was postcards up on Nana's refrigerator.

A few nights before I got up the nerve to start looking for an apartment in Los Angeles, I drove the forty minutes to the bar Rob used to take me to. Now isn't that funny? I mean, of all the places to go to, it's like I was running circles, all tangled up in a leash nobody was forcing me to wear. The whole thing was cute or sad, or both, like one of those velvet painting crying clowns.

So, anyway, I sat at the bar and that's when I met Nolan. Rob would have been proud. From the second I saw her, I knew Nolan wasn't what Rob would label lesbian or even gay. She was a young foxy dyke with plenty of style and obvious brains. With her baby face, Ivory soap, movie-house-refreshment-stand boy style, it was easy to figure she was some college dropout who liked easy days of wrangling espresso machines at the coffeehouse across the street. Wrong. Turned out Nol was way older and more responsible than she looked. A graduate degree in mathematics tucked in her back pocket, she taught community college and paid all her bills on time. Funny thing is, from the very start something about Nol reminded me of Nana, both of them built sturdy and solid like you could lean on them and trust them with anything you've got.

That first night I met her, Nolan and I got to talking and she told me about the Crystal Room on the other side of town. "If you can get past the Birkenstocks groovy name,

52

it's a pretty great dive bar." I followed her car there and she introduced me to nearly each dyke that packed the place.

Turns out one of the women I met was an ex of Rob's. No, not Traver. Vivienne was her name. Vivienne, linebacker strong with sparkle blue eyes, older-and-wiser Vivienne. Good thing I was still fresh out of college naïve because otherwise I might have never got up the nerve to talk with Vivienne. See, she's a superstar arty filmmaker with a fierce stomp and it was like everyone else was intimidated. Strong presence is family to me and I didn't know she was practically a movie star how famous she was, so it was only natural that Vivienne became a good buddy super quick. Didn't hurt any when she said Rob was a complicated mess of a boy. I kept buying Viv drinks just to hear stories about how problematic Rob had always been. She huffed and puffed and blew Rob's persona down.

Lord, I swear that night was at least half of a lifetime, how much changed. That was also the night I met Amy and we started some sort of halfhearted fling. It was all drinking and necking and boring at the bar and at the Airstream trailer she pretended to slum in. Her trailer park days were a joke, really. I mean, her 1948 WeeWind sixteen-foot trailer was in mint condition, like it belonged in the entryway of the Smithsonian right under the American flag from the Civil War. Turned out Amy was the type of stripper who could afford to travel first class to London and Manhattan on a regular basis. Basically her trust fund allowed her all kinds of play, but the play she liked most was pretending she was blue collar. Kind of Marie Antoinette in her milking maid regalia frolicking in that little playground of a faux village the king built for her and her friends. Add to my annoyance with Amy, she had a tendency to talk about this one other rich girl she played tennis with more often than I could stand hearing about, but whatever. Amy was a mighty fine kisser and we sort of hung out at the bar and at her place for a short while.

Yes, I started learning Crystal's better than I knew my own face. I'm going to nip your thought in the bud. No, I am *not* a bar girl. Allow me to elaborate. Get ready. I'm short, five feet two inches without my boots, and, damn right, I dig what elevator shoes made out of soapboxes do for my stature.

Let's start simple, what other spot in L.A. besides Crystal's could I land in to be around like-minded dykes? Sure, I could have gone to the Trader Joe's down the street from Crystal's, there were always plenty of dykes there. But, you know, I don't think grocers like it when patrons sit themselves down in a corner to kick and offer each other social networking. The problem of having nowhere else but Crystal's to go to is pretty basic at its core—boys own the fucking world.

As bundles of dykes spend our lives selling four quarters for a dollar, getting headaches from trying to bust past bulletproof plastic ceilings, disproportionate bunches of straight and queer boys alike with wads of disposable income buy the fucking universe.

Boys own most of the stores I shop at for food. Boys own the newspapers I read. Boys own the coffee I drink. In fact, the only girl-owned coffeehouse in town, way far far far away in Dorothy's West Side Boy Town, closed down because the collective boys were able to pay higher rent on the space than the owner and a handful of girlfriends were able to. What for years was a dyke coffeehouse in Boy Town turned into a picture-framing place owned by boys who frame boy art to be displayed in queer boy houses. Sure, we made fun of the seventies crunchy granola ambience of that lesbiana Georgia O'Keeffe–worshipping java joint, but still, we supported it and it employed some of us and a few girl bands played there the rare Tuesday night. You know, it might not have been perfect, but it was ours.

So, winding road to tell you what I'll now say simple, I was a regular at Crystal's because it was the only kick space in all of Los Angeles owned by a dyke and nearly exclusively frequented by dykes. Besides, I was particularly fond of places with blinking bright light Vegas-style signs out front. Crystal's was a blessed comfort zone.

At the pink house, Nana scolded quiet and hurt that I didn't spend enough time with her. What, didn't I remember where home was anymore?

I was certain I was just beginning to realize.

Nol helped me find a place in Silverlake, not too far from where she lived. My new home was an old apartment building single, a micro room with a bathroom attached at one end and a kitchenette at the other. I promised Nana I'd visit *very* often, gave her a million hugs to stifle her protests, filled four crates from the store's storage room with clothes, my pearl choker, a couple of photo albums, and my toothbrush. After I'd packed my car, Nana handed me her old shoe polish box filled with shine and neatly folded rags. Right then I knew I had her blessing to step on. I moved out of the pink house yet again.

I'll be honest, my apartment was beyond dreary. The only furniture I had was a twin mattress and telephone I bought secondhand, one antique 7UP wood crate, and three plastic milk crates. I felt pangs of homesick most every day, but I was confident in an inarticulate way that the move was what I needed to do. I comforted myself knowing I wasn't too far from where Nolan lived, Crystal's was just a skip away, mariachi music blared out my neighbor's windows, and Nana was within easy day-trip visiting distance.

My guilt wasn't soothed by the last of the aforementioned comforts. The early June sizzle hot sun down and the evening air calm, I could practically hear Nana thinking about how I had abandoned her and the home she had given me. One especially conflicted and lonely night I unpacked my pearl choker and clasped it onto my princess neck. Weeping laced her stinging hands around my wrists and bound me to my new home.

After a few weeks in Los Angeles, Weeping's dry winds began to rattle my apartment windows at night with ferocity more intense than I had ever experienced before. There were plenty of evenings when the dancing windowpanes would make me anxious with the knowledge that Weeping was nearby. Damn, that woman filled me with anticipation that was almost overwhelming. It was all too confusing. To avoid the contemplation that brought on my nervous-girl-in-waiting nosebleeds, I'd walk the couple of blocks down to Crystal's.

Rubbing so close to so many tangled lives made me feel young and overexposed and in need of a corduroy jacket with suede patches on the elbows. But really, corduroy just wasn't my style. I wore my pearl choker whenever I left the apartment, especially if I was going to Crystal's. Crystal's, that's where I was when, a year after I'd settled into L.A., a very red-faced Nolan left a frantic Edith at home and came searching for me.

5

ome on, Leticia, just say it, I look dangerously handsome tonight, don't I?"

Nol was wearing a wool pea coat, matching navy blue knit cap, and thick scarf. It was a late June simmering hot evening. I don't know how to play cards. Good thing I don't want to learn. I don't have a poker face.

"You look feverish, Nolan. Like you have the flu or something. You should let your better half dress you." I looked out toward the front door but didn't see Edith's giraffe poise and sleek ponytails.

"Better half? Watch it."

It wasn't the reference to her being the worse of the two that bothered her, and I followed lead. "Nolan, you know you and Ms. Edith are little old marrieds."

"Leti . . ."

"Nol, it's been like what, half a year, since you got together? I'm glad you two are happy. Sure as hell Edie and I weren't meant to be a couple, you know?"

"Yeah, you were even more insane together than you are apart."

"Why thank you. So, do tell, what's the occasion for your visit? It's rare these days for us guests here at the Crystal establishment to have the pleasure of your company during the week, married lady."

"Enough with the married stuff . . . you know Edie and I have an open relationship."

"Right, but you live together and you don't date other people—you're married."

Nolan continued in an almost chanting flat voice, "My relationship with Edith is currently a monogamous one, but the terms of our being together allow for us to explore other opportunities if they arise, so long as we remain honest with one another."

"I remember that contract. Did Edie make you hold your hand over your heart when you signed it?"

"Shit, Leti, stop already."

"Sorry."

Nol breathed deep. "I came by because Edith and I wanted to know if you're working tomorrow."

"Nope, Beatrice said I could have the weekend off. Why?"

"Edith is at home calling people to invite them to our Easter party. We called you at your place but your machine picked up. We called Bea's shop and she said you'd already left for the day. And Amy said you weren't at the trailer, so we figured you'd probably be here."

"Easter? It's almost July, Nolan. And don't call Amy's looking for me."

"I thought you two were hanging out again."

"It isn't the sort of thing where you call the trailer and ask if I'm there."

"Well then, what sort of thing is it? I mean, seems like you two are hanging all over each other like back when you first moved into town. How was I supposed to know I shouldn't call her place looking for you?"

"Nolan, come on, it's not like Amy and I are, ever were, or ever will be girlfriends. She doesn't keep tabs on me. I don't keep tabs on her. And, besides, she's still very attached to her bad habit of playing tennis with Malibu Barbie. I'm over it." I took a drink and remembered another important point. "She snores. I can't stand sleeping next to someone who snores."

"I'll make note of that. Anyway, we were thinking of having a valentine-making party but we thought that might be too strange, so we figured we'd have an Easter party instead."

"In July?"

"Yes, in July. So are you going to come?"

"A Valentine's party wouldn't be 'strange' exactly. Maybe Edie could hand out little bows and arrows to each guest if they promise to shoot me before having hors d'oeuvres." Nol gave me a cautionary stare. "Ah, come on, Edith would get a kick out of the idea."

"Like I was saying, princess," Nol smiled at my pearl choker, "Edith and I are having an *Easter* party. Look, are you going to come?" Nolan finally took off her jacket, sat down beside me, and stared ugly at my glass.

"Jesus, Leti, why are you drinking that?"

"Shirley Temple? You get a plastic monkey if you order a Shirley Temple."

She signaled Crystal over and ordered a kamikaze with a plastic monkey. She put her monkey to play with mine on my bar napkin.

"So, listen, Edith invited this yum dish she says has been coming to Foxy's on her shifts."

I played with the green monkey in my drink, "That doesn't tell me a lot, Nolan. Every hipster and peep-show connoisseur from here to Highland has been to Foxy's on

Edith's shifts at one point or another."

"The person I'm talking about shows up with Vivienne."

It was time to take notice. Vivienne. Viv-viva-Vivienne.

"Vivienne as in filmmaker, knock-your-pants-off, growl, whole lotta dagger, what-a-woman Vivienne?"

"Do you ever stop?"

"Nope."

"What other Vivienne would I mean? And look, I know for a fact that the person Edie invited is single. She lives upstairs from Viv. From what I've heard, I swear I'd snag the girl myself if Edie wouldn't kill me."

"Wait, if you and Edith are 'open to other opportunities if they present themselves,' why should your not-wife care if you hooked up with Vivienne's neighbor?"

"Because we think *you* would look hot fucking Vivienne's friend."

"Quit being gross, Nolan."

"You started it."

I took Nolan's monkey and hooked it onto my monkey's tail.

"Come on, even Viv thinks you should meet her neighbor. You and Vivienne have similar taste, right? I mean you've had at least that one ex, what's her name . . ."

"Rob."

"Right, you and Viv have Rob in common, right?"

"And that ugly coincidence is meant to motivate me into a blind date? Besides, these days Viv hangs with super-femmes—I don't think I could deal with claw marks on my back. Too 'Edie' if you know what I mean."

"Again, watch it. All I'm saying is that Vivienne is friends with this person and Edith thinks the person's cool . . . and when you're not such indifferent royalty, you respect Viv and Edie's opinions. Chances are you'll dig Vivienne's friend, right?"

"I learned about that in school, Nol. It's called circular logic and it makes for a really weak argument."

"Leti, you are a pain."

"Yeah, whatever, you like us complicated. So, tell me, have I seen mystery girl in here?"

"Hello, haven't I been telling you that you two have to meet?"

I asked slow and with more volume, "Have I seen her in here before?"

"No. I don't think she's been here before."

"Is she new in town?"

"No."

"Great, she just realized yesterday that she likes girls, right?"

"Some people just don't hang out at bars, Leticia. She's probably just busy being a grown-up and—"

The tail almost broke as I snapped her monkey off mine and dropped it in her drink, the sass in Nolan's voice was no longer amusing.

"Take off your hat, Nol, you look ridiculous wearing it inside."

"I didn't mean it like that. I'm not talking trash on your job, all right? Everyone knows you're smart. You don't have to prove anything with me, Leti. I mean, jeez, you graduated summa cum laude. That and you've read more film theory than I ever want to poke with a stick."

"Yeah, I can watch movies with the best of them."

"Shit, Leti, quit it. Besides, making those stupid little dogs look as good as you do at Bea's is an art form as far as I care. Look, all I meant was that your blind date is just doing what she does and it doesn't include this bar. That's all. She's content, smart, and cute to boot. Just like you."

"Quit flirting at me, Edith wouldn't like it."

"Yes she would."

"You'll get us killed."

Crystal was listening in and handed me a small cup of maraschino cherries.

"Don't joke, I wouldn't put it past Edie, she's a total nut, a smart and strong one. God, I love that girl."

Nolan held her head in her hands. I smiled and popped a cherry in my mouth.

"Nol, can you tie the stems into a knot?" I pushed the filled cup toward her.

"Very mid-nineties *Bar Girls*, Leti." She pushed the cup back to me.

"Tell me, what does this person do, being so responsible with her career and all?"

"You'll find out tomorrow."

"What's her name? You didn't tell me her name."

"K."

"K? What else? That's not her name."

"I don't know, Edith introduced her as K and I didn't feel like saying, 'Huh, that's your name, nuh-uh, what is it really?' "

"K? That's so pretentious."

"No it's not, you'll see. So, will you come to the party?"

"I'll be there."

Nolan told me to be at her place around noon the next day and hugged me good night.

A wandering neighborhood dog followed me from my parked car. Rabid dogs were the norm in my neighborhood, but not up in the hills under the Hollywood sign where Nol lived, so when the barking dog started running behind me, the 99-cent store plastic flowers with permanent gel dew-drops that I'd brought for Edie almost jumped out of my hands. I threw open the little white picket fence fast with the weight of my body and stumbled onto the path leading to Ms. Edith and Nolan's guesthouse cottage. Edith came over to me all gliding smooth and gave me a kiss on the cheek like you wished the girl you had a crush on in junior high would do at the soda machine. My voice cracked when I told her the flowers were for her. She smiled and smoothed my hair and I got tripped up as hopeless uncomfortable as if my baby-sitter was flirting with me. She took my hand to show me the bunny.

It took up nearly the entire picnic table set up at the side of the micro guesthouse she and Nolan shared. A huge mass of purple Jell-O molded into a crouching rabbit with red gumdrop eyes sat on a tinfoil blanket.

"I made it myself. Be honest, what do you think?"

"You are unreal, Bird. Absolutely unreal."

She gave me another kiss on the cheek, left the scent of lilacs to torture me, and wandered away to mingle.

Right then Amy showed up with tennis girl and a hickey. I would have loved to stick my tongue out at that catty tennis girl in her gray Prada uniform dress as she eyeballed my brown kneesocks and threadbare black 1940s housedress that I liked all ratty and old. But I refused her the pleasure of seeing me lose my cool. Instead I smiled and princess-waved at Amy. I think her tennis girl especially liked the pretty green Band-Aid accessory on my knee. She had prickly eyes I figured would melt away if I poured water on her. Both of them annoyed me. At least Amy was a good kisser. Somehow I knew tennis girl wasn't even the type to kiss, she was the type to be kissed and that annoyed me no end. Amy said hello but didn't really care about me until an hour later.

Candy heaven. Tall, dark, and handsome, K showed up. Nolan introduced us.

"K, I'd like you to meet Leticia, she works at the dog-grooming place over on Hyperion."

And I called Nol my best friend? What the hell kind of introduction was that? I had some quick work to do. Batter batter swing batter, I started up, zooming the words out of my mouth.

"Yeah, I've been working there for a couple of years now. I wasn't ever allowed any pets when I was growing up and I love to play beauty salon on all the queer hill boys' little royalty dogs, I even paint and glue doodads on some of the poodles' nails."

I kind of laugh-breathed, "It's not as if I had any experience grooming dogs. I mean I just went into Beatrice's Poodle Primp on a fluke one time after I was at Trader Joe's, you know Bea's shop is right next to the dyke Trader Joe's. Funny, isn't it, 'dyke Trader Joe's,' but that *is* the one place in this town you can always count on seeing some girls. Well, that and the Home Depot down on Sunset, at least one or two cute dykes there 24/7. But, like I was saying, I just walked into Bea's store and asked if she was looking to hire. She put down her Parliament, I swear that woman is always smoking one of those, and asked me if I had any experience. I didn't lie, I said no, and she said good because she didn't like kids who think they know everything. Then she winked at me. She's probably about seventy but she sure loves to flirt it up. Anyway, I'd just gotten my degree in film studies from the university and I'd worked so hard during school that I really wanted to do something that would be completely different, though studying was pretty easy and I enjoyed it, but I just wanted something different, I mean, what could I do in my field of study really except work at a video store or go to grad school."

Nol's eyes were all bugged out, looking like she might have to throw me down to the ground if I didn't shut up. If K hadn't been smiling and if I hadn't already been enjoying the head rush from falling head over heels, I would have spun upright to kick Nolan for prompting my knee-jerk rambling. Slow and calm, K reached out to shake my hand.

"It's very nice to meet you. Your pearls are quite striking, Leticia."

Yeah, what she said was hokey, but, damn, I was a sucker for a good line. And help me if I didn't blush even harder when her deep boy voice pronounced my name smooth perfect right.

Edith came over and K gave her a kiss on the cheek. That was a first. Edith kisses, not the other way around. Edie placed her hand all delicate ballerina prim on my shoulder.

"Did you see the darling little bunny, K dear?"

"Yes, Edith, I did." K smiled but didn't say anything more.

Edith sent Nolan to get us drinks, winked at K, and walked off to play hostess. Nolan brought us bright red Shirley Temples and, laughing as she walked away, said, "Happy Valentine's Day."

Happy Valentine's Day indeed. Oh lord, K was making me dizzy with how hot she was in her grungy androgy-boy way. She could flirt with the best of them. Did I mention charming? Ay, that four-hundred-watt smile when she laughed that laugh that was never forced. She had a deep scar stretching taut above her left eye and at her chin and I wanted to touch that smooth skin something bad.

Amy and tennis girl came over and stood too close to us. After they scooped part of the Jello-O bunny's jiggle head onto their plates and sat next to us, K suggested we go inside the house for a while to change landscape while we talked.

K kept her sunglasses on when we sat down on Nol's bed. At one point she pulled out of her baggy front jeans pocket an old yellow and red tin Kodak film canister. I watched as she unscrewed the lid and poured a small mountain of pills into her hand. She chose three—one red, one blue, one white—popped them into her mouth, and washed them down with a swig of beer.

Kind of mellow and damn cute. Good crush material, maybe some sex, but wáchale, girl, keep your emotions down, she's probably no good for long-term. My god, how many drugs does she do? No wonder I've never seen her out, she's probably doped up on her couch most of the time. I wondered how I could get her to take her sunglasses off so I could see if her pupils were dilated. That and if she had little stars in them like I knew mine did.

I started to feel shy. Sure, we were sitting on Nol and Edith's huge queen-size bed, but only because it practically took up the entire cottage. There we were, innocent enough, just talking, and my nerve was being strange. I mean usually I'd take the moment as an opportunity to at least kiss the girl, but I was feeling all out of breath and practically wished I could pull the blankets up around me and hide. K wasn't saying anything, she was just looking at me and smiling. I could barely stand the silence and the way I was sure she must be able to hear the blood rushing through my body, making me warm and almost too hot. What the hell was wrong with me?

"So, that Jell-O bunny sure is amazing, don't you think?"

My desperate attempt at conversation embarrassed me the second I heard my own voice. Seriously, what the hell was wrong with me?

K took her sunglasses off and, sly girl, had to rub up against my side as she took off her jacket. "Yes, the bunny is amazing."

"So, why didn't you tell Edith that you like it?"

"She knows I love it." K looked down at her lap, slid the glasses into her jacket pocket, and laughed quiet as she put the bundle aside.

"What's so funny?"

"Oh, nothing."

"Come on, tell me."

"Well," she looked out the window to the picnic table, "it's just funny, that's all."

"What's funny?" I was getting annoyed.

"My name, the Jell-O rabbit, all of it."

"I must be missing something, I don't get what is so funny about all of that combined." I was half ready to force myself out of my crush. Our conversation was driving me nuts.

"Nol and Edie didn't tell you my name? I mean, my real name?"

"What, it's not K?"

She laughed, "No, it's Berenike, I was named after my great-grandmother, my grandma's mother on my father's side. Having my name is probably no big deal in Greece, but growing up here it was nickname nightmare—Bernie, Ronnie, the worst was Veronica. For whatever reason, K stuck."

"I'm sorry, I'm still missing something. I don't get it."

"*Bunny*. Bunny is a nickname for Berenike."

It started raining outside. Completely strange for July. I've heard that on the East Coast there are thunderstorms in the summer, but in the desert it was plain weird. I don't think it was even humid out, but, boom, it was thundering and pouring in what just minutes before had been a solid hot blue sky. To say that the party was caught off guard, like chaos or something tragic ensued from the sudden change in weather, would be an exaggeration, but it was pretty amusing to watch everyone's reactions. Amy's tennis Barbie didn't melt, but what was left of the Jell-O sculpture started to. Edie was howling screechy and Nol rushed around, calming her down and dragging the bunny in with Amy's help. Everyone came inside and we were crammed up against each other all soggy like jarred peaches. The way we had to squeeze together to make room for our sudden company, K was practically sitting in my lap. As tall K sat near me and I talked to her long neck, damp warm air fogged the windows. I smelled clover and spice and warm tingle.

"K, I know this sounds like a lame pickup, but is that Old Spice you're wearing?"

"Yeah," she blushed. "Did I put too much on?"

"How could a girl ever wear too much Old Spice? Please."

"No, I'm serious, did I put too much on?"

"Is this a test?"

I couldn't figure out if it was cosmic or comic the way our conversations so easily turned.

"I was nervous knowing I was going to meet you today. Edie and Viv said such great things about you. I accidentally knocked over the cologne when I was getting ready. I'm usually very careful. You have to be when you don't have a sense of smell."

"Excuse me?"

"I said, you have to be very careful when you don't have a sense of smell."

"Don't be silly, you smell great."

"No, really, I have zero sense of smell."

"Seriously?"

"Seriously."

"How come?"

"It's a long story, I'll tell you sometime."

We would have long stories together. She would tell me sometime. We had a shared "sometime" to look forward to.

And Old Spice? I could barely believe the luck of meeting a girl who wore Spice same as the neighborhood boys did back on Walnut. Whoosh, K made me dizzy pleased with her tough boy cliché.

6

Every now and then I'd stop talking, but I wasn't running over K's words. She chose what she'd say real careful like. Her precision made me cautious, as if it was necessary to consider each move I made. I was completely anxious, actually. I'd never been with someone so comfortable with her own silence before. Even though K gave me her phone number before I left the Easter party, and even though I wanted to see her again so much I ended up giving some poodles at Bea's shop frightful shave jobs during the week, I didn't call K. It was scary to think of all her quiet on the other end of the line. Seven days wiggled by before we saw each other again.

And I said, "Please, I insist, have some. Please, I want you to take more."

"I want you to have it," K said.

Back and forth that dance went on about the sweet corn cake from our shared chicken dinner plate. Back and forth until everyone else at the table was nauseous from so constantly rolling their eyes at our gaga.

We were out with a group collected from Crystal's, clinking glasses for K's birthday at the Cuban place with the good sangria down on Virgil. Edith and Nolan had organized the whole thing a couple of nights after their party, the good nurturing parental types that they are. Unfortunately, Nolan wasn't nearly as graceful at coordinating social events as Edith could be. When Nol invited me to K's birthday dinner, Amy had been standing near us. Tennis girl wasn't around that night, so Amy's big ears were hanging over every word we said. She took what she heard through eavesdropping as her invitation, wrapped an arm around my waist, and said, "Yeah, I'm going too. I'll pick you up."

Her possessiveness was the kind one generally should cuss at, but I said OK but not because I was lame and glad to have Amy's transparent affection. Like I said, I had been waiting a week to see K. I wished K would offer to pick me up for the dinner or that I could figure out how to be smooth enough to offer to pick her up, but with her quietness and my nerves those two options just weren't happening. So I said OK to Amy's offer of a ride because I wanted sangria and I didn't want to have to drive so I could drink buckets full of the fruity stuff if I wanted. Amy made me itchy but otherwise she was a free taxi ride to the place where I'd get to see K.

The next night Amy picked me up, late, that passive-aggressive skunk, and we went to Edith and Nolan's to meet up before dinner. Ms. Edith provided enough green-bottled import beer to stock a queer boy's Wall Street party, but I didn't have any. Even though the sun had started to fade, it was hot and all I really wanted was sangria with lots of cold sweet chunks to sink my teeth into and gnaw on. Well, that and I really wanted for Amy to quit trying to pinch my ass whenever I'd get up from where we all sat on the bed. Amy's rude boy attempt at publicly

71

pissing on me like I was her favorite fire hydrant was old before it began. When we were about to drive the four blocks to the restaurant, Edith looked at me and asked, "Would any of you darlings mind giving our tipsy birthday girl a lift to the restaurant?"

She opened her cigarette case, loaded her cigarette holder, and stared her fire brown eyes directly at me. I lit Edith's cigarette for her like I'd done countless times before, snatched a cigarette from her silver case, tucked it behind my ear all James Dean, and unhooked the keys from K's jeans belt loop. I grabbed K's hand and pulled her toward the door and she smiled at me slow melted liquidy.

"I like you, you know that, Bunny?"

Maple syrup smile response.

We left the cottage with that smile deflecting the nasty razor vibes Amy threw our way.

We walked halfway down the block and K said, "Here we are."

I started laughing nervous tweak snort. Parked in front of me was the biggest cowboy truck I'd ever seen. I don't know how many tons. Just big. Like you could fill the back with water and have a swimming pool, an Olympic competition swimming pool . . . big, got it? I just about died. I really didn't even have that much experience driving, especially not some huge-as-a-house truck. As a college graduation gift, Nana had bought an old Pinto from a junkyard, and my cousin Jimmy and his mechanic friends fixed it up for me. That rusted little old reliable was what I was used to driving. And there I was, standing in front of K's monster cowboy truck, and I had to drive. K smiled wild and winked at me.

I figured for sure that the girl must be crazy when she let me maneuver her vehicle through the hilly streets barely wide enough for its hips. I hitched my skirt high and had Edie's cigarette hanging from my lips during it all because the "smoke 'em if you got 'em" posture was taking me over more with each passing second. Quick, I gained confidence in that truck. By the time we got to the restaurant, it was like I thought I was the Marlboro Man herself. I parallel-parked the truck in a spot near the patio and declared myself god as I opened K's door and offered my hand to her.

Everyone else was seated with drinks in their hands when we walked in. The marrieds had saved us seats between them, so K sat next to Edie and I sat between K and Nolan. Nol gave me a smirk like she figured K and I'd had our own little party already.

"What took you two so long? It was only four blocks," Nolan didn't really want an answer, but she was having a good time ribbing me with her elbow.

"She let me drive her truck," I whispered to Nol, and tried not to grin, though the muscles in my face wouldn't obey.

All throughout dinner K squeezed my knee to emphasize points, to respond to jokes I told, and to get my attention, as if she didn't already have that. Shiver. Tingle metal jingle up my neck made me smile. K poured me sangria and drank lots of water herself, "So I can drive you home if you'd like." I liked. We bickered sweet over who should be given the corn cake. When it was time to leave and K pulled my chair out for me, Amy "accidentally" kicked her boot at my shin under the table.

As a group we stood around on the sidewalk outside the restaurant. Smoking cigarettes and most of us standing wobbly from sangria. Nolan gave Amy a piggyback ride to the corner and back and almost dropped her in the gutter. Almost, but not good enough. Cars honked as they drove by.

"They must think we're cute," Nolan said, even though we all knew it was mostly thick-necked straight boys honking like the bunch of us were a freak show display.

Whatever. We were cute. And we all knew it too.

Hugs. Hugs. I swear it took us half an hour for everyone to hug good night. Why do dykes hug goodbye for so damned long? Hugs. Amy followed her hug to me with an extra hard slap on my back, kind of a "good ol' buddy" slap, but way more residual sting than that. Amy was playing mean like my boy cousins did when we were single-digit age. And right then, right then my girl Weeping came to say hello. She brought with her a bouquet of polluted murky air from near the curb. Air thick with car exhaust burned my eyes same as it had when my boy cousins played rude at me on Walnut Street.

Too many teeth still missing to hang with the grown-up mural boys, my rinka dink stink young boy cousins would always stop by the store on school nights before dinner. They knew the adults would be inside the house fixing food. And me, they knew I'd be alone behind the counter with a book to read. My peewee boy cousins threatened me into giving them sodas for free even though they knew their mothers had said they weren't supposed to have any at all. Gulping down grape Fantas, the glass bottle going click click click against their teeth because they were so sloppy. I'd watch them get messy down their chins with the amethyst sugar water.

"Ah, come on, rich witch girl cousin, we need more soda. Give us more."

If they said please real nice, altar-boy super-precious polite, sometimes I'd let them have another round.

They didn't intimidate me. I liked them coming around to sneak sodas. Considering the way the family adults wove my days in the store protective tight with manners and work, I enjoyed my boy cousins' rude visits.

Ernesta, my only girl cousin, sometimes she'd come by with the boys. She was the coolest of the group, twelve and real pretty with a little mole next to her eye and her front teeth crooked overlap. I always wanted to impress her some. She said she wanted to grow up to be a nurse, I could see her taking good care of people that way. I didn't know what people needed to become nurses, but I decided I was going to help her out. I even stole the doctor's-office-looking information booklets from the tampon boxes we sold in the store for her. Stowed them away in my little red rectangle vinyl purse and presented them as a gift in exchange for a looky-loo at her in her communion dress. Her mamá had hid the dress away the day it came back from the cleaners, and since my side of the family wasn't Catholic, I hadn't been allowed to go to Ernesta's communion. Money was tight so I knew that even when she got the portraits back, she wouldn't be allowed to give me one, not even a wallet-size. Basically I was dying to see my girl cousin in her dress, so she found the box of white sateen under her mother's bed and put it on for me. She was the most beautiful sight I'd ever seen. I told her so that day. She started coming to the store with the boys after that.

But then, a few months later, Ernesta's mother found the tampon booklets with their line picture diagrams of what she said was nasty dirty. Mamá and Nana Lupe stood up for me and said there was nothing nasty about a woman's body, insides or out. Still, my girl cousin Ernesta wasn't allowed to come to the store anymore. It was her I really wanted to visit, not her brother Jimmy and the other boy cousins.

See, when Jimmy was around the others, he was creepy rude to me. If it was just the two of us alone, he could be all right. Like the one summer that a bee in the plastic pool out front his house stung me, that summer Jimmy taught me how to swing a punch way back from where my arm meets my shoulder. He kept telling me to prove that I'd learned how to punch, to do it right then and pop him one if I even knew how to. He's lucky his pretty face looked so much like Ernesta's. I never hit him once. I told him to quit teasing me or he'd have to be my boyfriend. He laughed when I told him he had to kiss me. I kissed him, you know. Right after he laughed, I kissed him.

But seeing him with the other boys, I knew I didn't want him as a boyfriend no more. All of them boys and their sticky bellies pushing out from under their soda-pop-stained *Incredible Hulk* and *Dukes of Hazzard* shirts, they'd dare me to ditch my sweeping and stocking and meet them outside. And I had no choice. If I stayed in the store they would have called me a puss, the lowest of insults that could be thrown without receiving a slap across the face from somebody's eavesdropping aunt or old lady neighbor. Tiptoeing to not be heard by my family inside the house, I made my way through the store's red swinging doors. Out the front of the prefab stucco box and to the gravel parking area at its right. There they were. Standing in a line. Shoulder to shoulder. All staring at me.

"We're gonna have a pissing contest, girl cousin. You have to play."

I stepped into line next to Jimmy, the youngest and littlest of the boys.

Pushed my pale pink panties down to ankles. Stepped feet as far apart as possible. Lifted yellow taffeta skirt above belly button. The boys paid me no attention as they tugged their elastic-waist bell-bottom pants below their hairless little pistols. We pointed ourselves toward the side of the store. Pelvises thrust as far forward as possible without stepping out of line, we tagged the wall in front of us with all we had.

Them full of free soda. Me nearly empty from the start. A pathetic puddle formed threateningly close to the underwear around my ankles.

Practicing machos that they were, they each shook what they called their manhood once or twice before pulling their pants back up. Chests puffed and thumbs hooked in front pockets, gangster-proud expressions they copied from their older brothers, they looked at my little girl puddle and I felt my face start to flame up embarrassed. I yanked up my hanky spank cotton undies and ran quick back past the store's front door.

Almost unable to hear them through the blood pound rush in my ears, I pinched my arm hard to stay strong like Ernesta had taught me so I wouldn't cry as the boys hooted and hollered. Outside, my boy cousins slapped each other on the backs, congratulating themselves. They shouted thanks to god for not being born girls.

Amy would have fit right in with my boy cousins. The spot between my shoulder blades where she had slapped my back flat-handed stung. I smiled extra to deny her the pleasure of my pain.

Once everyone else had driven away, I told K I wanted to give her a birthday treat. We drove to the store to get supplies.

It was too early in the year to find any strawberries, so we bought bananas and whipped cream at the twenty-four-hour supermarket with the sticky linoleum. Paper bags brimming with props in tow, we tiptoed into my apartment. K sat on my bed. I stood at the kitchen counter.

I knew that if I charmed the food, K would be mine. And if I really flowed magic something fierce, it wouldn't be superficial "the path to the heart" stuff, it would be as deep and true as any old country curandera spell could be. I whipped up our faux strawberry shortcakes with as much cariño as I had in me, breathing deep and sending bliss into the food through my fingertips. K smiled the entire time she ate. Her sexy scar pulled taut, taunting me with its lovely smooth. She blushed. That was when I was sure that the goods had kicked in.

We sat on my twin bed eating our dessert, trying to balance cups of Earl Grey and not crash knees on the miniature cushion that her tall lanky frame nearly filled. With her second cup of tea, K swallowed a small pile of pills she poured out from her Kodak container. I tried to play it off casual and asked what they were. I mean, if they were innocent enough maybe I'd try one, but mostly I wanted to know exactly what K's trip was.

Turns out the pills were homeopathic decongestants, painkillers for cramps, and this stuff that she said helped her digest dairy. I found it almost scarier to realize that instead of being a junkie, K had a crunchy streak. Her potential alley-cat drug habit had been the only thing keeping me from forming a ridiculously serious crush. The steam from our tea fogged the mini-room and I was surrounded by little clouds of bergamot and Old Spice. I was doomed.

Whispering tired and eyes beginning to drag, until late in the night we looked at the photo albums I'd taken from the pink house when I'd moved. The next day Nolan had a good laugh when I told her about my dessert date.

"You didn't actually sit on the bed and show her your photo albums all night, did you?"

I didn't know what else to do. Words weren't coming easily with K nearby. Like I said, her silence was something intense for me. That night I stayed pretty quiet with her, tasting how settled calm she was without words. I usually exhaled talk, but that night I was worried to lose K in my stories. I liked my loop narration with so many screaming points a person could barely know what was most important to pay attention to, but K's quiet was speaking loud that night and I knew it was important to listen. Flipping pages and saying, "Oh, you don't want to see that one. Isn't my fifth-grade school picture a crack-up? Yes, that's Nana," was all I wanted to do. I held the blue-satin-covered photo albums in my lap so she could see the pages and I turned the glossy and matte and white-bordered photographs pasted on black pages when it was time. Having the photo albums to hold on to kept my hands from shaking nervously. K wanted to drink in each page's details for longer than the one before. The third blue satin book was not opened past halfway when morning stepped into the wings, readying its entrance. K asked if I would walk with her out to her truck.

I wanted her in my bed. Or up against the kitchen counter. Anywhere, but I didn't want her to leave. I wanted to know more than I already did. I wanted to touch her, to have her linger in taste until it was morning again. I wanted to understand her everything right then. At the same time I knew that the quiet would be too much for me if I didn't have a chance to be away from it. I wondered what K would think when she learned I talk in my sleep.

I walked with K down to the building's front door and I opened it for her. She said good night extra soft and slow and walked down the front steps toward her truck.

She didn't give me a kiss. No hug, not even a handshake.

The shared corn cake and strawberry shortcake charm and the bound photos, including the black-and-white of me that she thought was of my boy cousin Jimmy, after all that, K didn't even touch my arm when she said goodbye.

7

She gave me directions to her place in Korea Town and I said I'd be over in half an hour. I figure it's the sort of thing someone shouldn't admit to, but I was sniffing my favorite bright orange City of Orange Towing Company little boy tee-shirt, trying to figure out if I could safely wear it another day, when the phone rang again. Embarrassed that maybe K would know what I was doing even though she was only on the phone, not climbing in the window, I threw the shirt back in the hamper and ran to the phone. I picked up the receiver, took a deep breath, and said hello in a smooth voice a notch lower than my natural pitch.

"Ay, my baby, exactly how did you get a cold in summertime?"

"Ahhh, no, Nana," I cleared my throat, "I just swallowed water the wrong way."

"Don't go gulping your drinks like you always do, then you won't swallow wrong. So, Leticia . . . I've been wondering how you are."

"Nana, I'm doing very well, thank you." I took another deep breath, got brave, and used my most polite family voice. "Nana, may I please call you back tomorrow, I'm so sorry, it's just that I was running out the door to meet a friend for brunch."

"Brunch? Since when do you have brunch?"

"It's just that a friend invited me over for breakfast."

"Well, why don't you call it that then? What's their name?"

"Her name is—"

"Wait, is Josefina back home from the Philippines? Yes, that's just like her to make you a special 'brunch' breakfast. Josefinita is always so considerate, she still sends me Christmas cards each year, you know. When you see my Josefina, tell her I say hello and give her familia a special hello from me . . ."

"Nana, I'm not meeting Joey. I'm going over to my friend K's."

"K? Like the letter? Leti, why do so many of your friends have such strange names?"

"Nana, I promise, I'll call tomorrow. I love you."

"Of course you do. I love you too. Say hello to your friend, ésa K, for me."

Dial tone. As fast as I could, I brushed my teeth with the expensive fennel toothpaste. A clean bowling alley shirt buttoned up, my pearl choker snapped into place, I smoothed my hair so perfect sexy that Barbara Stanwyck's character in *Double Indemnity* would have been catfight jealous if she saw me. You know that scene in the grocery store, I can't remember if they've already murdered her husband or not, but she's so composed calm and she has her movie star sunglasses tucked strange into her crazy stiff blond wig? Well, I looked that tasty but a touch of punk and, dare I say it, even fucking hotter. I drove over to K's place north of old

81

Wilshire Boulevard's Miracle Mile. She met me at her building's thick iron security gate and I smiled electric like the telephone lines overhead.

There were three chairs at the kitchen table. Two were red and one was yellow. I sat in one of the red ones. I offered if I could help get the food together. K said no thank you and handed me a shoe box full of photos to look through while she fluffed a bowl of whipped topping with a fork.

"Hope you don't mind Cool Whip. Don't laugh, but I actually like it," her deep voice said.

Lord, the crush was hitting deep.

The photographs she had given me to look at slid from the box to my hands to the box again. There was one of her as a toddler sitting in a romper suit with a Raggedy Ann doll propped up against her side, her long taper hands were so fat and dimpled back then. And there were Polaroids of when she was high school age, posing tough with a group of boys her age in front of a tagger mural outside a train station.

The photo practically radiated with the mural's industrial oranges, reds, and blues, colors way brighter than the shades of plum, gray, and sailor blue that wallpapered the store's exterior when I was growing up. The photo's train station hip-hop mural and tags were a completely different flavor from the Gothic romantic sprays the grown-up gangster boys in my neighborhood threw down when I was little. But the proud swagger standing in front of the work was universal. A spray can tucked bulging in her oversized front pants pocket, the photographed teenage K wore her hip-hop khaki baggies slung low on her narrow skinny hips. Two oversized shirts and her smug stance made her as boy as the buddies she stood by.

"You didn't tell me you used to date tagger boys."

She stopped fixing our food.

"Exactly who do you think painted that mural?"

It dawned on me that the colors in her apartment were the same as the ones in the mural. Stoplight red and canary yellow chairs wagged their fingers at me and the cobalt blue plates she fixed the shortcakes on told me to open my eyes. The hot of embarrassment cooled into warm enticement.

I stared at the tags.

"My apologies. So, what was your tag?"

She came over and looked at the photograph over my shoulder. She pointed out the techno-burst safety orange spray name closest to the mural, "Casper."

"Casper? You're not exactly Swiss Miss," I said, staring at her dark curl thick hair, her yellow olive skin, and gypsy green eyes. "The only Casper I ever knew growing up was a Mexican blonde, you know?"

"What can I say, the next palest guy in my crew was coffee with barely a drop of milk Puerto Rican. Compared to that I was practically see-through white. They wanted to call me Blondie. Casper was a compromise."

"Why didn't they just call you Bunny?"

She laughed, snorting a little at the end, "Yeah, that would have gone over very nicely. Very tough name, Bunny. Casper did me fine."

Shuffling through those photos for the tenth time, there was one image in particular that snagged me.

I squinted at the one photograph and let it hold me captive. K said that some of the bananas she was slicing for the shortcakes were bruised. I said back, "Um good, I like them that way," and tried to be subtle but found myself completely obsessed with the photo I held warm in my hand. The faded Instamatic photo was a close-up of her. She was standing side by side with one of her crew. Arms up on each other's shoulders. Chins thrust up toward the camera all come-on bad boy.

I hunched forward toward the photo. In my hands I held a time when the deep ridged scars that adorned K's face did not exist. I wanted to ask what had happened to change the baby smooth face I saw in the photograph, but when K handed me my plate with a shortcake on it, my hands burned hot like I was holding something that wasn't meant to be mine yet.

"Leticia, your eyes turn gold when you're intense like that."

"Yeah, they're hazel."

"Right now they're not hazel. They're gold. Pure gold."

"Hmm."

Fast, I returned the photo to the shoe box, put the closed box aside, and politely ate K's shortcakes.

8

"What is it with those loco hazel eyes everywhere, K?"
Down at the detailing shop where K painted murals on the sides of vans, Old Man Charlie complained that all the girls she was airbrushing were starting to look alike.

"They all look possessed or something with those eyes. Cut it out."

And the hillside queer boys who took their babies to Bea's shop, they whined that I was primping each and every one of their bejeweled poodles with identical Bunny Pink nail polish manicures.

The way my bunny K and I were with each other, with each other's ideas, with each other's bodies, with our bodies together, it wasn't limited to teasing or rough or controlling like I had grown used to. I didn't have to bottom or top or be strong or coy. It was all that and none of that and the incredible everything in between.

During our early days of being together, K left love-letter tokens in my apartment for me to stumble upon. Fabulous little things like nuts and bolts and screws from Charlie's that she had spray-painted bright K colors. She would leave those gifts under my pillow, planted in the window box peppermint, between clean undershirts, in my slippers. Let me tell you, those small expressions of her admiration made me believe I lived on an altar, like I was a diva even though only my crackle voice carried the schmaltzy tunes I suddenly found myself singing all day long.

K, she glossed my life silver and gold and all found things that are bright, shining, and perfect. She listened to the winding stories that flowed out from me. I felt certain it was safe to trust my winding talky-talky way with her silence. Being with her was so surreal intense in its pleasure that at times I wondered when a more staid reality would insist that the Technicolor set needed adjusting. My bunny K, when I kissed her toes she turned papaya lush blush.

The first time I came up for air, Nolan asked how my vortex was.

"I need to tell you . . ." I pulled up a chair at the table Nol had saved for us at Crystal's.

"Stop." Nolan held her hand up all Motown. It had been weeks since I had spent time alone with Nol. She had called and said she was going to put my face on the side of a milk carton if I didn't come to meet for a drink that same night.

"Leticia, thank me however you want," thick eyebrows jumped full of suggestion, "just do *not* get all mushy. Oh, and don't ask Edith and me for help moving when you get the U-Haul," Nolan amused herself with the joke she'd dug up stinky corpse from the dead. "Wait a minute, you and K already had your second date a long time ago. What happened, were they all out of moving trucks when you two marrieds went in to get one?"

"You're loving this, aren't you?"

"I sure am, Married Girl."

"All right, Nolan, enough. Hey, where's Edie?"

"She wanted a night by herself tonight. She's probably flooding our bathroom with lilac bubble bath. She sent me out the door demanding I send you her love. Kiss. Hug. Love. OK, done."

"Thank you, darling."

"You're quite welcome, darling. So, what's K up to? Is she going to put a hit out on me since I stole you away?"

"She sent a hello and, no, she's not going to kill you. Charlie's been keeping her busy . . . I think she was kind of happy to have some downtime alone tonight."

"Why, do you wear her out?"

I kicked her foot under the table.

"Hey, watch it, don't scuff my shoes."

"Oh, Nol, you're so cute when you're upset. My little pumpernickel doll."

"Princess, you are beyond strange."

Nol and I sat around being bratty to each other, catching up with gossip and drinking ourselves to just this side of stupid. Even though I had to work at Bea's the next day, I didn't get home until nearly three in the morning. Still, once I got in bed, I couldn't sleep. I kept thinking about K. I missed her. I fought with myself for a long while, telling myself that it'd be pathetic to call her, I mean it was practically the first night we'd been apart for months, I didn't need to call to say good night, I could just wait until the next day to say hello.

Right.

I wanted to say good night. I'd probably wake her, but she fell back asleep no big deal, so whatever.

After six rings her machine picked up.

"Hello, K . . . it's Leti. I just wanted to say good night . . . K?"

I was a freak. I mean, here it was the middle of the night, she was sleeping and I was doing some sort of Hitchcock stalker impersonation.

"All right, I just wanted to say good night. Talk with you soon." I hung up.

It must have been the alcohol, but damn, I had unbearable dreams that night. Not really nightmares per se, but definitely not restful all the same. It was more like those dreams where you think you're awake because every detail is lifelike but then something just unreal enough to question the entire reality happens, like you get hung up on a cross or something and as you're dying you look up into the sky and see that the sun is purple and then you realize it's a dream and you can end it, but you can't wake up because it's like your eyes are glued shut. Those were the kind of dreams I had all night. By the time my alarm went off, I felt more frazzled than when I'd gone to sleep.

I knew what would perk me up. I took a washcloth cat-bath, got dressed, and ran out the door. I was going to be late for work, but life was short. Besides, I was always so reliable and hardworking at Bea's shop that she said I made her and her constant cigarette breaks look bad. So if I was late, then maybe I'd be making her look extra good. See, my being late was actually going to *help* my boss and her business.

I parked my car out front of K's building. Vivienne was opening her front door as I walked up the driveway. A sexy, sleepy tough burly smile crept onto her face.

"Leticia. You beautiful woman, you've returned so soon? What did you do, go to get me a cappuccino?"

"I would have brought something even sweeter than coffee if I knew I'd see you," I did my best kitten-girl voice for

88

her. My batting-eyelash flirting was more a cover than any-thing. See, flirting hard with Viv kept me from blushing even harder in reaction to her constant to-the-point and somehow completely melt-my-knees cruising stares.

"You'll break my heart one of these days." There was a faint echo of Rob in those words, or maybe Rob had stolen Viv's words. Regardless, as it happened sometimes, I real-ized that the Rob I knew in college had probably modeled herself after Viv. Lord, that made my knees melt all the more. To think that as hot as she was, Rob had learned everything she knew from Viv. What would it be like to be with Viv?

"*You* break *my* heart each time I see you, Viv. It would only be fair for me to return the favor sometimes."

"I'm getting old, Leti. I don't know if I can take this so early in the day." Miracle be known, a slight blush tinted Viv's neck and she laughed it away. "Seriously, though, I fig-ured you two would be sleeping until at least noon after last night."

"Last night? What do you mean?"

"Oh," Viv cleared her throat and fumbled with her keys in the door, "I just mean, K got home late. I figured you were with her."

"No, I was out with Nol."

"Oh, that makes more sense. I mean, if you'd gotten home that late you wouldn't look anything as fresh and per-fect and, did I say perfect, as you do right now."

"Come on, Viv, don't stop."

She laughed, "Sorry, little girl, I'm off to my studio. More later."

I got a goodbye kiss on the cheek before she walked away.

I walked up the entryway stairs and knocked on K's door. Waited. No answer. I knocked again and waited just a beat before unlocking the door with my own key. Like always, K had slid the safety latch into place, but with my skinny wrists it was easy to reach in and unhook it.

I sneaked across the floor toward K's bedroom, avoiding the termite-eaten planks I knew creaked. K was asleep, snoring ever so slightly. I sat down on the edge of the bed and she bolted up and stared at me, eyes wide and olive drained from her skin.

"Whoa, it's just me. I'm sorry, I didn't mean to scare you. My god, you should have seen the look on your face just now."

K slumped back down into bed and rubbed her face. "Good morning, Leti. I wasn't expecting anyone, that's all."

"If you were, it wouldn't be a surprise. I tried calling last night to say good night but you didn't answer," I snuggled up to her to get a hug.

It hit me. Instinctively I checked my choker with my fingertips as I pulled away from her quick.

"What?" K sat upright again. "What's wrong?"

"Nothing." I stole a look at my fingers. Of course there were no lipstick bite marks staining them. "K, you stink like lilacs."

She rubbed her nose and coughed slightly.

"That's what's bothering you? You sure are jumpy this morning."

"Well, come on, did you swap your Old Spice for Edie's perfume or something?"

"Leti, Vivienne and I went out last night and we bumped into Edith. That's all. You know how much perfume that girl wears, even I can practically smell it. I mean, she even just looks at you and it's like you took a sauna in flowers."

"So you did go out last night? I thought you stayed home. Where'd you see Edie?"

"I was going to stay home, but then Viv invited me to go

to Foxy's with her and it's been so long since I've hung out with her that I thought it'd be fun."

"Wait, you saw Edie at Foxy's? She was working last night? Nol said Edie had the night off . . . like she was just going to chill at home."

"I don't know, maybe she had the night off at first, maybe she got called in to cover for someone. I don't know, she was there working when we got there."

"I swear, Viv is so bad. I just saw her downstairs . . . she played so innocent about getting you home late, like she didn't even go out last night, she just said she heard you get home late."

"Yeah, well, Viv was at Foxy's with me, until about eleven anyway. She gets bored quick, even with Edie flirting like crazy the whole time, especially during her cowgirl routine. She wrangled Viv with her lasso."

"Wait, I'm totally confused. So then you and Viv both came home early?"

"No, no." K rubbed her eyes to get the sleep out. "There was this guy who showed up and started bugging Edie. You know how it is there, the bouncer doesn't even wake up unless the customers touch the dancers . . ."

"Yeah?"

"So when Viv wanted to leave, Edie asked if I'd stay and kind of keep her company. She gave me a ride home after her shift ended. That's why I got in so late."

"But Viv thought I spent the night. Why?"

"She probably figured you came over or Edie and I picked you up and she dropped the both of us off here. Honey, I don't know exactly what Viv thought, but it makes sense she was confused. I mean you and I have slept in the same bed together pretty much every night for a long while now."

"True. God, I'm getting a headache from all this."

"What, you can't take a story being told all loopy and

winding like you would tell it?" K laughed.

"You think you're so funny, don't you?"

"Yes, I do."

"Lord, I just wanted to say good morning, so 'good morning.' Meet up later tonight?"

"Sounds good, I can be over at your place by five-thirty."

"Perfect, see you then." I kissed K's neck and got a fragrant poison on my lips. "That is too strange, K. I haven't kissed lilacs since my Edie Torture Days. Go take a shower, it weirds me out."

"Sorry, you know I had no idea I reeked like her perfume. I would have taken a shower if I'd known. I promise I'll take one before I come over, swear."

"Thank you, stinkalicious boy, please take a shower."

I kissed K again, ruffled her hair a little too hard, and walked out the front door.

K and I built habits together and our shared routines soon shaped our lives. We knew which apartments were which nights' sleeping spots and where we would cook breakfast on Sunday morning. Thursday nights were reserved for Scrabble marathons. And fabulous ridiculous dizzy make-out dates marked each week. The apartments' ovens cooked so many duo effort complex recipes that they began to whine. Our homes were becoming each other's. In my closet were a pair of K's work boots flecked with floated-down particles of paint from her work. I massaged and whipped polish onto those shoes over the layers of bright-hued texture when dust spoiled their shine. I bought a toothbrush and nestled it deep in the meticulous order of her apartment's medicine cabinet. The curve of her back had become part of my sleeping attire. My right arm was the trim of her blanket. Each day together we would wake to the endless pleasing variations of twenty-four hours ahead.

I loved each millisecond of it.

Nana, she was not as perfectly thrilled with the changes in my life, but she was happy for me in her own way. To occasionally avoid Nolan's teasing "you have abandoned us" phone rants, I started screening my calls. One night K and I were at my place, the phone rang and I let the machine pick up, but when I heard Nana's voice, I knew I better answer. I was supposed to call her, if she called, too much time had passed since we last spoke. K draped across the bed to take a nap and I sat down with the phone at the foot of the bed on the matted shag carpet. Nana was something serious upset in her voice.

"Here it is Thanksgiving coming up and who knows if you even remember me, let alone if you plan to give thanks for family."

"Nana, I'm sorry, I know it's been a while since—"

"It's been too long, even longer since you visited."

"I know, I've just been busy, I'm sorry."

"Everyone's busy, Leticia, that is what life is, busy. I tried calling last week, but you didn't ever pick up."

"You tried calling? But there weren't any messages."

"You know I hate those machines, I hang up before that beep says I can talk. A machine telling me I can talk, no, I don't like that."

She "tsk, tsk, tsk'd" just like Mamá used to, "I called early, I called late, I called in the middle of the day. I called your work . . ."

I breathed out audibly at hearing that and Nana's voice turned even more fire.

"What? I'm not allowed to call your work if I can't find you at home for days? Your boss, Beatrice, she was nice to talk to. She wanted to hear how I was doing. She told me you weren't working. That was three different days last week. Did you quit that job and don't want me to know? I almost called the firefighters to go see if you died in your bathtub. If you were home, you should have heard the phone."

"I'm sorry, Nana, I've just been screening my calls."

"Screening your calls? Ay, the way you talk. Just like that, you decide you'll not answer the phone when it rings? What if there had been an emergency, how could I have told you? Eh? Tell me."

"Nana, all you have to do is leave a message, even just start to leave a message, and I'll pick up if I'm home." The air was thick and my nostrils sent burning licks of flame up into the front of my skull, building a steady ache.

"What if I had died, Leticia? The hospital doesn't have time to wait for a machine to decide to record. I'd be buried before you even called home—"

"Nana, please, stop!" The words jumped out in English, hard and loud before I could stop them. "Shit," I mouthed silent to myself, and slapped the mattress at my side. K propped herself up in bed and looked at me and whispered, "Are you all right?" I nodded and stared down at the carpet. The phone was completely quiet; I couldn't even hear Nana breathing.

"Nana? Nana, I'm sorry, I'm sorry for being rude. Forgive me, please? Nana?"

"Yes, yes, I'm here. Don't raise your voice at me like that again, Leticia. It's ugly to talk like that to me."

I bit my tongue and breathed out quiet, deliberate and slow, trying to remind myself that she loved me, that she missed me, that she was only upset because she missed me.

"But look, who was it that you went to that brunch with over the summer, what was her name, May?"

"K, Nana, her name is K."

"Like the letter?"

"Yes, I told you before, like the letter."

"But that's it? That can't be her name. A mother doesn't give a child a name like that."

"Her real name is Berenike, she's named after her great-grandmother." I hoped the trivia would earn some points.

"Oh, that's better. Still, it's such a different name, but that's nice, 'Berenike,' I like that."

Thank god.

"So, tell me, are you two still friends? Is that why you never call? Where is she from? Did this Berenike friend of yours grow up in Los Angeles like our Josefina did? Have you talked with Josefina lately? You know, you should call her mother and say hello to her, I'm sure she'd like to hear from you."

"K's from Pennsylvania, Nana."

"Pennsylvania?"

"Pennsylvania."

"That's so far away. Listen, did she move out here with her family?"

"No."

"Well, where in Pennsylvania is she from? Is she one of those Dutch girls?"

"Nana," I was too stiff nervous from my previous screwup to let my guard down. I couldn't gauge if Nana was trying to make me laugh or not, so I kept my answer simple, "She's from the city, from North Philadelphia."

"North Philadelphia, all right, North Philadelphia, I've seen that on the television news. It's a big-city version of our Walnut Street. But no Mexicans, Puerto Ricans, though. Yes, maybe a little tougher, maybe a little dirtier on the sidewalks too, like that stinky Los Angeles so far away from me, but where she comes from, it's like Walnut more or less, right?"

"I'm not sure exactly, Nana. So, Nana, how have you been?"

"Fine, fine, but look, this Berenike girl, is she nice to you? Is she a good friend? Because you know what Mamá used to say."

"Yes, I know, 'Better alone than in bad company.' K is good company, Nana. She's a very nice person, you'll like her."

"Well, I guess she sounds like a good girl. Is she there right now? It's rude you've been spending such time with her and I've never even heard what she sounds like. Put her on the phone."

"K," I put my hand over the receiver, "my grandma wants to say hello."

I held the telephone out to her apologetically. She shook her head. I nodded mine. K cleared her throat and took the telephone from me.

"Hello, Señora Torrez, it's very nice to meet you."

I couldn't hear her, but I knew Nana well enough to know what she was saying. It went something like, "Yes, hello, Berenike, it is nice to say hello to you also, but you know, you need to have Leticia bring you down to Orange someday, she needs to visit, ay that girl, she doesn't visit enough, but if you two come down, that way I can meet you for real. Leticia says very nice things about you, Berenike," and Nana probably went on to confirm all the background information about K that I had just provided. Twice K said, "Yes ma'am," and once she said, "Thank you very much." She said, "Yes, I promise. Yes, you too, Señora Torrez," before she handed the telephone back to me.

"Nana?"

"Your friend Berenike doesn't talk much, does she?"

"No, Nana, not much."

"Does she have something wrong? Like a speech problem

or something? Is that why she's so quiet? Is it my English that made her not want to talk? My English works just fine, you know."

"Yes, Nana, I know, your English is perfect. K's just more quiet than we are, that's all."

"But she didn't ask me anything, she didn't tell me anything, really. Is she shy?"

"No, not shy really, just quiet."

"It's just a little strange is all, how quiet she is. She's polite, though. Her family taught her right. Look, I'm glad you've met a special friend, Leticia, but don't you forget your family. You only get one family. And someday the doctors will be calling you and your 'screening' to tell you I'm dead. They'll be driving me around in a hearse to bury me before you know it."

"Nana, please don't joke that way."

"Did I say I was joking?"

9

Just after K and I celebrated five months of our "we" "we" "we" "I can't get enough of being with you" "where can we fuck" togetherness, Nolan called and left a message saying that K and I needed to practice spending social time with other humans again. Nol said she and Edith could cure our annoying isolationistic smoochy disease, but only if we admitted we needed help.

"It's not like we need a twelve-step program or something, Nolan," I told her when I finally called her back.

"If you don't get treatment soon, you will. Besides, the four of us need to do something crazy. We're all getting old. If even Princess Leticia is settling down, we must be getting old."

According to Nolan, it was "time to cherish and revel in our fleeting youth." She told me her idea and I had to admit that a road trip was enticing. It was so "Lucy and Ricky with the Mertzes" zany that none of us could resist. Nolan's contagious false concern was as good as any excuse to skip out of town for a few days, so the four of us put in requests for some vacation time at our jobs and we were off. The launching of our we've-got-something-to-prove, "we're hipster queers and we're here!" trip to San Francisco was complicated only by the white soccer-mom minivan rental we took turns maneuvering up the coast's winding freeways.

After eight hours and four million pit stops for Edith, the kind of woman who needs to luxuriate in cigarette breaks and stretch her slim muscled limbs often, we drove across the Bay Bridge and toward the Castro through the Mission District. The sun peeked out from behind the thick cloud layer and squinted my vision. I tried to keep the sudden glint out, but the bright rays amplified as they mixed up with Mission terra-cotta mud air. That pulsing vapor poured over me and hardened cold and thick. My eyes froze shut. Still, I could see. Oxygen bubbles in my veins filled my line of vision. The backs of my eyelids, back into myself, that was the place I found myself staring at.

Five years old with Nana, in line for food at the Kmart cafeteria, standing on "Spanish"-style burnt sienna tile floors. My tennis shoes on a floor like the kind some local historians claim lined the rooms at missions up and down the coast. Go to the San Juan Capistrano Mission on California's southern coast and for a nickel you can purchase a handful of birdseed. Feed the birds. I used to think they were pigeons, those birds, but Nana told me they weren't. They are swallows, I think. Those birds are said to come home every spring to fill the mission's echoing walls with their sad song, a reminder of the pain those buildings brought when they were built heavy on clay earth's back.

Swallows. Missions. Five years old and I stood in line for a blue slushy drink to swallow down my thirsty throat. I was with Nana, my feet wiggling on a burnt sienna Mission tile floor.

Actually drinking the slushy was only half the treat. The slushy cup and accessories were pretty great. A Hush

Puppies dog wearing a floppy blue ski hat was drawn on a wax paper strip rolled and melted at a seam to form the cup. A dome plastic lid crowned the cup. And through the lid was pushed a multipurpose plastic red straw that had a shovel-like spoon on one end. Choosing the color of slushy to get was also fundamental to the process of enjoyment. I had my red scratchy sweater on, my favorite one with the shiny flat gold buttons. And I was wearing my long blue flowered skirt with the elastic waist, a clean yellow tank top, and lavender Velcro sneakers with yellow treads. Puffy plastic E.T. head decals adorned the outer edge of each shoe. But back to the details pertinent to my hugely important decision of which color slushy to request . . . I was wearing a red sweater. The color red framed my head. Considering that detail alone, it was clearly mandatory to order blue or purple, not red cherry, for my tongue stain slushy. A blue tongue would contrast most with my sweater and be stick-out dramatic perfect. No question, I wanted blueberry gorgeous blue.

There was a man in line ahead of us and I could tell he didn't want a blue slushy. He had his cigarettes, the fire-lit tip directly in front of me. As he reached to the bowling ball laminate countertop for his cup of Dr Pepper, he leaned his smoking hand back, to counterbalance himself.

And me, I never was good at obeying American body space waiting in queue rules. My pigtails were bouncing, I was eager. Doodley-doo, I wanted that blue. Blue slushy. My tongue begged to be blue slurped. I edged toward the counter to hold on to something solid and stable as I pulled my torso up and strained my neck to see the slushy machine. My thumbs latched under the counter, dry gum wads avoided. The ridges of my fingerprints gripped the top of the counter. Doodley-doo, in search of my slushy I got too close to that cigarette hand man.

It seared through my entire body when the lit end of the cigarette made contact with my right hand. My right hand, the hand that was just learning how to hold a pencil and write my name. My right hand. With my downward gaze I saw the mission red tiles and I knew I was a bad little Indian girl. Almost as bad as Weeping had been when she was young. The round burn on the back of my hand was red and instantly began to blister. I bit back hot tears. Blink, blink, they were gone. Nana was standing right behind me, getting change out of her purse for my slushy. I could have and probably should have told her what had happened, but I didn't. Make a scene and I wouldn't get my slushy. Why would I have wanted to induce that reality on myself? No way, thank you very much. When I got home, I'd make sure my young rude boy cousins saw my blue tongue. They'd be jealous of me like they should be. They didn't get a blue slushy, but I did.

Nana and I left the store with the slushy. Ah, that blue slushy. We got to the car to begin the ride home. We had the Buick then, the tan cigar-long station wagon with automatic windows, its interior beginning to fall apart. A cloth liner covered the cushioned ceiling and I pushed my fingertips up into it to make indents in the flesh so soft it was like a woman's, my cousin Jimmy had said. Nana got in the car and I quit messing with the ceiling. My burnt hand rested on the door's cushy elbow rest, my left hand held the slushy. I was saving my drink. I wasn't going to sip a single icy granule until we got on the road. It was to be savored, that fine wine.

Nana, about to pull out of the parking lot, looked toward her rearview mirror and spied the burn.

"Girl, what happened to your hand!"

"Nana, it's nothing, that man in front of us in line, maybe he burnt me with his cigarette, I guess."

My body's yellowed water gathered under glowing angry skin.

101

Nana turned off the car and unlocked the automatic doors with a fancy silver switch on her door panel. She opened her door, walked around the back of the Buick to my side, opened my door, and pulled me out of the car so fast I didn't have time to even think about possible protest. With the wrist of my throb burn hand in her grip, she yanked the slushy from me. The cup's plastic half dome lid was ripped off and thrown on the clear plastic floor mat where my feet should have been because we should have been driving home. At that very moment, we should have been nearly to Walnut Street and my drink should have been gliding down my throat.

Nana poured the entire slushy beautiful blue slushy onto my burn. The spoon straw fell to the ground and was covered in slushy that splashed from my hand to the asphalt. When I reached to pick up the straw, Nana scolded me.

"Girl, that is nasty dirty, you leave it there."

"But, Nana, you told me it's bad to leave trash on the ground." The hot tears couldn't be bitten back with my mouth moving to talk. I started to cry.

"Ay, fine, here, put the straw with the other trash on the floor mat. But you be sure to wash your hands careful when we get home."

And wash my hands I did, but it made no difference. The burn hand stayed bright blue.

For days to come, my stinky little boy cousins made fun of my hand.

"Look, girl cousin is a Smurf. Stinky blue Smurf hand ugly girl."

Eventually, the burn healed.

Edith had driven us through the Mission and she was weaving us around the Castro looking for a parking spot. Edith and her raven black parted-down-the-middle hair slicked into aerodynamic smooth ponytails behind her ears, her beyond long mascara lashes clicking behind oversized tortoiseshell dark glasses. Hot coal brown eyes shot at anyone who got in her way. Damn she was dangerous heaven, that woman, my Bird Edie.

At Ms. Edith's side, Nolan was first lady in the front seat. Her feet propped on the dash and her 50/50 button-down uniform shirt wrinkled as she napped. I saw Nolan comfortable and remembered the sleep I barely got the night before we slid onto the road early in the morning. The coffee fuel had worn off. K sensed how tired I suddenly felt. She took my right hand and massaged its lines like she was getting ready to tell me my fortune, or maybe she was going to tell me my past. I stared out the window and leaned my head against dew moist glass. I took my hand from K's and looked for a scar. There was no visible trace of that day when I was burned.

Our minivan traveled up one steep road and down another over and over again as we wandered around and pushed ourselves to near exhaustion. We danced down the roads and at a few different clubs where we threw enough attitude to not get stared at like we were new. In the downtime after we'd had breakfast the next day, we browsed a queer bookstore and sipped their free chai with soy. We went to a sex club Rob had always talked about full of nostalgic stars in her eyes and K and I attempted fully clothed sex in a play scene jail cell's hanging leather harness.

"No antibacterial wipes, no clothes coming off," I said.

Besides, there were too many straight boys walking around and I didn't want to give them a Penthouse thrill.

103

Our clumsy fumbling in dark corners, into buttoned jeans and under tee-shirts, melted Edith's "I'm too sex-radical for this shitty place" holier-than-thou stripper attitude, and she caught a fit of giggles that only dried up when Nolan and I told a bouncer to fuck off for not letting us over into the happening section of the club. The section with thumping music and well-maintained toys, that section was restricted for queer *boys* only, the bouncer said. As if the jerk had a right to tell us what we were. Nolan and I nearly got the four of us thrown out before Edith initiated our haughty voluntary departure. Leaving the sex club was fine by me. There weren't enough dykes in the house anyway. Weren't we in San Francisco, Girl Central, for God's sake?

Our eight feet made the way down to Market Street and we sat in an old movie-house balcony with seats so sunken-down broken-springs that we might as well have sat on the sticky floor. We strained our necks up toward the screen to watch women with big hair walk their cats, drink herbal tea, and hang out with all their ex-girlfriends. The projector broke just as one of the women suggested to her most recent ex, the one she still slept with though they were "just friends," that they throw a vegetarian potluck dinner party and invite all the people they had ever met through the personals. We groaned full of pain and went for a drink at the tiny city's equivalent of Crystal's.

The place was wall-to-wall delicious dykes and good ambience. A Ms. Pac Man arcade game blinked in the corner. Tall messy overflowing shots of tequila were served with sides of rocky salt in little paper cups, the kind you get at the doctor's office to take a pill. K and I necked and messed around in a curtained caboose seat over in the corner near the video game. The caboose curtains stayed open a little and our clothes stayed mostly on. Playing like we were just talking was half the fun. Two tired corporate-tower types who were totally out of place in the tough vibe of the bar, probably trying to reclaim some fire in their relationship, they tried to be subtle as they watched us out of the corner of their eye. Our sex wasn't exhibitionism, it was public service of a kind and it made me feel high and mighty and sleepy-eyed just-been-loved. After those two women left, K and I settled into seats at the table Ms. Edith and Nolan held for us. A couple shots of tequila in me, I turned toward the flash of Nolan's camera and without even trying I had down pat the "ooh girl, look at me now, I'm so bad-girl rock star Joan Jett and the Runaways" look I had worked so hard to cop for Traver back in school. Nolan got the roll of film developed at a one-hour place our fourth day there and K promised she'd put the photo of me up on her refrigerator when we got home.

"Rebel girl," K said, the picture in her hand.

After one night of no sleep and only a couple of quick naps in the minivan, we were trying to decide if we should find a motel or what and then Edith spoke up. I think we all thought she was going to object to resting her regal tresses on a polyester motel pillow, but instead she said we could sleep at her parents' place the rest of our trip.

"At your parents'?"

"Yes, at my parents'."

"But don't they have a single in the Mission? We'd be in the way, Edie, wouldn't we?"

"I am certain we will not be in their way."

I should have known something was up. Edith held her head extra high and she kept biting her luscious orange lipstick lips.

10

Edith called her parents and we were on our way to meet the familia Contreras.

Now, Ms. Bird had always said that she was from the heart of the barrio and none of us had ever questioned that. I mean, why should we? Edith seemed a self-made star. All the glamour she threw around was easily bought with the money she made at Foxy's. And all her pronunciation and presentation? So what, most anyone could read books and put on airs. That Edith came from tough barrio roots was completely within the realm of reason.

So, when Edith drove our minivan up a seriously ritzy sloping Nob Hill road and parked in front of a pristine art deco luxury apartment done up in fancy crystal Christmas lights, I wasn't the only one who was confused.

"Shall we, ladies? Let's take our things up, my parents are expecting us." She opened her car door and started stepping out.

I'd never seen Edie nervous before, but there was no confusing what she was feeling right then. Nervous.

"Wait a minute, Edie. This is where your parents live?" Nolan's forehead wrinkled confused. She held on to Edith's shoulder.

"Yes, this is where my parents live, why else would I have just said 'Let's take our things up'? Come on, let's go." She turned to get out of the minivan again.

"Hold on." Nol's strong hand held Edith's shoulder tight. "This is kind of a shock. You've done a pretty good job feeding us stories about who you are if this is where your folks live. Do they know anything about you . . . that you're a stripper . . . that you're about to bring your girlfriend and your two dyke friends up to their pad? Is your name even Edith?"

"Nolan, quit being ridiculous. And let go of me, you are leaving a bruise."

"I'm serious, Edie. Tell me."

"Yes, Nolan, my parents know I am a dancer, but they do not know I dance at Foxy's, they know you're all my girl-friends, they do not know that you are my *girlfriend* and that Leti and K are *girlfriends*. But I want them to meet you. And, yes, you prick, my name is Edith. Happy?"

"No, not exactly happy, but at least I'm clear about where we stand." Nol's fingers turned white from gripping Edith's shoulder so hard.

I couldn't believe it when quiet K snapped, "Nolan, back off, Edie didn't have to bring us here, she wanted to. Consider that, would you?" She was shaking visibly as she spoke.

Nolan pushed Edith away as she let go of her shoulder. Nol turned around.

"Stay out of this, K."

"Nolan, how am I supposed to stay out of this, I'm sit-ting right here and you're practically acting like you're going to start throwing punches. Shit, Nolan, I'm not just going to sit here."

107

"Then get out of the van if it bothers you, K." Nol's broad shoulders were tense and ready to throw some hits indeed.

"Calm down, all of you, fucking calm down. This is too bizarre, just calm down already." My stomach was starting to hurt from the tension.

"Ladies," rubbing her shoulder with a manicured hand where Nol had gripped her, Edie turned around to K and me. Mascara was making little dark ponds under Edith's eyes, her lips were trembling and the tip of her nose was red.

"Let's unload our things now and go on up, please," Edith said in her smooth voice like nothing at all out of the ordinary had just happened.

11

Her laugh was a rapid, shrill thing. Tinkling and frequent and loud like a wind chime's machine-gun song. She worked so hard each and every second to try to prove that she was happy and that she could laugh pleasantly from cradle to grave.

Her brown eyes were overly bright from the moment we stepped into the *House Beautiful* foyer where nothing was to be touched and everything was insured. The almost buglike roundness of Mrs. Contreras's eyes hinted at the hyperactive thyroid it seems she had grown accustomed to, addicted to, and was only sometimes inclined to medicate. See, when she took the pills her doctor prescribed, she inevitably gained weight. Those Chanel skirt and jacket suits stopped fitting quite right and the manic efficiency she's known for turned tar pit thick and confining slow. Simply put, no mania and she lost the edge that kept her on top of her social circuit. So instead of taking the pills that coated her small bony frame with a slim layer of cushion, her cosmetics consultant advised her how to minimize the bulging discs of her carob eyes.

Edie's mother scared the shit out of me. Truly, Mrs. Contreras terrified me.

"Thank you, sugar."

"You are such a jewel, sweet thing."

"Oh my," laugh laugh laugh laugh laugh, "what an absolute joy!"

It took true effort to hold up the props of such a layered performance.

I learned quick that Edith's corporate lawyer daddy was more than happy to share an invented reality with his wife. By the time the seemingly nameless French Swiss live-in maid had served our dinner, Mr. Contreras was high-volume crass on his fifth gin sour. Nolan smelled his gasoline breath and I guess she just couldn't resist picking a fight with the person who looked so much like Edith and who obviously wouldn't mind yelling back a little bit. Nolan put the banana peel down in front of herself and slipped on it, staring at Edith and her daddy the whole time.

"This sure is a nice place you have, Mr. Contreras. And here we always thought Edie came from the Mission District, isn't that funny?"

"The Mission? What a damned insult. Edith's grandparents still live there, but I can't fathom how they bear it. The whole area smells of tortillas and menudo, and that damned ranchero music with its ludicrous polka insanity, too many damned lazy beaners without any ambition."

Edith stared at her plate. If I hadn't been momentarily paralyzed cold by the sudden assault, I swear I would have reached over and fucking torn the guy's tongue out. Mrs. Contreras cleared her throat delicately and laughed a little chime.

"Henry, darling, we needn't discuss this at dinner. May I have the help bring you another drink?"

Mr. Contreras didn't even look at his wife.

And Nolan, she gunned her engines all over again, "Mr. Contreras, I'm shocked to hear you call anyone a 'beaner.' It seems so self-deprecating. You and Mrs. Contreras are Mexican by heritage, aren't you?"

Nolan put her hand on Edith's.

"I am Hispanic, thank you very kindly, and, young missy, I have had just about enough of this interrogation."

I wouldn't doubt if he left a dent as he slammed his drink down on the oak table. Fuming Man shot a stare at Nolan's hand deliberately holding his daughter's and he glared at Edie.

"It is a shame that your associates have not learned from your example of fine upbringing and etiquette, Edith."

"*Henry,*" Mrs. Contreras's laugh laugh laugh laugh, "perhaps we should all call it a night? Yes?" She wasn't waiting for an answer. "I apologize that we have only one guest room, but I'm sure you little darlings will be quite comfortable. Two of you can sleep in Edith's old bedroom. Now, Edith sugar, you be a nice girl and let your friend Nolan sleep in the bed, I'll have Marjorie bring out a bedroll for you to set up on your rug. And K, Leteesha," hearing her say my name made my teeth ache like when you're chewing gum and you bite into some of the tinfoil wrapper by accident and it zaps a filling, "there are two twin beds in the guest room. Oh," laugh laugh laugh laugh, "K darling, you'll just barely fit your tall self in one of those beds, but I hope you'll be able to forgive us for the inconvenience just this once."

It must have exhausted Mrs. Contreras, the way she lived. Still, she needed pills to sleep at night, her frantic forward movement only numbed by Percodan, Vicodin, or Valium, though Valium made her a bit too groggy the next day for her taste and, of course, "important ladies simply don't have time to be drowsy, now do they?"

Her life was such an obvious one to map out. See, after she disappeared into her suite for the evening, Mrs.

Contreras got dolled up in the cheetah print silk chemise the catalog guarantees to "bring out the beast in him." She offered herself to her husband, who lay in bed, gripping his Mikasa Park Avenue highball tumbler once again filled with gin and ice. His liquor presence was a constant weight on her as she smiled and squirmed, but nonetheless she managed to lift her legs so as to display her gym-sculpted calves at their most flattering and thinning angle. Less than five minutes after he entered the room, her Henry was snoring with the tumbler still in his grip.

She drew herself a warm bath, not too hot because that depleted the skin of its natural moisture, gently cleansed, conditioned, exfoliated, and shaved. After patting herself dry, she lathered on the thick lotion her husband's assistant orders for her from a Parisian spa. Then she poured herself mineral water from the little refrigerator next to the vanity and swallowed the two pills she placed under her tongue with her sculpted nails.

Sleep came slowly even with pills dissolving in the belly that rose and fell in unison with two scarlessly augmented breasts each time she took a breath. She lay down in bed beside her husband and she thought of the cuticles that should have been trimmed, eyebrows that needed tinting, a bikini line that needed to be waxed, funds that she would raise for the Responsible Women of the Bay Area society group. The following day would take such energy. Henry and she would arrive at their Manhattan apartment by four and the dinner guests from the New York firm would join them for cocktails at six-thirty. Dinner preparations would need to be supervised. Marjorie never seemed to get things quite right if she wasn't watched closely. Gin sours would need to be refreshed.

"And god knows," she reminded herself not to crinkle her nose up in wrinkles at the thought, "someone will think it a charming idea to voyage off to Rockefeller Plaza to watch those hopeless fools ice-skating."

Mrs. Contreras shifted under the down comforter and thought of her daughter, that difficult child of hers. Why Edith wasted her time with friends who were so lacking in refinement, well, it simply frustrated her no end. Eyelids finally heavy, she pulled on her cobalt blue sleeper's mask filled with soothing potpourri. "Cobalt blue will bring you the deep sleep you need," her spiritual healer told her as she paid to have his Mercedes and Bel Aire home painted orange for cosmic radiance. Eyes closed but thoughts still buzzed forward at a maddening pace. Desperate to drift out of thoughts, Mrs. Contreras reached under her pillow and shook two Valium out of the pillbox she kept tucked there. Her drugs eventually wrapped their soft warmness around her and Mrs. Contreras slept.

The world in morning-after-downer slow motion, Henry booming at her to stop her dilly-dawdling, just before she walked out the door the next morning, Mrs. Contreras wrote in her pristine hand,

> Darling Edith,
>   How divine to see you! And to meet your perfectly delightful friends—what a pleasant treat!
>   Father and I are on our way to the city.
> Always affectionately,
Mother

"Jesus mother fucking Christ!" Edith growled loud in the kitchen, and a heavy crashing sound followed.

K miraculously remained asleep at my side. I jumped out

of Edith's bed, tripped on the unused bedroll next to the bed, and slammed my knee into the nightstand. K barely stirred as I cussed up my own storm and limped down the hall as fast as I could. When I landed in the kitchen doorway, Edie spun around to face me. She stared at me a long second, unclenched her fists, stretched her giraffe neck tall and proud, and forced a robot calm smile.

"Good morning, darling. Did you sleep well?"

"What just happened, Edith? Are you all right?"

"Unfortunately, silly me, I just accidentally dropped my mother's favorite teapot. I was going to start some breakfast for us, but I guess we'll need to go out for coffee instead."

The bone china teapot she was referring to, its destroyed remains made a pathetic pile of shards on the kitchen floor catty-corner to where Edith stood.

Edie was mighty good at talking about the embroidered curtains while the elephant sat on the couch.

"Edie, hello, what the fuck is going on?"

"Leticia, I told you, I simply was going to make some tea when—"

"Never mind, Edie, never mind. You're all right, I mean, you didn't hurt yourself, right?"

"I am perfectly fine, Leticia. Thank you for asking." Tears broke past the mask she was trying to secure in place. "I am completely fucking fine." She shoved her left hand toward me.

I took the crumpled piece of paper from her grip and read Mrs. Contreras's note.

"She left it for me on the kitchen table." She pointed to said table.

Four hundred-dollar bills were tucked under an apple on the table.

"I guess we can get triple large cappuccinos with whipped cream if we want," I sat down on a chair next to the crisp pile of cash.

"That is not amusing."

"I know it's not. I'm sorry. Really, I'm sorry."

And I was. I mean, sure I wouldn't cry if my family wanted to throw money at me, but hush money, even coming from your mother, is still hush money just the same. It was too clear that Edie's perfect mommy and rich daddy and little princess darling triad was truly fucked up. The extent to which they were probably fucked up, I didn't even want to think about right then. I didn't want to think about it, but the entire scenario was far from foggy no matter how much I tried to ignore it. The night before, Edie had told K and me that we could sleep in her old bedroom, the canopied bed would be cozy enough for the both of us. She wouldn't even step foot into that pink wallpaper, innocent darling, every detail in place too-perfect-to-be-true room. Nol had slept in the guest room and Edie on the couch. Her mother had been extra careful to not wake Edie on the way out.

Edie stood in front of me in the kitchen with her hair messy, not beautiful like it used to be after she'd spent the night tangled up with me. My Bird crying for real tore me up something bad.

"Edie, come here."

She walked over to me and sat down on my lap, draped her arms around my shoulders, sank into me, and cried humid silent sad. I held Edith close and felt against my chest the heartbeat I thought I'd live the rest of my life never knowing again.

12

Eventually, Nol and K woke up out of their deaf zombie sleeps and the four of us went out for morning coffee. Her composure completely regained, Edith winked at me when she ordered a triple café mocha with extra whipped cream and chocolate sprinkles.

As ridiculous as it was, even once we had sat down at the cramped coffeehouse table Nolan continued to act like Edith was invisible. Add to the fun, ever since their spat in the minivan the day before, Nol and K hadn't exchanged a single word. It was creepy how corpse silent K had become. I was the only person still on speaking terms with everyone. The silence decided that we would drive back home that day, but only after one last field trip that I insisted upon.

At the Fishermen's Wharf there's a penny arcade. And in the penny arcade, which kind of smells like piss and sea salt combined, there is a photo booth. You know, the passport photo kind of booth with a swivel stool and a curtain and you look into a square that is the camera and several quarters later you get a strip of film with five little photos framed in white borders. I wanted photos of the four of us together.

I got my quarters, pushed my girls into the booth, and stood closest to the curtain so no one could leave. I told everyone to smile. Edith doesn't know how not to prime herself up when a camera is pointed at her. Instinctively, same as beauty pageant contestants with slippery Vaseline on their teeth, Edie poses pretty. And K smiled because she wanted to make me happy. Nol only smiled in response to the fact that I tickled her right after I dropped the quarters into the slot. Pop. The flash glowed once, twice, thrice, four times and then Nol got ticked at me for tickling her. She pushed me aside and stormed out of the booth. I left to talk with her.

In the split second it had taken me to follow her, Nol up and disappeared. The camera booth flash-popped its final spark from somewhere behind me. It was foggy like a Loch Ness sighting that day. Visibility was pathetic. I searched the wharf but couldn't see much more than a foot around me in all directions. Nol was gone.

The hazy blur sun eventually disappeared into the water. I was full of popcorn and the video games were full of my quarters by the time Nol resurrected herself. K was first to drop her shaved-ice and greet Nol's return.

"Where have you been?" K was past the point of fuming quiet.

"No one said you had to wait."

I was fed up with being the patient all-loving mediator.

"If we'd known you were going to be such a brat when you got back, we would have left you here to rot in fucking salt water taffy."

What I said wasn't supposed to be funny. The three of them, they couldn't stop laughing. At me, not with me. I was

117

pissed. When their laughing subsided, the score balanced out even. Everyone was upset. There was no way any of us could have driven the eight hours home that night without wanting to kill someone.

When we settled in at Edith's parents' place for the last time, we remained not too far from some mission somewhere. It was less night than day, late or early depending. K nestled close to me at my side. I couldn't sleep. I didn't want to quite yet.

Thinking.

Of what 2 a.m. meant. It was once Weeping Woman gone away into the coming dawn, night-light-glow cinnamon hot chocolates as a child with Nana when I was not feeling well, gossiping with Joey when we brushed our teeth after all-night giggling study sessions, dirty-talking with Rob in the brushed cotton of her bed, tipsy stomps home to my apartment with Edith from Crystal's, tossing and turning in bed all alone.

Thinking.

Of the woman at my side before she fell asleep. Thinking of K's eyes. Damn, help me, those dark green eyes looking up at me with the city lights outside the window making shadows down on her. Our bodies lit ice fires together, but even at our highest mutual peaks of emotion, we shared grounding calm. It occurred to me that with her I believed I would change.

Thinking.

Of the times life has filled up so much of my dreams with its pulse that I would wake in the middle of the night, unable to go back to sleep. That jumbled tired of being awakened by my own mind's illusions, it was like the static wind whipping power lines outside our theatrical sleeping place. There were no thunderbolt charges in the sky and the mist was barely heavy enough to be seen on the light coming from outside, but the air was in motion and I felt a shot go through me. Weeping Woman, she kissed me slow and steady and all of a sudden. My lips stung pleasant, her kiss was unexpected like a memory I hadn't lived yet. Everything in her presence was different from the countless times she had visited before, but I knew what to expect. Her copper grin was mine to taste sweet chocolate with each breath in. She firefly-sparked me and set my skin tingling. My girl Weeping's metal whisper echoed in the layered shadows of the room.

13

If time is subjective, the drive home from San Francisco took at least fifty hours longer than the drive up. The minivan returned to the rental shop, Nol and Edie stormed off together to their house. K and I went to her apartment building to get some sleep in a much deserved familiar bed.

When we opened the door to K's apartment and stepped inside, I almost blacked out. Literally.

"Good god." I was coughing and trying to unlatch the French windows with one hand, the other hand clamped over my mouth and nose.

"Leticia, what's wrong with you?" K stood just inside the door, her duffel bag still in hand, staring at me like I was *the* hysterical woman.

"K, don't just stand there, open some windows." My cheeks covered in wet tears that formed to wash away the stink of natural gas collected in the apartment.

"Is it gas? Oh god, I'd told Viv that old stove was no good. She didn't believe me, but I told her . . ." K's voice trailed off into the kitchen. "Man, don't come in here. I'm dizzy already."

Quick, the windows were open, K had turned off the stove valve and we were sitting light-headed in the entryway stairwell, waiting for the apartment to air out.

"That's really dangerous, K. I mean, you can't even tell when the whole apartment is dripping in a gas leak?"

"I know, it doesn't make me happy, trust me."

"What if I wasn't here? What if you'd gone in and gone to sleep? You could have died, K. It sounds so five o'clock news, but you really could have died."

"Yeah, I guess that could happen."

"K, you could have *died*."

At least half an hour passed with us sitting there silent before we went back inside.

"At least we're not at Motel Contreras tonight," K said as I threw my bags down in her bedroom and tucked a black sheet up into the French windows' hinges to keep the city lights out.

After taking a few deep breaths heavy through my nose to reassure myself the place really was clean air, I started to relax. It was warm perfect to lay down all stretched out lazy in K's bed. I felt myself twitch like you do when you're falling asleep and it feels like you're jumping off a tall building. Right then K jumped up and out of bed. She turned on the bright overhead light.

"I'll be right back."

"K, come on." I pulled the blankets over my face to block the sixty-watt.

I heard her digging through her duffel at the foot of the bed. Then her heavy barefoot stride wandered off into the kitchen.

"Leti, come here for a second."

"K, I'm sleeping."

"No you're not. Come on, just for a second. Please."

"Cripes, K." I thumped my feet out of bed and onto the cold wood floors, stomping to the drafty kitchen.

"Look." K was smiling and pointed to the refrigerator.

Without much more effort than one of her smiles, that girl could melt the grumpiest of my moods. I leaned up against the sink next to her and admired the refrigerator.

"Rebel girl. Leti, I'm keeping those photos of you on my fridge forever."

"Why is it that, coming from you, the promise of being up on a refrigerator for eternity is romantic?"

"Because you know how much I adore you."

We went back to bed.

I woke up with creases from the sheets on my face and in the skin of my stomach. K was still sleeping, her face turned toward me on her pillow.

I kissed her slow and steady with my stare like Weeping had kissed me the night before. I kissed the scar above K's brow and kissed twice the one closer to her ear. Illuminated even in the shadows of night, the scars were shooting-star burning streaks of snow white on her skin.

When she rustled out of sleep and her eyes focused up awake, I decided it was time to ask. The answer I had waited months to pursue was given very matter-of-fact.

"The scars are from a car accident back when I was seventeen." Her eyes turned a shade of pine new to me.

Snap of the fingers, I was painful nervous, chatty nervous.

"Really? I was in a car accident when I was a kid too. That's where I got this scar on my lip from," I pointed to the barely noticeable bump on the downside of my upper lip's cupid bow.

"Lord, I was a monster about it when it happened. Nana Lupe and I, we were coming home from a parent-teacher conference after school one day. We were in the big old Buick. I climbed from the front seat to the back seat, you know, it wasn't the law to wear seat belts back then and I was just going to hop back forward to my seat real quick once I had what I needed from the back. I was jumping to the back seat to get this natural science report on owls that I'd gotten an A on. My fifth-grade science teacher, Mrs. Doherty, she had told Nana about the report during their conference. I wanted to show Nana the scratch 'n' sniff sticker Mrs. Doherty put on the report for getting an A.

"We were coming up to the tracks, about to cross into our neighborhood, and Nana saw real late that the crossbars were coming down. She slammed on the brakes right when I was climbing over the bench seat to the front again. The train rumbled past us and my face flew into the steering wheel."

I made myself stop talking. I stared at K for a long time but her faraway eyes told me she didn't want to say anything. K kissed my forehead as I squirmed in under her arm and put my head on her shoulder.

K's silence. The way I silenced the whispering secret I really should have shared with K right then. Silence. All the silences combined were more than I could handle. I kept talking.

"K, remember those plastic string things people used to wrap their steering wheels with? Well, Papá Estrella had done that to the Buick's steering wheel. But a real long time before that day. And the plastic was all hard from sun exposure. The pointed tip of one of the strings cut straight through my lip.

"The crossbars went back up but we didn't move for a long time. Nana was fussing all over me. I didn't cry. I kept

123

telling her real professional, like I'd seen the ambulance guys do on channel 5's *Emergency*, to give me a tissue so I could hold on to my lip with my head tilted back and make the bleeding stop like how Mamá Estrella made me do when I got my bloody noses from the heat.

"Nana keeps telling me, 'Take your hand away from your lip. Let me see. Let me see.' When I let her see she says I have to go to the hospital. All that crying held back, trying to act all grown-up with blood pouring tacky down my chin and throat, making my mouth thick bitter, I insisted hard, 'I do not need to go to a hospital. Give me a tissue, now!'

"Nana looked in her bag and found me a McDonald's paper napkin and started to drive. Toward the hospital.

"I was something awful once we got there. When they started putting in the stitches, I kicked and bit and spit at the doctor. He told me to stop or he'd have the nurses strap me down. I kicked him in the gut and he kept his promise, one nurse even held my forehead down with the palms of her hands.

"Nana was embarrassed. The day it was time to take out the stitches she told me to behave while she removed them because she'd already had enough of my misbehaving. I'd been watching television with Papá when she told me to go sit on the bathroom counter. She snipped the little black threads and started to pull at them with Mamá's eyebrow tweezers. The dull tug of the thread inside my lip felt like the needle sewing me up. I didn't think it out, it was more like instinctive defense or something, but I kicked Nana, hard, I kicked her very hard.

"Her face froze up and she put the tweezers down on the counter real slow. 'You can take them out yourself, Leticia. Don't you ever kick me again.'

"I sat on the counter and stared at the wall a long time. I

124

wanted to cry, but I was determined to play tough. I didn't want to apologize because I knew I hadn't decided to kick her, it just happened, a knee-jerk response. Nana wasn't going to come back and help me get the stitches out. Finally, I stared into the mirror and pulled on the thread. But I couldn't stomach it. So I went into Papá's barbershop room and used his detail hair scissors to clip the thread real close up against my lip. The rest of the stitches stayed inside and dissolved away eventually, I guess. But that's probably why I have my scar. I didn't heal up proper because the stitches stayed in.

"K," I looked up at her face and saw that her eyes were shut. She'd barely moved the whole time I'd been talking, her breathing so in tune with itself, I wondered if she was dreaming.

"K? Are you sleeping?"

She was absolutely quiet.

"K?"

"I'm awake."

"So, were you nasty bad when you got your stitches?"

"I don't remember," she said so low I barely heard her. I rolled onto my side and propped myself up on one elbow, watching her until she opened her eyes.

"How can you not remember something like that, K?"

She sat up. Her long back against the wall. Pillow in her lap. Hands elegant folded on the pillow at first. Then one reached out and touched my lip. At the scar. The hand joined its mate again on their pillow pedestal.

"I don't remember, Leticia. I was in a coma so I don't remember. I wasn't conscious when I got stitched up."

I felt smaller than whatever is the smallest thing in the universe for pushing the subject to the point it had landed at. But still, we hadn't reached the story that had me running scared, I could deal with anything but sharing that story with K right then. I sat, my mouth glued, my eyebrows knit up, waiting to see or hear or feel whatever came next.

"You know how I told you I used to do murals before I moved out here?"

I nodded.

She had been heading off with one of the guys I'd seen in the photos when it happened. No, they weren't on a date. They were off to go check out a wall, not some sort of Pink Floyd figurative kind of wall. A real wall, solid and tall with loving concrete smeared smooth over bricks. It was a rarity, that wall was, as most of the walls in North Philadelphia were raw brick. That concrete wall, it was out at an intersection, a busy intersection clogged with buses and people walking by, lots of little stores and apartments up above them. Anything done on that wall would be seen. It had just been painted over fresh white when they were off to see it. The wall would be theirs, they had decided.

They should have just walked, the wall was only about a mile away from their families' block, but her friend had just gotten his license and bought his ride. He wanted to cruise K down to the wall in his new baby.

So, he double-parked his car in front of K's building, he honked the horn, she trucked her lanky teen self on down and hopped in the car, and they started out on their short drive.

Halfway down K's block was when it happened. My K's eyes turned a marshy lily pad green when she thought of the oak trees lining the sidewalk. You know, in Philly they have things like that, huge, practically ancient, solid trees. Where it happened wasn't like here with palm trees swaying so scary toward the south sun they look like they should snap somewhere in their middle.

Maybe the guy had been playing with the radio, trying to find appropriate tunes. Maybe the sun hit his eyes just so.

Maybe the rickety little tin of his first car's steering chamber was shot. K, she'd been sorting through spray cans in a cardboard box at her feet, looking forward to that night when they would return to use the paint. Her daydreaming plans pulled her attention and so she hadn't buckled into the car's body yet. And then the car drove into an old oak tree at the side of the road. A seat belt gripped her friend unharmed in his place, but K went through the windshield. Her body flew forward and up, she went into the windshield and out of consciousness.

Her friend left her slumped body halfway in, halfway out of the car. It wasn't due to lack of concern that he walked away from the scene, don't get his motivations wrong. Things get all messed-up crazy at moments like that and he thought he was doing the right thing. But the mamás on the block, they dropped their brooms on their swept stoops and screamed loud for God. K's friend walked dizzy-faced down the street to K's building. One of the mamás hollered up to her balcony for her boy to call the ambulance. Another mamá called K's dad at his work. K's friend finally made his way to his destination and tapped the entry door's heavy brass knocker. When K's mother answered, the boy sat down on the front steps, staring at the ground, and pointed his arm toward the car crashed just out of sight.

The ambulance arrived as her mother walked casual down the street. When she got to the car and realized the accident wasn't just another one of her girl's pranks, she fainted. K on a stretcher and into the back of the ambulance, smelling salts, the EMT sat K's mother on the bench seat as the sirens started up and he used a little flashlight to check K's pupils. He pushed on K's skinny boy chest to make her breathe and he filled her with pointy fluids to keep her blood moving. His partner drove to the hospital as fast as the laws of physics allowed. What a sick irony. K was dying from a car wreck and the ambulance had to drive like the devil to keep her alive.

At the hospital, they hooked K to machines of nearly every kind that go beep in an emergency room and they stitched her up. There was the gash above her eye that peeled back flesh to expose an oddly clean and bloodless white skull. There was a jagged rip where glass had wedged itself close to her right jugular vein. Little snags and holes could be found here and there and everywhere. They stitched her up and she didn't so much as twitch with the thread going into her skin.

Two weeks followed in slow motion, though that part was still her parents' memory, not hers. K's mother and father talked her through her coma with words like "Don't you leave us, little girl, you stay with us, you hear, we love you something awful bad, our precious girl." A garden blossomed in K's hospital room from all the flowers her mother brought clipped from her window boxes. Snapdragons and pansies and tea roses made the air sweet, but even if she had been conscious, K wouldn't have been able to tell. Severe brain swelling killed the connection between K's olfactory receptors and her brain. Stitches oozing and bruises turning ochre, her body lost all its baby fat and grew gaunt in its hospital bed. Once K finally did wake up again, her parents overprotective loved her with vanilla ice cream banana protein milkshakes and shoofly pie and Italian water ice whenever she wanted.

K kept her eyes shut as she talked to me. Or was it that she was talking to herself? I felt I was listening in on something so personal that I wasn't sure she was actually speaking aloud. I was without the words to tell K exactly how much her story terrified me.

That night, K and I slept like stone statues painted deep-ocean gray. When K went to work the next morning, it took me hours to wake up. Midday I yanked myself out of bed, splashed cold water on my face, brushed my teeth so hard it made my gums shine, and drove numb to my place. The carpet in the hall of my building suctioned on my feet and made each step a trek. When I got in my apartment, I went into the bathroom and brushed my teeth again with an extra amount of peppermint paste on my brush. I needed the mint burn to keep me awake. I rinsed the toothbrush but still didn't feel awake clean enough.

I have this bad habit that kicked in right then. There was a tag on my thumb. Not the kind that has a price on it. I think I must have paper-cut myself. I didn't remember that sting you get when you paper-cut yourself and I knew the slice never bled, but there was a tag of skin from one side of the cut left as evidence. I noticed the tag. Dry, hard, air-exposed, getting ready to fall off like an umbilical cord two weeks after the baby's been born.

I was a scab eater when I was little. Took scrapes and cuts forever to heal. As soon as the edges of the scab started to lift naturally, all on their own, I had no choice but to peel it off, still raw and clinging at its center, and chew it like jerky before swallowing it guilty and full of proud excitement for what my body could produce, knowing that no matter how many times I ate the scab, another would start up in its place. The opportunities for eating scabs decreased considerably as I grew older and more cautious and probably less fun to climb a tree with.

So there was this tag on my thumb and I brought it to my mouth and took it between my teeth and bit it. The second my tongue wrapped around the tag, I tasted apple. Bittersweet green apple.

The tart apple still in my mouth, I put a circle Band-Aid over the dot of blood on my thumb and walked to my 7UP wood crate nightstand and lit the candle I kept there. The

129

special candle, the one in the tall pink glass with the Virgen de Guadalupe image on its label, the candle with the prayer to the miraculous Virgen printed on it.

Virgensita, full of grace, let me be with you, blessed are thou among women and blessed are thine eyes. Blessed Virgen, bless us now and at the hour of our death. Amen.

I stared into the blue-tipped candle flame in front of me and wished hard for the Virgen and her bad-girl sister Weeping Woman to keep far away from me as they waltzed in circles with their papier-mâché cousin Lady Death. No matter how perfect powerful they thought they were, I wasn't going to let them ladies play me like a fool.

I grabbed the thickest of my blue-satin-covered photo albums and opened the book to its last page. From under the bottom image in the final plastic pocket, I took out the photograph. The photograph. Of my mother.

Doily edges of the yellowed black-and-white photograph mirrored the ones on her blouse. She was young in the photo, beaming a young love smile. My mother's happiness captured in that image was something innocent like picture shows try to create and seldom get right.

My sophomore year of college, when I was home for winter break, I had found the photo in an old shoe box. It was hidden away with other personal doodads that Mamá Estrella had kept tucked far back on the top shelf of the pink house's linen closet. The top shelf had always been her shelf. The middle one was for towels, and the bottom held extra toilet paper and soap for the bathroom. That visit home, nine months had been lived since Mamá passed away and still I waited until Nana went to run errands before I got brave enough to reach up to the top shelf and pull down that box to look into it for the first time. The photo of my mother, it was in there with some other photos, a mother-of-pearl crucifix I'd never seen before and little love notes Papá had penned early in their marriage.

For hours that day at the pink house I had stayed glued to the floor in front of the linen closet, staring at the crumbling photograph of my mother. When Nana came home later that evening, she found me asleep on the carpet with the open shoe box next to me. She had the photo in her hand and was crying dry tears when I woke up. Nana handed me the photo.

"She loved you very much, Leticia. She still does."

Nana walked away and I heard her in the kitchen fixing a cup of tea, thick with honey I was sure.

Asking questions about my mother and father only ever made the women in my family silent and the men weep. Result is, I don't know much about my parents. But from looking into the only photo I have of my mother, I do know that she was beautiful. And proudly satisfied. And that she and my blue-eyes father must have loved each other something bad.

The Virgen candle flickered warm in my tiny apartment. My mouth was fresh with the taste of candied apples. Unraveling once again was the story I'd pieced together from years of overheard whisperings and daydream elaborations.

See, it was spring break, still called Easter vacation back then, and my folks decided to leave their college books behind to go to Joshua Tree for a few days. Like a lot of their friends, they felt confident that the vast cacti and arid moonscape was where they could stock up on love and peace and the fulfillment of euphoric hippie dreams. My mother was bulging with seven months of me. She was radiant even under all that dry dust that coated her waist-long black hair and patched bell-bottom jeans. Barefoot. Nipples pushing through the thin gauze of an unbleached white cotton peasant blouse with lace at her tiny wrists. When the flash popped bright, my mother was smiling at my father, leaning up against their VW Bug. Sleeping bags, backpacks, and food from Mamá's store piled high in an old wooden 7UP crate on the back seat, crammed up against the side windows. My mother's arms rested across her front, under heavy breasts and on top of an equally heavy, tight belly.

She was driving the last stretch of road back home from the desert. She liked driving, with the windows rolled down it was almost like flying the way it tangled her hair up in the wind. She had been driving for an hour. She was so pregnant and so easily tired. She asked my father if he wouldn't mind taking the wheel. He smiled, "Of course I don't mind, Rita." She pulled to the dirt side of the road and they traded seats. My father pulled the car back onto the narrow highway. My mother fell asleep at his side. He drove. There was a car. On the wrong side. Of the road. Toward. Crashed into their. Car. Her body. Her body. Very still. Body. Shaking. Screaming. She was not screaming. Screaming. That was my father before he too became still and joined my mother.

Mamá, Papá, and Nana temporarily closed down the store to be by my mother's side at the hospital. My mother's comatose body was kept on life support for a month while I incubated, getting ready to be born twenty days early by cesarean delivery. The day I was hatched, Nana gave my mother one last lullaby kiss good night. Me safe in her arms, Nana then gave the doctors permission to turn off the machines.

What I had learned about K when she told me her car crash story, it tapped deep down past my bones and filtered itself into my blood. When K told me about her scars, my mother and father turned up high-volume the story I knew I wouldn't speak. See, I could talkity-talk static ramble voice just like Mamá with the best of them, but there were some stories I preferred remain silent.

14

hat's a strange way to say it, K. You mean to tell me
you didn't invite Nol?"

"That's up to Edith."

"Nol's our friend too."

"Yeah, but Vivienne said she wanted Edith there."

"Why just Edith specifically?"

"I don't know, but if it's such an issue maybe just Edith
and I should go. You think screenings are pretentious anyway. You and Nol could have a night out at Crystal's or
something."

I picked up the phone to call Nol. K walked out of the
room shaking her head disapprovingly.

Quiet snazzy happy was the main course between K and
me . . . except for whenever Edith or Nol came up in conversation. Two months of licking wounds hadn't healed the
aftermath of the San Francisco dramathon trip, not between
K and Nol and especially not between Edith and Nol. Lesbiana paper dolls with no ability to let go, Nol and Edith
still paid rent together, shared linens, and were "trying to

work things out." K and I were sure the whole situation was hopeless, but it wasn't up to us to decide. And it wasn't up to me to exclude one so the other could feel comfy. I invited Nol to join us for the Valentine's Day debut of rock star Vivienne's latest film.

The night of the screening, Edie and Nol came by my apartment to pick up K and me.

"Shall we, ladies? I don't want to be too late." Edith tapped my doorframe impatiently with her high-gloss glitter nails.

Bird wanted to be fashionably late, of course, but not so late that everyone would already be engaged deep in conversation and wouldn't notice her entrance. I knew this fact about Edie's demands from when we dated. I was always ready half an hour before I needed to be. Between the two of us, Edith and I covered an hour of estimated departure time. I checked my watch and saw that, predictably, Edith and Nol were nearly thirty-five minutes later than Edie had promised.

K and I grabbed our jackets and walked out to Nol's old but still shiny sporty coupe. Nol was sitting in the passenger seat waiting for us. Nol's car, but Edie was driving. Typical, that girl was such a control monster. So anyway, Nol was in the passenger seat and when she saw us coming she reached to unlock the doors for us, but that didn't stop Edith from pushing a gizmo on her key chain to make the car do the same thing in response to her command. The car beeped a cloying hello, we got in, said hello to Nol, buckled up, and Edie pushed the car into fourth gear before we were half a block down the street. Got to be late just the right amount.

I used to think about Edie's habitual tardiness a lot when I sat around waiting for her. She must get off on adrenaline when she has to rush around and drive fast to avoid missing events entirely. Considering her skinny, high-metabolism, cigarette-smoking, caffeine-pounding self, my theory seemed simple enough. The trees whizzed by us. Houses were a blur. We'd be late, but not "too" late for Edie's grand arrival at Base.

Yes, "Base." Annoying name, right? See, the art space that represented Vivienne's work in Los Angeles was once an old military base helicopter hangar. I'm sure all the art scene people were quite smug about the site of the gallery. Ah, the perfunctory killing machine transformed into a place of cultured society. Anyway, the Richie Rich who bought the place during the Carter years snagged nearly a fourth of the base around the hangar for all the fancy cars that came carrying fancy pants. There was plenty of space to park, so we did. Good thing we were in Nol's car, the security would have detained us if my Pinto or K's truck had been our chariots. We got out of our relatively socially appropriate car and walked to the industrial wall rolled up on the east side of the hangar.

Oh lord, the perfect people were present in droves. It was all about fashion, baby. How that scene managed to do it all was beyond me. I mean, it must have been a full-time job to find perfect hip clothes in vintage stores, have perfect hair, and talk perfect small talk as perfectly as they did. Considering the perfect glistening luxury and classic automobiles they drove when most of them were in their twenties and thirties was brutal enough. It was no wonder Viv wanted Edie to make an appearance. With her high-elegance drag vibe, Edith fit in perfectly.

It didn't take much for Edith to be a fashion diva worthy of being declared the perfect people's queen. She looked perfect indeed in her dark denim blue jeans, starched and cuffed high above her black trouser socks, a men's white tuxedo shirt, a thick black belt, and "Sunday best" grandpa-style black dress shoes. Her skin was perfect, her oiled glossy braids and spit curls were perfect, her deep red lipstick was perfect. And although I was still adjusting to the disclosure, she was rich. In that context, at that very moment, Edith was perfect.

I stared down at my own outfit, caught my reflection on the polished interior of the hangar walls, and hoped all the beautiful people thought I was doing the "retro-grunge goes to a dinner party" thing. Let them eat cake for all I cared.

"Bird . . ."

Edith flashed a perfect smile at someone she recognized. They waved. I smiled at the woman and waved too. She looked a little confused, we'd never met, but she smiled the same smile and waved to me. Fakers, they were all a bunch of perfect fakers.

"Bird," I whispered through the diseased smile I decided to leave on my face for camouflage and protection, "I finally figured out why everyone looks so damn good at these events."

She smiled at another person she recognized. Smile. Wave. I smiled. Waved.

"What were you saying, sugar?"

"Viv's films excluded, of course, but you know, the work here usually is so ugly that the gallerists and artists invite the beautiful people to distract attention from the horrible art. Besides, everyone knows that the beautiful people will buy stupid and ugly art because they love to have it in their homes, it makes them look even more beautiful and slightly less one-dimensional by comparison."

Edith couldn't afford to be amused.

"Why did you bother attending tonight?"

That Edie, she was begging for a kiss.

"Did you see where the wine is?" She strained her neck trying to find it.

"I'll be right back."

I wove through all the beautiful people, rubbing my

ragged clothes against them for fun. Enlighten their world a little. I walked to the table with the communion wine, stinky aged cheese, and soggy crackers. Nol was at the food table, tucked into a corner, leaning against the wall with a plastic cup of wine in her hand. I popped a chunk of cheese in my mouth, quick decided better of it, and spit its nastiness out into a napkin. I searched for a wastebasket, left the napkin balled up on the table, picked up a little plastic cup prefilled with the thick sweet wine, and took a spot of wall next to Nol. She smiled at me and we both stared off into the sea of art happening.

K was talking with Vivienne. Edie was fielding courtiers. The lights dimmed and Viv's cinematic queer extravaganza was projected against a slab of drywall. Nol and I walked outside to catch some fresh air and become cold in the February crisp. Viv found us later and announced the divorce.

15

Their ceremony had been in Vegas and they had both been wearing Elvis costumes because they were performance artists, but whatever, they had been married. Had been. The married couple was no more.

Soon I would be K's neighbor.

At one point, before either K or I lived in Los Angeles, her building had been quite the place. Back in the day. You know, the onion-skin-thin mythical day everyone talks about, the glorious desirable good old days.

Back in the day, the late 1980s and early 1990s to be exact, K's apartment had been a building stocked with fierce dykes full of swagger and style. They were artists, musicians, and the professionally hip. Their presence had filled the worn-down beauty queen eightplex 1920s building with legends that baby queers still tried to link themselves to over drinks at Crystal's.

Word was that the building's parties had rocked with a good time better than any club's offerings. There was always some sizzling hot famous dyke wandering around the courtyard glassy-eyed with a cup of coffee in the morning. Soap operas played out on a daily basis. Fights for real and knives for fun and laced tea parties where everyone smoked the kind of tea your mamá don't drink. Sounds that couldn't quite be described came from behind common walls. And, cherry on top of the fantasy pie, the rent was the cheapest in town.

Of course, the rent had to be cheap. Where else could a group of avant-garde dykes take over a building except in gang warfare turf? But just because the building's rent was inexpensive didn't mean the place was dilapidated pathetic. A charm dream through and through, just the opposite was true. Every door still had crystal doorknobs. A birdbath filled with clean water was in the courtyard. And when a girl wanted to step out for a night on the town, she was only five minutes from downtown. With each person that moved out, fifteen others wanted to move in.

But you know, even legends start to get crow's-feet after a while in the sun. With the years that had gone by and the latest married couple that moved out, numbers had shifted and only two dykes still called the place home. K and Vivienne, and K hadn't even moved in until after the gold plating had begun to chip off the building's luster. Her upstairs apartment had only been hers for two years, since she met Vivienne.

How K hooked up with the apartment, that's one worth telling in itself. It started when a lump of money so big that her folks told her to get a will came through from her friend's insurance company after the wreck. K was twenty then. She left her spray paints in Philly to travel. Went all around Europe with a backpack strapped to her body. Her parents had thought she'd lost it, seeing as she was practically the first one in their family to ever leave Philadelphia. She settled down in New York and then San Francisco and then Houston long enough to spend a lot of her money. In El

Paso she bought her cowboy truck with the bundle of dollars she had left and drove toward the Hollywood sunset.

Why Hollywood? Simple: talk isn't cheap. The boys K hung out with in Philly had always talked big about where there was tricky tagging and murals done up good. Always proceeding "I know more than you" brag was gospel praise for certain low-ride detail shops. So, long before K drove her slow truck toward the sooty Hollywood sign, she knew where to go to see about work if she ever landed in Los Angeles.

Charlie's Design Shop. Old Man Charlie had a reputation as strong as his old man macho iron will. If you wanted your low-ride done slick, especially if you cruised a van, it was Charlie's you went to for airbrushing. He was a retired pachuco, apparently quite the rude boy at one point, but he'd long ago become a family man with a golden reputation for honest business. Still, he'd never lost any face with his old street corner brothers. Everyone knew Charlie could still paint up the meanest-looking murals if he wanted to.

K took the photograph of her Philly train station mural to Charlie's the day she drove into town. That Charlie, he didn't believe she had painted the mural.

"¡Chale! That's man's work. Forget it," he had said, shooing her out of his garage.

K drove away calm from that first meeting with Charlie. After a few errands, she settled into her motel room for a nap. Late that night, she drove back to Echo Park, fed Charlie's security dog raw steak to make friends, and did up another version of her Philadelphia train station mural on the parking area blank wall of Charlie's shop. Having met him once, she knew Charlie would rather a curvy Aztec warrior woman instead of the lanky hip-hop girl she'd put in her mural at home. Standing atop the peak of a blue mountain with a silver desert stretched out before her, the woman in the mural K did up that night was insane perfect in detail.

The next day, K walked in to say hello to Charlie. He had her airbrushing the walls of pimped-out low-ride vans for a healthy pay that same afternoon. K's mural, it added fresh gleam to Charlie's local fame.

It's a winding road, but the mural is how K got the apartment in Viv's building. See, one of the building's old legends worked in a shop tuning cars across the street from K's work. That woman and K, they started talking out on the sidewalk during their breaks one day. The legend was moving to North Carolina to live on acres of land and start a printing press with her girlfriend. K needed a place to live. Introductions to Vivienne were made and that was that, the next week another dyke went off to be a farmer and K moved in.

Still, K wouldn't have ever moved in if Vivienne hadn't approved. On top of being one of the building's original glory players, Viv was the manager. Ever since the early revered days, she was careful about how she held the reins on the place.

I've told you about Vivienne. I swear, the night I met her at Crystal's, it became impossible to think that Prince Charming fairy tales were entirely made up. Mercy, Vivienne had a deadly Colgate-bright gruff smile. She didn't wear the smile for just anyone, only those people she deemed worthy of being on her good side. When I saw that smile aimed in my direction, I got the kind of crush I knew would be nothing but heartache if I ever let it lure me in. That said, Vivienne wasn't the reason why I wanted to move into the building.

K and I had been together more than half a year, my little apartment continued to be depressing small, the apartments in K's building were big one-bedrooms, and K and I, we still liked each other. I had all the convincing I needed. So, I talked with Vivienne about moving in and focused on

141

not blushing through all her strong-arm flirting. She handed me a fine-pointed red pen to sign the papers and made sure the apartment was cleaned up and painted real nice in pure white. As K and I unpacked a U-Haul a few weeks later on the first day of March, Vivienne threw Trader Joe rice pilaf at us and hummed the wedding march.

"Good luck, girls," she anointed in the baritone that made my ears blush warm.

Boxes piled up on the creaking wood floorboards in my new living room. K and I squatted, leaning up against the wall, and played with dust balls in our tired post-moving mood. Strong spring winds teased the closed French windows that lined the north wall. I unlatched the tall rectangles open wide and blocked them from swinging shut with unpacked boxes pushed up against them. Gale winds moved out bits of the previous tenants' breakup and finalized my move in.

Always practical, K reasoned, "At least if it rains and your place floods, it's a short swim to my place."

"The wind is going to work, just watch . . . and, besides, it flooded on Walnut when Nana was a kid and she did fine canoeing down the streets to deliver groceries. So there."

"But, Leticia, what if Weeping decides to take this as an invitation?"

"Don't you use my telling you about her against me. We'd be lucky to have her around. But she doesn't come until nighttime, remember? I'll shut the windows before then."

K stood up, dusted her jeans, and said she was going to go enjoy the warmth of her apartment. I promised to be over soon. She walked down my entryway stairs, across the building's pathway, through the clanging of the security door at the base of her stairs and up her stairs. I heard her poorly aligned front door shut with a solid thud. The heavy tread of her footsteps faded in and out through our common wall.

I unpacked my telephone and answering machine and found the jack in the kitchen. With the phone hooked into the wall, I plugged in the answering machine, put it on the counter under the cupboard, and deepened my voice a notch to record myself saying hello in the slow pace of an outgoing message. My head was so close to the answering machine that when the telephone rang, I jumped and hit my skull on the underside of the cupboard. Rubbing what was going to become a lump for sure, I answered the telephone.

"I'm not cold, thank you very much."

"That's very good to know, Leticia." It was my boss Beatrice's scratch of a husk hello.

"Bea, sorry, I thought K was calling."

"I figured out that much. So, how is the move going?"

"Good. The U-Haul's returned and boxes are all over my living room. Everything good at the shop today?"

Day-Glo graphic detail, Bea told me how anatomically revealing one of the hill boy's cropped shorts were when he dropped off his bichon frisé to get a brush job. I swear Bea would never retire just so she could have a daily opportunity to outdo the boys with her catty remarks.

"Anyway, I was just calling to make sure your new number was working. I guess it is. Monday you have a Maltese wash-style-dry, a Pomeranian style, an affenpinscher trim, three nails booked, first one at ten. And by the way, one of the daddies says if you dare put Bunny Pink on his girl again, he'll have an Oscar-worthy Bette Davis conniption. He says six months of the same manicure has damaged his girl's image. Bring some coral pinks or something, all right? Happy Home and hello to K for me."

"Thanks, Bea. See you Monday."

I called K and asked if I could borrow a sweater to wear while I unpacked a few things.

"It's kind of cold with the wind coming in."

Laughter through the telephone echoed in the wall.

"I'm getting in the shower. You could just close up the windows and come over here. I'll keep you warm." Her best perv throaty laugh. "Hey, did someone call you a minute ago?"

"Yeah, it was my other girlfriend. She said to say hello to my old lady for her."

No response.

"Oh, come on, *laugh*. I'm tired, I'm doing my best."

"You sound tired."

"Golly, thanks. Anyway, Beatrice called to say hello. I just can't wait to primp up the yippers on Monday."

"You know you love glamming them up for queen boys to flaunt at Bark Park. And you know you do good work."

"Thank you, K."

"It's just true is all. Look, I'm freezing in my towel . . ."

"Didn't you just tell me it was warm over there?"

"Warmer than the apartment of a loopy girl who keeps the windows open in the middle of a windstorm."

"Watch it, I'll send my girlfriend Weeping over, she'll mess you up something good."

"Yes, dearest," she loved playing tired old couple with me. "Whatever you say, dear heart. Come and get a sweater if you need it."

"Thank you, poopie."

That got her to hang up.

I didn't want to go and get the sweater. I wanted her to bring it to me. With a kiss. I wanted my tiara, damn it.

The rusted pipes rattled as she showered. I unpacked and hung my clothes. When I heard her turn the water off, I tapped on the closet wall three times. "I love you." She tapped three times back. We were sick, truly embarrassing sick.

With the windows closed up for the evening, I turned on a night-light in the hall. I walked down the stairs, across the walkway under the bright searchlight of a police helicopter flying overhead, up K's stairs to her heavy front door, and into her warm apartment that smelled of apple soap and chamomile shampoo.

K pitted and sliced the olives. I warmed the tortillas and slicked them in hot oil. She shredded half a pound of cheese. I crumbled the walnuts. She slid the tortillas in red sauce and filled them with the olives, walnuts, and cheese. I rolled the bundles into perfect little factory cylinders. She sprinkled cheddar and olive bits onto the top. I tried to light her 1950s oven, but it burped a devil scary fireball at me so she took over the task. I set the table with two good forks, two blue plates that matched each other's color best, and squeezed lime wedges into two wineglasses of bubble water. The enchiladas melted together and we clinked our water in a toast.

"To good neighbors."

Dinner, my toothbrush from her medicine cabinet, the curve of her back, and my arm wrapped heavily across her belly. Bliss.

The first time I brought home a paycheck to my new apartment, I passed go and immediately proceeded to the 99-cent store with bars on its windows at the corner of our block. I'd been cradling the idea for a while and I was thrilled when I finally bought a shrink-wrapped collection of oversized bejeweled rings. Two of the rings lived at my place and two at K's. Their plastic shiny golden bands with

145

sugar-cube-size tinted glass stones stayed on a hook at their respective front doors when we were out, and when we were in they adorned our hands as we waved our diamonds about in reference to our mansion's west and east wings. No matter which apartment we were in, those rings were a mighty fine accompaniment to my pearl choker. And seeing K with her gigantor ruby and amethyst rings, it was almost too Liberace sexy to be true.

Once I got to wear both of the rings at K's place for an entire day. I woke up lazy late in her bed after she left for work, threw on my sweats, shoes, and a fisherman's cap for a touch of tough in case Vivienne saw me as I walked next door. I hung my ring up on its hook to leave and realized my keys were at my place on the kitchen counter. I had carried an armload of groceries for dinner from there to K's the night before and she had let me into her place. And, of course, it was autopilot for me to lock the bottom lock of my door from the inside as I walked out. My door would be locked. No keys.

I considered crawling from K's tiny bathroom window to my bathroom window just a foot away. But there was no ledge, it was a story up, and a rotted baby palm tree where I suspected mice lived would catch me if I fell. The potential accident was imagined to its final rescue scene in manager Vivienne's strong arms and then I remembered that Vivienne was in New York being glamorous with her girlfriend at some film festival she was showing in.

K was at work. The groceries were at my place that week. The television was at my place. My wallet was at my place. Beatrice Poodle Primp was closed for self-declared holiday. I had all day with no plans.

I put on the west wing's jewelry collection, sat in K's kitchen, and looked through her shoe boxes of photos. That one close-up of K before her accident, damn, that photo gave me the shivers so bad that I put the shoe box away almost as soon as I'd opened it. I walked the rather long two neighborhoods away to Crystal's, hoping to manage a drink on the house.

I hadn't even ordered my Shirley Temple yet when this burly biker grandpa lady dressed in leather chaps with a whiskey sour sat down beside me.

"A good joke always lasts at least thirty seconds," she told pasty beautiful Crystal behind the bar. "If not, no matter how good it seemed so far, it's guaranteed to crash."

Grandpa took a swig from her drink, put the glass down on the bar, covered the rim with her little white bar napkin, and walked outside for a cigarette.

Crystal mixed my drink in a short glass and stared her laser eyes at me.

"Twenty-nine seconds by my count."

16

I almost busted a hole through the teasing common wall. After a month, putting on and taking off shoes repeatedly to retrieve miscellaneous things from whichever apartment K and I weren't inhabiting for the night got completely old. Vivienne said she wouldn't tattle to the owner if we tore down the wall so long as we promised to patch and paint it over if we ever moved out. I could tell from the glint in Vivienne's eye that it got her hot to think about seeing us in white undershirt working clothes, dusty with drywall and probably needing to borrow her power tools for the chore. I chipped away at a tiny spot of painted plaster with a hammer and flathead screwdriver. The task bored me as quickly as I began. Sleepovers in alternating bedrooms charmed us suddenly and our common wall remained intact.

Silver lining, K and I added tool-belt sex to the variety pack.

My princess feet decided they didn't like treading on vinyl floors faded and stained nasty, so I installed linoleum in my kitchen. Chalkboard black squares with little flints of white. For one prissy week I made K take her shoes off when she came over to eat in my dinette. Before going to bed, I wiped the floor clean with a paper towel and Windex while she watched and pointed out spots I had missed. It was a dee-lish game.

I responded by supervising K as she painted her kitchen apple red and her closet cobalt blue, minus a far corner of the high ceiling that she couldn't reach, not even after threats of a good spanking. To compensate for the blotchy white corner high up in her bedroom, she spray-painted her bedroom door silver. The silver was the same color she used to detail the hair of the Aztec princesses she painted on vans down at Charlie's shop. Those fierce Aztec women stood at the top of Aztlán pyramids with their lightning-bolt-licked long blue-black hair whipping in a wind definitely not produced by the vans' slow motion as boys cruised down the street. The silver was clearly a good choice for the bedroom door. It kept things nice fired up.

There were no special long-term rules to obey for most of our improvements, but when K painted the bathroom cabinet bright orange, she warned that I'd have to bake chocolate chip cookies Vargas Girl style if I got toothpaste globs on the cabinet. Done. As she licked melted chocolate from my garter belt thigh, K told me I better start watching it with the toothpaste.

We made Vivienne downstairs proud. She thought our homemaking efforts were amusing or cute or something patronizing like that, and as a gold star of approval she gave me money for gardening supplies. Just as I was squatting down to fix up the ground in the courtyard for forget-me-nots, Vivienne found me.

"Don't know if you want to bother with that."

I figured she was flirting so I ignored her and waited for more promising bait.

"Leticia, the owner just called. They sold the building."

"What?" I looked up so fast that I lost my balance and landed on the seedling flats.

For the first time in fifty years the building had changed hands. And Vivienne wasn't manager anymore. No warning. Snap, just like that, a residential civil war began.

I suddenly knew where evening soap opera plots got their nerve. It turned out that a young queer boy turned skinhead wannabe, the only creepy tenant in the building, was the new owner. He hadn't ever been a welcome presence in the building, but Vivienne had always told us just to ignore him because having to deal with the fiasco of evicting him would be too much headache. Skinhead had sneaked his way into the building a couple years back to be roommates with a previous tenant, one from the famed days, and then he stayed when she moved out. His roommate left because it was easier to find a new place to live than to fight for the apartment once he started beating her on Fridays for fun. He paid his rent on time and he generally left the rest of us alone, so Vivienne just flicked away his attempts at confrontation. Unfortunately, that was no longer an option. Apparently, having just one apartment was not good enough for him, so he pulled his billionaire daddy out of the sky. Daddy bought the property for Skinhead to manage. Abracadabra, the building was the plaything of a supposedly gay, most definitely entitled, homophobic neo-Nazi who had taken a liking to using "dyke" as if it were an insult.

As Vivienne said, "That fussy snot needs to go to queer school."

The situation was fucked. I wanted to live there. Third Street was my home. I mean, I adored our building and I felt a trace of family in the neighborhood. Having grown up on Walnut Street, it was easy to gauge just the right amount of tough to show the Third Street gangster boys. Just the same, I'd quick figured out who would nod nice to my smile hello but then whisper rude in the fast Spanish they assumed I couldn't understand. "Are those girls in that building cousins? Aren't any of them married? They're not whores, are they?" I bit my tongue and tuned it out in my hunky-dory honeymoon mood. Our block was perfect as far as I was concerned. The police helicopters that flew above our neighborhood nightly, rarely on actual calls and usually just for oppressive kicks, lit our bedrooms with what I chose to dub romance mood lighting. Trumpet-backed mariachi singers and polka-beat band music poured into my apartment the entire weekend long. That was just like Walnut exaggerated a little, I told myself. But then Skinhead hammered a Confederate flag plaque into a post next to my mailbox. My bliss smile was staked deep down into the mud when that plaque appeared.

A week into his reign, Skinhead evicted my downstairs neighbor to create a "recording studio" so he and his guitar-toting thug friends could practice Jethro Tull and Jefferson Starship songs at full volume Monday through Friday late at night. Warbled renditions of "Aqualung" and "White Rabbit" shook the building with Skinhead's confused bumper-sticker politics. During his frequent "rehearsal" get-togethers, his charming buddies literally let their dogs, three pit bulls and one ratty mutt as mean as she was ugly, go loose. And as a special favor, Skinhead's heavy combat boots stomped back and forth on the hardwood floors under my bedroom whenever I'd finished getting ready for bed and was about to fall asleep. When I'd call the pink house to say hello, he would turn his amps up extra loud so I could barely hear Nana on the other line. Fucker played "Brown Sugar" predictably on those occasions. A sense of humor in the wrong hands is a dangerous thing.

Nana sent me two nature sounds tapes, rain, and ocean waves, to flood the downstairs music and marching. It was a gross combination. Wet sounds mixed with the rhythm of neo-Nazi boots didn't exactly rock me to sleep. When K said, "It gives new meaning to 'white noise,' doesn't it?" I found it hard to laugh.

All of this and I'd only been at what should have been the epitome of dyke fantasy land for just under two months' time. Translation: a joke gone bad far earlier than thirty seconds in the grand scheme of things. Not all punch lines are delivered as slowly as the requirements of fine comedy demand.

Time to pokey on out and onto something new. I lit a candle and asked Weeping to help. That girl, she must have held a collection at her office for us because before my angry tears and K's frustrated near-complete silence could dry, I found a highlighted page from the *Weekly*'s real estate section folded up and slid under my front door.

There was an old bungalow ready for rent a hopscotch-jump north of downtown in an affordable neighborhood. Elysian Park. I didn't know much about the area. The off chance that Elysian Park was named for the mythical Elysium fields of paradise was hook, line, and sinker.

Early the next morning I woke up and rattled the hot water pipes with my shower right after I heard Skinhead settle down to sleep. I buttoned on a classy blouse that Vivienne lent me from her collection of ex-girlfriends' clothes. She gave me her lint brush to use on a pair of abandoned slacks from graduation. The pants ironed, I dug out a handbag from a shoe box tucked in my closet's far corner. I spit-shined a pair of high heels tissue-wrapped and stored away for so long that paper lint stuck permanent on the heels. After practically shredding a pair of knee-high nylons with my hangnail hands, I damned a gold barrette to hell in a handbasket.

Lickety-split, I was at a real estate agent's office to fill out an application for the bungalow. I played Emily Post perfect, my smile was real nice, and I shook hands professionally. The agent took the application from my hands that listed K and me as "roommates." My four sheets of paper went on top of about forty other applications for the house. I *was* going to get the bungalow I hadn't even seen yet; I approved of no other outcome.

Realtor man gave me directions to go look at the house. On the way, I passed a few billboards in Spanish. They were literally good signs, the place felt like home already. I drove past the landmark diner the real estate agent had told me I would pass if I was going in the correct direction. I turned right at the third antique lamppost on the boulevard, found the house, and parked my car in the drive.

The unlocked house was being painted a truly hideous off-white streaky cheap paint color, but I was in love. I scratched out a note and tucked it out of sight on the high shelf of the bedroom closet.

"This is now officially Leticia and K's home."

As I drove away from the bungalow, my heels kept snagging on the floor mat carpet under the clutch, so I pulled over, took my shoes off, and drove the rest of the way back to the Third Street apartment barefoot. My car parked, I held the heels in my hand, ready to hit one of Skinhead's roaming pit bulls if I had to, and ran up the entry stairs to my door, keys ready and working fast in the lock. Not two minutes passed and the phone rang.

I answered with a telemarketer's measured charm. By the time K got home from work that evening, we had been chosen to rent the place.

I called Nana and gave her the news.

"I've lived my whole life in one house. You must have ants in your pants, Leticia."

"Well, if I do, so does K." It was time to get brave. "K and I, we're going to live together, Nana."

Silence.

"Nana?"

"Yes, yes, I heard you. Look, you come pick me up the day you're moving. I'm going to help you two girls."

"Nana—"

"You don't call often enough. If I'm not there when you move, I might lose track of where you live these days."

"Thank you, Nana."

That "Thank you" contained level upon level of nuance. Nana knew.

"Don't thank me. I'm not lifting any heavy boxes."

17

We parked in front of the store and walked around its side to the pink house's back porch door. I pulled on the sweater I'd brought along to cover my tattoo. I knocked once, unlocked the door, and let us in.

"Nana . . . ?"

"I'm in the kitchen. You girls come in here."

K smiled like she thought Nana's bossy was cute.

"Wipe that grin off, K. Do not encourage her."

We walked into the creaking-floor Pine-Sol clean kitchen, Nana started to tell me to take off my sweater to be more comfortable, and my girl K, oh she was smooth, she offered her hand to Nana.

"Thank you, thank you." Nana took K's hand and stood upright. Both feet firm on the ground, she strained her neck back all the way with a confused smile at my androgy tall girl. K smiled polite.

"Very nice to finally meet you in person, Mrs. Torrez."

"Yes, yes, Berenike. If you girls would come visit like I tell you to, we could have met a long time ago, no?"

"Yes ma'am."

"Enough of the 'ma'am.' You make me sound like some little old lady. Call me Nana, same as Leticia does."

"Thank you." K smiled and turned red.

"Yes, yes, call me Nana." Nana rubbed the back of her neck. "Ay, Berenike, you are tall. You sure don't look Puerto Rican, do you?"

"Puerto Rican?"

I stood there silent. I'd never clarified what had up to that point been a calmly clouded issue. I wasn't about to start unfolding the laundry then.

"Yes, Puerto Rican," Nana used her extra careful English pronunciation to clear away the accent she thought was causing confusion. "You are from North Philadelphia, right, Berenike?"

"Yes," K's light clicked on bright, "oh yes, and a lot of my neighbors back home are Puerto Rican, but my family's from Greece originally."

"Oh, that's why you're so tall, I guess." I could see Nana's wheels turning, *Do most Greek girls have hair so short and wear boys' clothes?*

Nana started shuffling and as we walked to the car, she took quick inventory of K's Sears catalog construction site pants, steel-toed work boots, and baggy long-sleeved men's tee-shirt.

K stood tall and humble handsome beautiful perfect in the line of friendly fire.

Nana sat on the lawn in K's yellow kitchen chair guarding the boxes K and I dragged down from our apartments. Nana was won over something good when K brought that golden throne down for her to command from. "Bend those knees, Leticia, lift from the knees, didn't you learn anything working all those years in the store? Leticia, you aren't listening to me, look at how Berenike does it, she knows the right way to pick up heavy things." K was sweating just as much from all the boxes she was lifting as from making sure every i was dotted that first day she met Nana face-to-face.

On one trip down the stairs, K's kitchen table balanced precariously between us, we found Vivienne talking with Nana.

"Good luck with your new place." Vivienne gave me a hug and K a slap on the back, Viv was so unbreakably old school like that.

Nana spoke up, "Leticia, Vivienne told me how she helped you two find your new place. How nice of her, did you already tell her thank you for how sweet thoughtful she is?"

Big bulldagger fierce cool artist Vivienne, she blushed and laughed shy in a way I swear sounded like a giggle. I never ceased to be amazed by Nana's power.

"Mrs. Torrez, it was nothing, I just saw the ad, that's all. I was happy to help them out." Viv stared at her hands like they might attack if she didn't keep a close watch on them. "So, look, I'm no good at goodbyes, I mean I know we'll still see each other around, but, well, look, don't be strangers."

"Thanks, Viv."

"Take good care, you two." She walked away.

Nana pointed her hand at K and me. "You better start moving those boxes, they aren't going to grow wings like some Greek myth monster."

Big show-off.

"I don't think they'll grow wings anyway, but who

knows." Nana looked my way and nodded her head once, a crisp move matched, thank the heavens, with a smile. "These days, I guess anything could happen."

K ran upstairs and got Nana some iced tea.

"Thank you, Berenike." Nana smiled sweet and real as she tapped K's shoulder with her glitter dust wand.

It rained toward the end of that moving day. Gray and gloomy. Windy to boot.

The moving truck was returned and paid for. We swept the worn wood floor of the bungalow silky as talc. Boxes were stacked in corners. I was in my new home. Our new home. K and I, we had a home.

Nana bossed me which boxes should be unpacked first, how they should be opened, what needed cleaning, and how nasty badly it needed it. In the midst of this quality-time fun, K grabbed her jacket and said she needed to go run an errand.

"Right now? But there's so much to do here." I needed her to stay, Nana was sweeter in her bossing when K was around, and besides, I didn't think Nana would approve if K wasn't there each second helping.

"I'll only be half an hour. I'll be right back, I promise."

"Can't it wait, K?"

"No, it can't, but I'll be right back. Promise."

"Leticia, if Berenike needs to go do something, let her. She's a good worker, she'll be back to help before you know it." Nana handed K her truck keys.

My god, that girl had it easy with Nana.

"Thank you, Nana. See you ladies soon."

A quick half hour later, true to her word, K was back. Wet from the constant drizzle outside and smiling a suspicious grin, she asked me to come outside for a minute, saying that she needed my help with something.

"K, I have stuff to do."

"Leti, come on, trust me."

I walked out and saw her truck pulled in backwards into the driveway. Crouched in the bed of the truck there was a clear-plastic-tarp-covered green couch, big and square and squishy-cushioned. Let me clarify the color of that huge creature dredged up from a 1970s lagoon. The couch was bright green like a hollowed-out emerald with a flashlight-glaring electric squeal bright at its center. Even with all the bright color K's style had introduced in my day-to-day, the couch was almost more than I could handle. The couch was so ugly it was almost beautiful, but not quite.

"Wow, I'm amazed." At least my response was honest.

"Aren't you surprised?" K smiled big and proud, staring at the couch like it was our shining new baby and she was about to pass around cigars.

"Yes, I am surprised."

"Edith was thrifting at St. Vincent's last week and she told me about this couch. It sounded too good to be true, but when I went to check it out, sure enough, there it was. That same day I put a hold on it for us." She gave me a kiss on the cheek and put her arm around my shoulder. "Happy housewarming."

Nana came outside. "What are you two girls doing out here, come inside already." She saw the couch. "Oh my."

"Isn't it beautiful, Nana?" K smiled even brighter.

Nana mailed a look in my direction. Her face smiling but her eyes ever so slightly signaling uncertainty, I had seen that look plenty of times growing up. Pretty much as soon as I started dressing myself, I saw that look on her face every day. She didn't mean any harm, she just thought K's taste was a little strange.

"The couch is eye-catching."

I coughed to cover a laugh.

I helped a beaming K lift the couch and lug it inside. We put it against the only wall in the living room long enough for its a-family-of-seven-can-sit-here-and-be-cozy length. The front door closed, the couch's plastic tarp removed, cushions fluffed, I realized how deep-down green our new furniture really was.

"K, I hate to tell you, but I think the couch smells like mildew."

"No it doesn't." K's face dropped as if I'd said *she* smelled like mildew.

"I think it does, honey."

I wasn't telling K to be mean. I just couldn't go and sit down on the thing and pretend it didn't smell like a dank basement corner. Nana put the brakes on what was about to build into a little green tiff. She said she didn't like the couch where it was.

"Why do you girls want your backs to the windows? You can't see the pretty field across the street that way."

"Nana, K doesn't like the field."

K stood up. "Maybe Nana's right, maybe we shouldn't have our backs to the field like this." She looked out the windows.

"Puleeze, K. Nana, K's scared because I told her that's where Zeus buried Alcmene."

"There's people buried over there?"

"No, Nana. Zeus buried Alcmene in Elysium. I think our neighborhood gets its name from that story. You know, mythology."

Nana nodded like she already knew that. K was puffing up a little.

"I'm not really scared, the story is just kind of eerie."

"Scaredy-cat," I laughed.

"Leticia, leave Berenike alone. If your story bothers her, it bothers her. But maybe if she doesn't trust that field, she should be able to keep an eye on it, right?"

"Nana, what are we going to do, put the couch smack-dab in the middle of the living room just so it can face the windows?"

"No, no. Look, the couch goes in that corner." She pointed to a narrow corner near the bedroom hall.

"We'd practically have to walk over the couch just to get to the bedroom if we do that."

"That corner is where the couch goes so you can see out the windows."

"Nana, the couch won't fit there is all."

"Leticia, if you don't want to put the couch where it should go, I don't care, just quit arguing at me."

"We could make it fit there. It'll just have to be at an angle." K loved having Nana on her side.

I rolled my eyes and pushed myself up off the couch.

"I'm outnumbered. Nana, where do you want the couch moved to?"

Nana pointed to the corner again. K and I lifted the mammoth object and I felt a sharp something jab me in the knee. An upholstery staple hooked into the knee of my jeans and, as we set the couch down in the designated corner, tore a gaping hole in the material.

"Damn it." My face burned fast with Nana's disapproving quick look. "I mean, *darn* it. Look, Nana, the couch tore my favorite jeans."

"You can stitch it up easy. Besides, why are you wearing your best jeans on moving day? And those pearls you have around your neck. Pearls aren't for moving day."

"Nana, you know the pearls are fake. And these are my favorite jeans, I like to wear them, that's why I'm wearing them."

"But you shouldn't wear good clothes on moving day."

K jumped in, "I'll sew them up for you, Leti, they'll look like brand new."

My arms were shaking from the weight of the green creature as I plopped down on the red chair across the room. Nana tested the couch, nodded approval, and watched the early May skies rain outside.

"How does that saying go? April showers bring May flowers," Nana crackled in English at K. "Flowers for you girls come June instead. May flowers in June for my two girls."

18

Red and orange lining paper went in the drawers and on the kitchen shelves. Snow white paint was put on the trim and doors. The walls were done up blue like the outside of a robin's egg before it flakes away into rainy sky gray. Silver construction site plastic tarp was hung as curtains on some windows for a touch of punk Martha Stewart–goes––dyke Home Depot. The green couch was sprinkled with baking soda like Nana said to do. Once the lounge machine was vacuumed up, our baby was summer fresh. Finishing touches, K put the photo of me from San Francisco up on the fridge in a frame made out of black duct tape.

"Can we put this up too?" K held the group photo-booth shots from the wharf penny arcade.

The black-and-whites were copper-tinted to imitate old-time photographs. It was impossible not to have nostalgia wash over you looking at photos like that.

"Maybe the living room needs some panache?"

K pushed a silver thumbtack into the wall next to the couch, found a small binder clip, clamped it to the top of the photo strip, and hooked the metal clip onto the thumbtack. "Perfect."

Each surface was scrubbed anew. Our home glistened sweet as rock sugar. K and I, we had a gingerbread house.

And everyone knows that candy goes with gingerbread.

I had smirking daydreams about the delivery accidentally being signed for by one of our apple pie elderly neighbors. Neighbor old Alma Sue next door would have really dug that. Alma Sue, she had the hots for K since the day we moved in. Why else would she have given us so many apricots from her tree? Why else would she have baked us that coffee cake? Why else would she have said, "Oh, he's so handsome," to me about K when I introduced them to each other? I mean, come on, my girl can look boy, but really.

If only Alma Sue knew.

It was such a difficult decision. So many colors and sizes and shapes to choose from. Glad I wasn't born with one because I got to decide nearly exactly what mine would look like. Candy delicious or serious or hideous pretty? Would I harness it in leather or vinyl, glitter plastic or a tight pair of boy briefs?

The first time I tried to order it on the public library computer, the site crashed. The second time, my credit card was declined. The third time, I canceled the order. It was too much fun, the anticipation and teased-out adventure. The fourth time.

Our first Thursday in the house. That's when the package arrived. To be able to receive packages was one of the solid benefits of living in our new neighborhood. Back at the Third Street apartments, a wrought iron remote-access security gate had fenced us in. On the rare occasion K or I'd get packages there, we'd receive yellow notices in our mailboxes telling us to come to the closest overcrowded postal office annex to pick up the delivery. Vivienne had told me to get used to the inconvenience. See, after the 1992 uprising burst into action two blocks down from our building, the neighborhood had acquired a reputation for potential implosion and the UPS guy didn't want to hang around any longer than he had to. Where our gingerbread house was located, an almost intimidating calm prevailed. Our new neighborhood's most politicized excitement in years was the package that arrived the Thursday after K and I moved in.

Frantic eager for her candy, K bruised her sweet knees on the hardwood floor.

The candy, it got hid away on May 10. Mother's Day, Mexican style, it was the same date each year. And each year Nana and I celebrated it at the pink house as predictably as the calendar had 365 days. Pumpkin pie from the bakery and Cool Whip topping from the supermarket freezer case. A prayer said to thank the Virgen for her motherhood. I gave flowers to Nana for raising me. And always a silent moment after I handed the flowers to Nana during which I knew we both thought of my mother.

Leap year. Nana said we'd celebrate at the gingerbread house so she could see how K and I had unpacked everything.

K set the alarm clock for before the sun came up. She mopped the cracked wood floors and I made every surface shine. We straightened the chairs around the kitchenette table and clipped mint from the window box for fresh iced tea.

Taking my sloppy cleaning clothes off to get dressed proper for Nana, I knew every move had to be extra careful like. The week before, my baggy jeans, recycled tee-shirts, pearl choker, and sharp-edged bob hairdo had dragged me down into a funk and put me in tears. My change should have been simple, but it wasn't. Preparing the new version of myself for presentation to Nana was like I had lost the notes for a chemistry lab but was going ahead with the experiment anyway, hoping that the elements would meld without too harsh an explosion.

Weeping Woman tattooed warm under the sleeve of my white Hanes undershirt, I got the iron its hottest and took the handsomest of my newly rag-picked grown-up dress shirts from the closet. I ironed the button-down with creases perfectly parallel to its ochre and olive green stripes, pulled it on, and buttoned it up. Cleanly knotted my new skinny navy blue tie and held it down in place nice and trim between buttons with a red paper clip. Fixed the collar of my shirt around the tie and tucked its tails smooth into new dark brown slacks. Got out the new good belt and slipped it into place. Took Nana's blessed shoe polish kit out of my closet and super careful polished my oxfords to shine as mirror perfect as had my patent leather Mary Janes when I was little. Made my cropped barbershop clean-cut boy haircut shine with the same kind of forest-scented pomade Papá had used and I crafted the tuft of bangs at my widow's peak into a subtle swirl that waved into the air.

Once my shaking hands had gotten me dressed, I told K that I still had so much cooking to do, I wondered if she would mind driving down alone to pick up Nana. No, she didn't mind, but she saw right through my jitter excuse. Kiss, hug, "I'll be back soon." "Thank you, K."

The food was ready long before K returned with Nana. Too nervous to sit still on the electric green couch inside, I waited out front on our garage-sale-find wood picnic bench. When K's truck pulled up the drive, I stood to greet Nana polite the way I was raised to do. I smiled, but she busied herself getting out of the truck and she didn't see me.

Looking down to watch for raised cracks in the concrete walkway, Nana led the procession with her careful stride. K

166

walked a respectful step behind. With one foot on the first porch step, her hand on the railing, Nana looked up at me to say hello.

She stopped her movements forward and she stared at me. Unlike back when I'd shaved my head in college, this time there was no way for Nana to make-believe that my new look was old-fashioned medicine. My tie clip sparked sunlight into my eye, but not before I saw Nana with her smile gone, mouth agape, maybe disgusted, definitely bothered. Shock harsh loud enough for the whole block to hear, she said, "Dear Mother of God. Is that a boy or a girl?"

19

My head ached from the screaming silence that followed Nana's arrival that Mother's Day. To describe the day as completely without words would be a slight exaggeration. Nana did say, "Thank you for picking me up, my Berenike," before she walked past me to get into the gingerbread house. But from that point on, nothing else was stated verbally.

Nana and I, we knew the routine of spending time together exactly. I gave Nana flowers. A moment of even more densely layered quiet followed. Nana led a silent prayer to the Virgen. K and I set the table with the pie and whipped cream. We sat in each other's company. Without words. There was no need for conversation, but the dense silence of Nana's obvious frustration made the air so thick I found it difficult to breathe. That painful silence, it was nothing like the quiet I had learned to share with K. The quiet of that Mother's Day punctuated every breath and punctured my confidence.

Nana made it perfectly clear, she did not appreciate my carefully honed boyness. Raw deal. I mean, Nana couldn't care less that K was so boy. But with me, ay no. No go. See, as far as Nana could tell, K had always been able to pass as dude if she wanted to. Not me. Nana remembered my girl as well as she remembered the endless days she spent crafting its precise style. Nana hadn't ever braided little K's hair. She hadn't ever taught K to bow humble girl into the Virgen's flowing gowns. Basically Nana didn't look at K's boy and see years of upbringing being actively denied.

When K and I returned to the gingerbread house after taking Nana home, I was beyond exhausted. But I couldn't sleep, not for a long time. I stayed awake. Thinking of boys, of myself, and of all the intersections in between.

In the 1950s bar days, there was a word most dykes would have hissed my direction in an attempt to describe me. Ki-ki. "That one's ki-ki, a neither-nor," they would have said loud enough for me to hear, to try to shame me out of their world. "One night she's a femme prowling pretty for a butch, next night she's a tom cruising for a lady. Never know which you'll get, not when she dresses in the morning, not with the way she talks, tells a story, acts. She's trouble, that one." I'm tough, I could have taken the sneers, but thing was, time had come I wasn't even willing to play the tidy-shift role of ki-ki.

I'd seen signs at intersections that read "Diagonal Crossing Allowed." Those signs fascinated me. See, even when diagonal crossing is permitted, I've noticed that the vast majority of people walk lines perpendicular to the well-traveled roads. Why? Fuck if I know. What I did know was that my life depended on me crossing the street diagonally, sometimes in a winding circular pattern for that matter.

I wasn't a boy, not entirely at least, but at times I wasn't a girl either. Rob would have accused me of being a traitor for claiming part boy. Rob and her blue rosette teacups, she was always ranting and griping and smoking her cigarettes real mean when she talked about how much it bothered her to see hard-core bulldaggers we knew taking hormones and getting the fat removed from their breasts and then cutting their names in half. As if "Rob" was the name her mamá gave that delicate little flower.

Regardless, there were times I was at least part boy. A femme boy deep down. Shy sweater fag, my cardigan on hand to comfort me in the cold world. Bookworm queer boy at heart, K told me on more than one occasion. Certain moods and I was the most enviable of drag princesses, eyelashes all a-flutter and my fingers tickling the air with each gesture. Sometimes I was full of flirtatious swagger, but that playful swag could turn fierce snarl for defense if need be. Never, I promised myself one line I wouldn't cross, never would I be the mean kind of boy that laughed me back inside the store's red doors when I did no good at hot afternoon sour pissing games. Of course, there were plenty of times I was such a fairy lady that I ceased to be even part boy.

Yes, Rob would have accused me of bringing the communal growl down for saying I'm part boy. And pre-Stonewall dykes would have wanted me to call my game. What kind of dyke was I anyway? Good question. Simple and complicated all at once, I wasn't a pigeon to be tucked away neatly into a hole. I didn't wear a fixed category without feeling pain. I was more, or less, or something different entirely.

20

No dogs barking. No stomping feet or rattling pipes. No wind tapping upon the windowpanes. No voices speaking or laughing. No helicopters overhead making the walls vibrate. No explanations offered. No compromises. There was the house all quiet and there was Nana's voice in my thoughts.

"Flowers for you girls come June instead. May flowers in June for my two girls."

What Nana meant by what she had said the day K and I moved into the gingerbread house was beyond me. June was one hopscotch-jump away. The field across the street had plenty of tall grass filling it, but flowers? May flowers in June? Sure, literalism could be thrown out the window, but then what?

I was home alone watching the sun go down fast. K was late at work getting some regular's van perfect for a low-rider contest down at the South Vermont drive-in. Soon she'd be home. She would be tired, speckled with paint, annoyed with macho, and probably deserving a good shoulder rub. But that wouldn't be until later.

I called Bea at home.

"Can I take tomorrow off?"

I didn't offer any excuses. Maybe it was the uncharacteristic drone flat of my voice, but for whatever reason Bea said "Fine" and told me to feel better soon. I said, "I'm not sick, Bea." Again she told me to feel better soon, more gravel in her voice. I said thank you. She said good night.

Sitting on the floor in the middle of the living room, I stared through the front windows' streak and bubble dripping patterns at the weedy grass field across the street. I promised myself to go over to the field someday, just to stand waist high in its tangle, to listen for stories its earth could tell. Listen. The living room creaked in discomfort. The balance of the room's weight was all wrong.

I stood up, walked to the living room's corner, and leaned my scrawny boy body against the green couch island's monstrous side. Four wooden feet trails scratched into the floor as I pushed the couch up against the living room's window-lined front wall. The couch's back flush against the windows and the room became right.

The San Francisco photos K had tacked up remained on the wall next to the heater where the couch had been moments before. There was plenty of room on the windowsills near the couch's new spot for the photos, but I decided against moving them. Somehow it was soothing that the five little black-and-whites were distanced from the emerald forest.

I sat backwards on the green couch, its thick cushion flattening my chest, my knees digging into the cushion-meet-backboard. My forehead on the bottom row of wood-framed glass. My fingers tapped the window's melted panes of sand. A chilled whisper from outside pushed in through the gaps in the old windowsill.

My girl Weeping came by to pay a visit. At least she and I were still on speaking terms.

Nine times I'd called Nana since Mother's Day. She didn't answer a single time. Not even when I called with the secret code ring she'd taught me a decade before other people knew how to screen calls. Six rings, hang up, two rings, hang up, call back and she'll know it's me and answer for sure. No answer. A week had passed that way. I was concerned, maybe there was an emergency, maybe she was sick in bed, maybe I should call an ambulance. I called K at work.

"I've called Nana's a million times, she still won't pick up, maybe I should go down and see if she's all right?"

"Don't overreact. She's fine. She needs some time to adjust. Just give her a couple more days."

"But what if there was an emergency, what if she fell down or something?"

"Nana is indestructible. Don't worry about her."

Me, all grown up, I sat in my gingerbread house on the giant green couch K had bought for us. Me, all grown up, I wanted nothing more than to talk with my nana. Me, all grown up, next to the window like when I was little in my sofa bed at the pink house. Me, all grown up, goose-bumped from Weeping tickling the air same as she'd done each night after Mamá had tucked me in.

Hot zing whirlwind, jack rabbit fast, I knew how I could smooth things out with Nana. The way I was smiling wide all of a sudden, Weeping promised everything would turn ginger peachy.

June flowers, first on my list I would order a sheet cake from the Armenian bakery down the street.

21

When I asked to see a book of cake designs, the grandma at the family bakery asked, "You mean the children's cakes?"

"Yes, I guess so. The children's cakes, please."

She shook her gray curls disapprovingly to let me know that I most certainly did not match her young-mother children's-cake-buying requirements. Whatever, I looked sharp in the starched tuxedo slacks and crisp white Calvin Klein button-down duo that I'd found in perfect condition at the Willy's. I may not have been a mother, but I was one hot boy mamasita.

Careful not to touch me, the grandma handed me the cake design photo album. Flip of several sticky plastic pages, cake number 25. The design was almost perfect. Instead of the Hansel and Gretel duo, I wanted two miniature Gretel figurines with their pink ponytails. Little baskets held at their sides as they walked down a pathway in front of a plastic gingerbread house, those two Gretels would be as fab as me and my K.

The bakery shop woman asked if I was sure I didn't want Hansel and Gretel. "That is what the cake design calls for." I took quick estimate of the situation. She was in her late seventies. Her grandkids were watching television in the corner of the store. Translation was necessary.

I explained: "Oh, but you see, the cake, it's for my two little girl cousins' birthdays. They're sisters. Their birthdays are just one week apart and we're having a combined birthday party for them. You know how little girls get so jealous, if they don't see one little girl doll on the cake for each of them, they'll throw a fit or something and my uncle will get so angry at them for ruining their own party."

"So then I'll put two pairs of Hansel and Gretels on the cake, one pair of the boy and girl little dolls for each of your cousins." She eyed my reaction suspicious.

"Hmm, but then their two brothers might act up and try to make them cry by saying the cake is really for the boys' birthdays. Which wouldn't be true, of course, but you know how boys are."

I didn't cringe once under her stare that stated loud and clear, "I know you're lying, you genderless freak cake vampire."

"Oh," she closed the conversation, and took the photo album away from me like if she didn't, and quick, I would have flown off on my broom with her property, and maybe a couple of her grandchildren, to my bat-filled cave.

Yellow carbon receipt in hand, I walked out peeved that I didn't have the nerve to tell her I wanted "Happy Housewarming, K and Leticia" written in screaming bright blue frosting across the cake. When push came to shove and I tried to attach words to who I was in relation to the person I shared a house with, I found myself unable to speak quick enough to save the day.

Neither of my languages provided words carved precisely

for what K and I were for each other. "Girlfriends" felt so squeaky clean that it made me itch. And "partnership" was like we had an office together and shared letterhead stationery. "Lovers"? I don't know, yes we loved each other, but I felt so overly schmaltzy or skanky focusing only on the connotations of that word. "Familia" worked most of the time, but it hurt to remember that Nana believed true family was the one we are born into, period. So what was left? "Marriage"? Were K and I really married? A pristine white dress that would require us to have maids, maids who could help us lift millions of layers up and out of the way when we needed to piss? And the whole part about being "given away." Hell no.

Rituals of union, that night while we were getting ready for bed I told K I wanted to have a housewarming party. K was washing her face at the sink. I tapped her on the shoulder, she moved aside so I could spit some runny toothpaste down the drain. Never one to be silenced by something as minor as a toothbrush in my mouth, I continued talking.

"I want to go all out for our party. But it'll be pretty easy, I mean, we'll just need to go grocery shopping early Saturday. I ordered a cake, you're going to love it, it's really fun, I want it to be a surprise, but I know you'll dig it. Anyway, we can pick up the cake Saturday noon . . . everything will be set up by Saturday night, easy."

"You already ordered a cake?" K wiped Ivory soap water off her eyes.

"Yeah, it was no big deal, I just went down and chose one, the lady at the bakery, though, now there's a story." I handed K a towel. "You still have a lot of soap around your ears."

Apparently she didn't care. She took the towel from me without so much as a "Thanks" and stared at me as she dried her face.

176

"We've only lived here a few weeks and you decide, without asking for my opinion, that we're having a party?"

I know you're not supposed to swallow toothpaste, but spitting seemed like horrible punctuation right then. I swallowed a good mouthful of peppermint toothpaste drool so I could respond.

"K, it's not like you're supposed to wait years to have a housewarming, the whole point is to have it soon after you move in."

Even though we used the nontoxic hippie saccharine-free kind of toothpaste, the sensation of gulping the thick chalky mess down made my eyes water up nauseous.

"You don't have to start crying, Leti. Never mind, all right?" K threw her towel over the door and walked out of the bathroom. I heard "The party sounds fine" echo in the hallway.

"It sounds fine?"

I followed K into the bedroom. She'd already turned off the lights and was in bed, pretending to be the World's Fastest Falling Asleep Girlfriend.

"That's it? K, I thought you'd be excited. I mean, the party's kind of to celebrate us being together, you know?"

K's lack of enthusiasm pissed me off deep around the edges, not all the way to the core, but still our spat was not making me a happy little newlywed. Playing more petty than I'm proud to admit to, I informed my suddenly selective-hearing girlfriend that the party was going to be a garden party across the street in the empty field she loved so much. She took my teasing hard, regained her ability to communicate, if you can call it that, and told me back off, she really didn't like that spooky field and she wished I'd stop annoying her about it already.

You know the exacerbated cartoon characters with hot steam coming out of their fuming ears? That was my girl that night. Very slow and controlled, K got out of bed, buttoned up a pair of jeans, tucked in her white undershirt and pulled on her boots. Charades, right? Phrase that sounds like "getting dressed"? Second word rhymes with "running away"? I mean, she was pulling a prank, right?

K said quiet and monotone, "I need to get out of the house for a little bit."

"What? K, we're going to sleep. Come on . . . Where you going anyway? Crystal's? I'll come with you, we can talk more there . . ."

"I won't be too late."

It felt too late already. Not trusting what dumb reaction my body might have if I moved a muscle, I stood still and watched from the bedroom as K walked out the front door. My soggy toothbrush still in hand, toothpaste dripped pathetic onto the floor.

K's giant Tonka cowboy truck rattled out the drive. When her truck pulled down the street past the point where I could hear its motor rumbling, it hit me what was going on. K had really left me standing alone in the late dark of night. I was fucking raging red fired up.

An hour passed and I got annoyed that no one was around to applaud my tantrum. It was too late to call anyone to gripe so I decided to calm down. The more tired I got, the more I started feeling a twinge of guilt that K and I'd been at each other's throats over something so stupid. I could own my half, I'd made a decision that was pretty big considering we'd never even really had friends over for dinner, let alone hosted a party. OK, so I may have made things more complicated than they needed to be. But where the hell was K? How was I supposed to say sorry and hear her side with her galloping off into the dark? Our first tiff and it wasn't like we'd pulled on each other's hair or written rude things about each other on the bathroom stall, but still I didn't like remaining on bad terms with K.

Fidgety and wired drained, waiting for K to come home, I poured myself some wine. One glass down, I pulled out the typewriter Nana had given me when I'd gone off to school. My typewriter wasn't the bulky deadweight beautiful one that I grew up being careful not to bump into in the pink house's dining room. No, that luscious machine still lived on the rollaway typewriter table in Nana's care. With its round keys and zing paper advance lever, I'd wanted that antique toy something bad, but it was a fixed anchor in the pink house. Never saw anyone use it, but I'd always known better than to mess with that old typewriter for fear of harming it. Nana made sure no dust ever dulled its gloss-black iron body. The pink house typewriter was sacred special.

Now, the typewriter Nana had given me, it was the plug-in beep-at-you when you misspell kind. When I flipped the on switch, it buzzed mad at me for waking it up so late at night. The way words appeared so fast on the crisp white page, it was like I was confessing to my Dear Diary invisible confidante. My second glass of wine beside me, I brought the machine to its knees.

Zeus and Alcmene, those two wild kids in love, their story was the kind of tearjerker that made soap operas lick their Kleenex commercial endorsement lips. Zeus and Alcmene, theirs was the Unrequited Love story. Sure Zeus flitted about, he wasn't as faithful to Alcmene as he should have been, but he had enough light in the attic to know he should stand awestruck when profound love graced him. And with Alcmene, that was precisely what went down.

See, Alcmene was Zeus's first and sweetest love. She was smart and fierce graceful and she told that old fool Zeus when he was wrong. Alcmene, damn, her beauty was so intense it hurt to look at her just like it stung to look into the sun. Alcmene. She grew old. She grew wiser. She grew stronger in her brilliance. Alcmene was human. She died.

Pained to the depths of his immortal thunder, Zeus nearly flooded the universe with his tears as he lamented the necessity of placing his love in a grave. In all the heavens, in all of humans' land, in all of the oceans' depths, Zeus knew that only one small section of paradise radiated brilliantly enough for Alcmene's burial.

Sparkling green and golden flowers and blue crystal air even amidst Zeus's storm, the Elysian gardens promised a calmer grief as she took Alcmene's body from Zeus's cradling arms.

Alcmene was honored eternally in Elysian fields. Our gingerbread house was tucked in Elysian Park. I'm a goofy girl, what can I say? The whole thing moved me. My typewriter humming warm, I crafted up a storybook to give to K. I figured the gesture was just pushy and weird enough that she'd have to laugh and forgive me for my end of the evening's drama. On the book's construction paper cover I glued down a coupon photo of a Franklin Mint porcelain gingerbread house. The little book I made for K, that love letter was romance perfect.

When K's truck pulled up the drive, I hid the storybook fast under the couch and stood to give her an apology and a mighty fine kiss. Second she opened the door, my plan imploded.

I'd had two glasses of wine, and no matter what my greeting, I was beyond being subtle.

"How is Edith?"

A third glass of wine might have been in order.

"Edith?"

"You're wearing a cloud of her perfume and cigarettes, K."

"Edith is fine. I swung by their place to say hey."

"I thought you were going to the Crystal Room."

"I never said that."

"So, you went to Nol and Edie's to tell them how much I annoy you?"

"Leti . . . let's drop it. Please. Edith sent a hello. She says they'll be here on Saturday."

"What about Nolan, she didn't say hello to me?"

"Nolan wasn't home."

That Saturday as I got dressed for the party, K strode up to me with a handful of my boy underwear in her hand.

"Should we leave these on display for the guests?"

Remember *The Newlywed Game* with Bob Eubanks? If I was sitting on one of those stick-to-your-thigh orange vinyl love seats and Bob asked me what one thing I did at home that peeved K most, I would have to answer it was the way I left my underwear everywhere. Well, she disliked the way I swept up dust from the floor with my hands if I suddenly got grossed out from a fuzzy layer while walking across the room, which happened often, but she'd only laugh real short at me when she'd find me compulsive like that. It was the underwear that predictably got her crescent green eyes dart sharp.

I didn't leave the underwear around gross guy style, nasty and dirty thrown down on the ground, waiting to be put in the hamper by the wife-slave. As if. No, my whitey-tighties were on doorknobs, the bathroom cabinet knobs, and a few were usually draped over hangers on the shower rail and here and there. All of them, no matter where they were, they were bleached nice white. My dirty underwear was clean, thank you very much. And they were turned right side out so no one would have to witness the private side of the fabric unless they wanted to. See, K and I only dragged ourselves to the coin fluff-and-fold once every three weeks or so. I didn't have enough pairs to last me that long, and even if I did, they would stay creepy stained if I hid them in a hamper and let them sit until we were ready to do our chore. Woolite and I were buddies. First week at the gingerbread, K had told me she was going to scream if she had to remove my underwear from the bathroom sink one more time to spit out her toothpaste. She accused me of some twisted form of exhibitionism. Maybe, but to me the whole situation was too tame to really be that. Anyway, K hated my damp underwear hanging around the house to dry and she had them held out to me the morning of the party.

"I think they make dandy decorations for a soiree."

Party preparations stress out a quiet girl like K. Either that or my comment just was not funny.

I hid the underwear away on hangers in our bedroom closet, all the clothes pushed to one side on the hanger rod so the wet underwear wouldn't touch K's jacket. Basically the underwear was out of sight by the time Nolan and Ms. Edith came at noon to help us set up the house for festivities.

"What a perfectly charming boy you have here, K." Edith kissed my cheek and straightened my tie.

Nol nodded and smiled my direction. "Nice. Now us boys can stick together and defend ourselves against Ms. Edith glamour girl."

Edith glared at Nol. Doomed dynamic duo.

With them lying low since the San Francisco feud and us fussing over fixing up our nest o' love, it was the first time Edith and Nol had seen the gingerbread house. Edith approved of the minimal decoration and pure blue walls. Even though she didn't say anything, I could tell she hated the green couch, especially amidst the clashing walls. I felt protective of our couch right then. Tough beans if Ms. Edie didn't like the green monster. Besides, considering it was her big mouth that told K about the poor couch, Edie had no right to vibe the couch and its ugly.

Nolan asked what was up with all the silver tarp on the windows, were we running a meth lab in our free time? Haha, Nol, they are called "curtains." "Curtains? No, Leticia, that is the stuff you build a freeway underpass house with." Edith called them "charming window dressings." Laser bolts charged the tense space between Edith and Nolan. It'd been five months of them "trying to work things out"—the forecast did not predict sunshine.

After putting down bags of groceries in the kitchen, Edith opened the clasp of her gold lamé handbag and slipped out a shimmering little box. The present was all sparkly paper and silky bow.

"You got them something?" Nolan stopped loading drinks into the refrigerator.

Edith sh'd Nolan.

"I mean, we got you something, gals," Nolan smiled too big.

K stood next to me as I unwrapped the paper careful not to tear it. An audiotape. *Maria Callas—"Medea"* marked on its cover in Edith's rounded flowy cursive.

I looked up at K out of the corner of my eye but she didn't meet my glance to exchange looks.

"Thanks, Edie. It's so sweet of you to get us a housewarming gift."

Edith waved me away with a smile. I took a deep breath in to prepare for the upcoming lecture.

"I've heard of Medea before, but who's Maria Callas?"

"Darling," Edie must have gotten tons of gold stars in Snooty Pronunciation 101, "you don't know who Maria Callas is? My goodness, how dreadful."

Ms. Edith leaned up against the counter, manicured hand to her face in exaggerated shock. She rippled her brow, a signal of her true desperation—she made it a habit not to emote through face contortions on a regular basis for fear of wrinkles developing.

"You absolutely should familiarize yourself with Callas's music, Leticia. Maria Callas was divine. Quite the royalty of opera. Haunting voice. Stunning, really. And the woman could outdress Coco herself."

Nolan started unpacking the drinks again to move out of the way of Edith's sweeping gesticulations.

"I just recently stumbled upon one of her albums for the first time. I took one look at the photograph of Maria on the jacket and knew I simply had to own her music. Then I had to go and purchase a record player. Remember that, dear?" Edith shot a look at Nolan, who had been doing her best to ignore Edith's storytelling.

"Yes, how could I forget, Edie?"

Edie froze Nolan's futzing with her stare and looked back at us. "Can you imagine how difficult it was to find a functioning record player authentically retro enough to complement my aesthetic sensibilities?"

Nolan could hardly control herself by that point.

Onyx-lined cat-eyed divas do not like being snickered at. Ms. Edith made it short.

"K, you are familiar with Callas. Please tell these two that I am correct in saying she is fabulous."

The thought of K listening to the same melodramatic music that pleased our Ms. Edith was beyond me. I mean, to think that they had anything in common beyond surface-value friendship was almost amusing.

"You know about Callas, K? I didn't realize you were such an opera queen."

"Maria Callas is practically a Greek icon, Leti. I am Greek, remember?"

"Yeah, but you didn't really grow up very Greek."

I realized immediately, but not soon enough, that my comment didn't deserve being said.

"K, I was just surprised, that's all. So, tell us, Callas is pretty fab?"

"I don't feel like talking about it right now, but, yes, she is."

Nol looked over at me, concerned. She wasn't used to seeing my girl and me bicker snap tone at each other. Hell, I wasn't used to it either. It was wrong, really wrong. I promised myself that the uncomfortable between K and me would change back to la-di-da happy, and soon. I smiled, don't worry about us, girl. Nol didn't seem convinced.

"Perhaps some things are best left unsaid. Just listen to the tape." Edith waved a hand toward K's boom box.

I handed the tape to K and she put it on for us while we cut vegetables into sticks. We listened to Callas. Edith sang along to Maria's soprano drama quotient. Lord, Callas had some lungs and attitude to boot. I listened, but I was nearly certain I didn't like Callas the way Edie did.

We were fixing up the living room when, no time like the present, I wiped nervous hands clean and told them my plan.

"You guys, I was thinking the other day—"

"Oh, honey, you have to be careful doing that . . . did it hurt?" Nol stopped arranging flowers in an emptied-out Jack Daniel's bottle she'd brought.

"Nol, seriously, I have something important I want to tell you guys . . ."

"Sorry, go on."

"Anyway, I was thinking that maybe it's time for me to do something *more*, you know? I mean, working at Bea's has been nice and all, but it's just a job and I feel like I need to make a move, do something grown-up. I think I figured something out that would even make Nana happy . . . I can't stand that she's so uncomfortable around me all of a sudden. I mean, Mother's Day was painful, wasn't it, K?"

"It was intense." She fluffed the green couch's cushions.

"So, I was thinking . . . what could I do that would be long-term good, that would be a mature step forward? I wondered, is there something I could do that would even make Nana proud?"

They were all looking at me, waiting as I paused for dramatic effect.

"I've decided I'm going to open a store." I clapped my hands and smiled big, even just speaking my plan made me giddy.

"A store?" Edith put down a platter of food, sat in a red chair, and searched through her handbag like it was the Grand Canyon and she couldn't find a prized piece of lint she'd dropped.

"Yeah, like the mom 'n' pop Mamá Estrella had. I mean, I grew up in it, I know all about having a little store. I think it'd be great."

Booger to Edie and her bad attitude. She wasn't going to piss on my parade.

"And where exactly would you open this little store?" Edith pulled her monogrammed cigarette case out of the purse and slid a Dunhill into her trusty holder.

"I don't know, Edie, I bet I could find a storefront somewhere nearby. I mean, rent's cheap around here. There's always stuff up for grabs."

"Darling, you need capital to open a business. Exactly how do you think you'll manage that?" Edith licked her glossy orange lips.

Nol saw my hands go from happy clap to discontented wring.

"Nifty magic trick, Edie. You sound just like your father." Nol knew she was going to get shit for saying it, but I was happy she did because I needed someone backing me up.

"I am simply being realistic, Nolan."

"Fuck you" was stamped on each syllable of Edith's response.

"Well, I for one think it sounds great, Leti. If it's something you decide you really want to do, you'll figure out whatever details come up."

"Thank you, Nol."

K didn't look up from banging on the green couch cushions to say, "But you do have to be realistic, Leti. Edith has a point. You've never run a business . . . it's not like your film studies degree was preparation for opening a shop."

"K, the couch is as fluffy as it's going to get."

She turned to face me and crossed her arms on her chest defensive tough boy.

"K, I was raised in a store. Remember? And besides, not knowing exactly how to run a business is the best part of my plan—I can ask Nana for her help. It'd be a perfect way to show her how much I appreciate her, how much I respect where I've come from, what she's taught me."

K's flat stare stung hard.

"I can't believe you're being like this, K."

"Being like what? I just don't want you to get in over your head."

"Not to be too arrogant, but I'm not exactly stupid, you know."

"Leti, I'm not saying you're not able. Look, just take some time to think about it."

"I'm going to do it, K."

Dead quiet so loud I heard ghosts in the other rooms demanding my immediate attention. As I turned to walk to the kitchen, Edie started to light her cigarette. The girl had nerve, really she had a bundle of nerve.

"No smoking in the house, Contreras."

I tried to just breathe and trust that everything would smooth itself out. Party guests showed up soon enough, the four of us put on our happy faces, and I changed the music. It was a small gathering and I didn't want to scare anyone away with a depressing opera blaring on about golden fleece, impossible dreams, and a strong woman using her life to make the one she loved happy and then being made to suffer for the love she gave deep from her fire. No, didn't need that in the background of our housewarming.

K's boss Charlie, his wife, and their Cal State L.A. sweatshirt–wearing daughter were the first ones at the door. As much as Charlie loved the work K did down at his shop, he was still an old-fashioned macho and you could tell that it was his wife and daughter who had persuaded him to come hang out with the dykes for the evening. Señora Gomez brought food like she figured we would forget to buy any for our party. She reminded me of my family ladies, strong fierce but still sugar enough to give as if the pot of gold at the end of the rainbow was hers. And as for Charlie's daughter, even though you could tell that Charlie thought she was his little angel perfect girl who he'd walk down the aisle one day, K and I often wondered if she didn't eyeball our dyke-o-rama life like she wished it was hers. There wasn't room for it to be appropriate to ask Mindy straight up if she liked girls, but she sure did seem happy to be at our house, hanging out with the gang from Crystal's, all of whom, even Amy and her stiletto-heeled inflatable doll tennis girl, were thankfully on their best behavior. Well, Amy was a pain, pulling my tie too tight and mussing up my pomade when she came in, but whatever, she was easily ignored after that. The best part of the evening was watching Bea sit down on the couch with Señora Gomez before I had a chance to introduce them. It wasn't every day Bea thought she might have the chance to meet a lady from the East Side she hadn't already hit on a million times over, one with awesome deep smile lines as a bonus.

After I clarified things for Bea and settled baby Gomez in with a soda, the phone rang. It was Vivienne. She hoped we had a good time but she couldn't join us because she was off with her newest girlfriend to go shopping at St. John and Bergdorf Goodman on Fifth and Fifty-seventh.

"We'll miss you. Have fun in New York."

When I hung up the phone, K asked who called.

"Vivienne."

"Is she coming over?"

"No." I repeated Vivienne's story verbatim. "Think it's true?"

"Fendi baguettes mix well with Viv's whips and chains. And you know all the fancy girls hope they'll be Vivienne's next feature starlet. Besides, Vivienne loves flirting with you." K raised her eyebrows like the long-lost lanky Groucho girl and put her arm around my shoulders. "She'd be here if she could."

"Oh yeah? So how come she never put me in one of her films?"

"You're going to be in a film?" Nolan walked toward the refrigerator for another beer and nodded her head toward the side yard. "Hey, did you invite K's girlfriend from next door?"

"No, but, you know, that is such a good idea." I put my drink down, unwrapped K's arm from my shoulder, winked at Nol, and went over to Alma Sue's.

Neighbor Alma Sue answered the door in her pink terry bathrobe, *TV Guide* in her hand. I asked if she'd like to join us.

"Oh, you girls. You don't need any old folk dragging you down, but thank you."

"Alma Sue, you do not qualify as 'old folk.' Can't you come over for a little bit? Just for some cake?"

She declined again, giggling, and swatted me hard with the *TV Guide*.

I went back home. "K, your girlfriend hit me. I think she wants you to go over next time."

Later when we sang "Happy housewarming to you" and sliced up the cake, Nolan and I had K take a corner slice, with a pink frosting rosette on it, over to Alma Sue.

"Be sure to raise everything but the roof for me," Alma Sue told K, pinching her dimple.

The girl came back blushed to the neck and ears.

The roof stayed in place. K and I flitted about keeping our guests fed and with drinks in their hands. Rather, I flitted and K smiled and pointed people to the food and drinks. The party ended early and we sent Nol and Edie home when they offered to help clean up. I needed downtime with my girl. I needed to sit next to her and feel calm and to hook into what had made me want to have the housewarming to begin with. Cups and bottles and plates still scattered around the house, K and I sank into the green couch next to each other.

"The party went well, Leti."

"Yeah, I think people had a good time."

"They did."

"K, I'm sorry. I don't want us to fight anymore."

"I'm sorry too."

"Maybe it's stress from moving in together or something."

She didn't say anything, just pulled me in for a tight hug.

"Omigod, I almost forgot, I have something for you, K. Close your eyes."

When she obeyed, I reached under the couch, wiped a dust ball off the tiny book, and put the gift in K's hands. She opened her eyes, saw the coupon for the Franklin Mint porcelain gingerbread house on the book's cover, and smiled.

That smile. I had been missing that spectacular smile something bad.

"K, before you read it, just remember how much you used to think my teasing was charming, OK?"

She opened the book, saw the "Zeus and Alcmene Go to Vegas" title page, and she actually laughed her deep laugh.

"You are impossible, Leti. Through and through, impossible."

That night we fell asleep curled up close for the first time in too long. Even though it was relatively early when we went to bed, we still woke up tired and lazy late Sunday morning like we'd never get out of bed.

"I don't think I'd survive a wedding." K looked wiped out, like bad dreams had nibbled at her all night long.

"But what about all the gifts we'd get at our showers?"

"No amount of Crock-Pots and antibacterial dish towels are worth it. Besides, Edith already gave us that tape. We're set."

"Speaking of that tape, what a fucking weird housewarming gift, don't you think?"

"I put it in your car tape deck."

"You did? When?"

"Last night, on my way back from Alma Sue's."

"Why?"

"Because I knew you didn't want it in the house. You can

play it if we ever drive somewhere with Edie. It'd make her happy to think we listen to it."

"I don't especially want the tape in my car, but fine. Still, think about all the other very Edie things that Ms. Contreras could have gotten us instead. Like a porcelain cat looking into a fishbowl for the mantel or a fuchsia squash-shaped ashtray for the kitchen table, you know? But she gave us that tape. Weird housewarming gift, don't you think?"

"I don't like vintage store knickknacks. Too trendy."

"K, you're not answering me. Fucking strange house-warming gift, don't you think?"

"If you say so."

"I say so. You can't mean to tell me that you—"

Our phone rang.

A sudden field of chills from neck to ankle told me not to screen that call. The second ring sliced through my sudden cold haze. The phone was next to the bed, the answering machine was in the kitchen, but the nerves prickling my skin told me there was no time to leap out of bed and turn off the machine. Shivering, I picked up the phone on the third ring, just as the machine beeped.

"Hello?"

My voice amplified through the machine in the kitchen and echoed metallic tin throughout the gingerbread house.

"May I please speak to Miss Torrez?"

Limbs cold, ears numb in response to the words spoken to me, my thoughts swam to keep from drowning.

Tell me, have you ever seen those gingerbread wishing cookies? Do you know which ones I mean? They're small and you're supposed to put one in the palm of your hand, make a wish, and press down on it with the fingers of your other hand. If the cookie breaks into three pieces, the wish comes true. I used to practice with those cookies, getting stomachaches from eating entire bags in a sitting, cautiously perfecting the science of holding them just right so they'd break into three.

The voice on the other end of the line continued its professional declarations matter-of-fact. In one gesture, the ground shook and my gingerbread life shattered into pieces far greater than a perfect three.

22

Weeping, look at Nana with her hands held out in front of her, clasped around invisible fingers. Are they your hands she holds? No matter what I'm told, I can see Nana is still clinging.

It is my throat Nana's hands are clasped around. I can't breathe in here. This cube with no air. I want to overwhelm the acrid plastic smell of this room with birds-of-paradise from the pink house's backyard. Remember how Nana used to send me out there with a box of salt to shrivel up slugs? I would watch them be pickled. I would squat down low to the ground to hear their antennae throb. I would squeal with delight and horror and love and disgust. I want a box of salt to make it all better again.

My headache builds steady. With this tension at my crown, I can practically feel how Nana used to pull my little girl waist-long hair too hard when braiding it up fancy style with ribbons. The Dippity-Do dripped cold slime down onto my ears. As she braided, I fiddled one hand in the middle drawer of the dresser next to the mirror. An entire drawer of my hair things. The little purple brush with hard black bristles and rhinestones on its back was my favorite. I am almost willing to promise Nana's god that I'll grow out my barbershop boy haircut if he promises to make her better again. I want a headache from a too tightly woven braid.

Headache. Six shining pills and still it throbs. The hospital room is too bright and me too hot. Fear. Fermented ear. Can't hear through the pounding in my head. I shake.

I shouldn't tease Edith and her theatrical style as much as I do. See, in my family we have dramatic flair to beat the band. Nana was in the produce section. Caught by the Granny Smith apples as she dropped her shopping basket and followed it to the ground. Dropped.

Nana raised me. I think she always will.

23

When the phone rang that Sunday morning after our housewarming, K knew something was wrong just from looking at me. While I mumbled information into the receiver, K went to the kitchen and turned off the answering machine. When she heard me quiet again in our bedroom, she came back to bed with cups of tea for us.

"Who was that?"

"Nana's in the hospital. She's already been there for a while. They didn't know who to reach. It was just coincidence that Ernesta, remember, I've told you about my girl cousin Ernesta, she's a nurse's aide now, fucking good girl Ernesta, always at the right place at the right time, saving lives, being good, I wish I could be a little more like her, she works at the hospital, it's just lucky that Ernesta was at work this morning and she saw that Nana was there and she told the doctors she was family and she told the doctors my name, that I lived in L.A., that they should call me because I am Nana's next of kin. The doctor told me to get to the hospital as soon as I can. Nana had a stroke. She was at the grocery store after church and she had a stroke. She had a stroke, K."

K was handing me clothes and holding her truck keys before I could remember how to blink the eyes staring at the phone in my hand that chanted a robot's "If you'd like to make a call, please . . ." over and over again. K hung up the phone. I let her help me stand. Instantly I was dizzy with a headache that for days to follow would refuse to return to the hot little section of hell it came from. K held up her keys.

"Leti, as soon as you're ready, I'll drive."

"No." I said it short and angry and my headache grew even hotter for being so sharp with K. "I'm going alone. Thanks, though, K."

"Leticia, you're in no shape to drive . . ."

"I am going alone. They wouldn't let you visit her anyway . . . 'family only,' you know?"

"But she's been like family to me, Leti."

"Right, like family. The hospital won't care. They don't consider you and me family."

"But you don't look good to drive, I'll drive. I'll just wait in the truck for as long as it takes."

I took a deep breath. She was trying to help. I would have been upset if she hadn't. I couldn't explain why, but I needed to be alone on the drive down to Orange. To collect myself, to prepare for seeing Nana in a hospital bed, to think of how I could apologize for upsetting her on Mother's Day. I sweetened my tone.

"K, I'm fine. Besides, I don't know how long Nana will be there. When I get to the hospital, she can tell me what the doctors recommend, but I just don't know right now, the doctor didn't tell me over the phone. And you know Nana would feel bad if you were waiting in the truck. She'll probably want me to stay with her to keep her company. I mean, I want to stay with her to keep her company. It'll be good to sit and talk with her. But I promise I'll call home later today so you can talk with Nana, all right?"

"I'll wait by the phone."

"You don't have to. If you don't talk with her today, she'll be going home soon enough and we can fix her a nice dinner or something. You could do me one favor, though."

"Anything."

"Call Bea and let her know that I won't be at work tomorrow. Tell her Nana's in the hospital and I don't know how much time I'm going to need to take off, but I understand if she needs to hire someone else or whatever, it's just that I can't say exactly what day I'll be back to work . . ."

"Bea will understand. She's not going to fire you."

I finished getting dressed, grabbed my car keys, and gave K a quick kiss. Wrinkle serious, she watched from the front door as I walked out. Determined to ignore her concern and get on the road, I went about my departure brisk pace, picked up the newspaper from the driveway so Nana could have something to read, threw it in the back seat, and got in the June-summer-sun-baked car. K didn't go inside until I forced a twitch smile and waved goodbye.

The gingerbread front door finally closed, I put the keys in the ignition, turned on the engine, and jumped scared. Maria Callas's faltering soprano rushed the small space with the final act of *Medea*. Nearly about to vomit in the car's overwhelming loud and hot, I turned off the engine.

Weeping, that's when I heard you gasp for want of cool air in the back seat. You drew in a deep breath and pushed my eyes closed. You looped your arms around me all chain-linked. I bowed before you and kissed your hand, gracious lady. Clicked my heels. A safe place, you knew I desperately needed an intermission, a changed reel, distraction. And, hence, a simple waltz, you lulled me quiet with hush girl stories of borrowed catastrophe. Thick velvet curtains pulled back to reveal a scene no small fraction my parents' and no doubt also K's. Flicker, twirl, flicker, silver screen black-and-white, I started the car. Young love at my side. And you wilting in the heat. I buckled my seat belt and told K to do the same. She said "in a minute" as she opened the glove box to look for a tape to replace the one you loudly protested you wanted to listen to. I took my sunglasses from the dashboard and put them on, only to take them off again once their warmed plastic began to cook the headache-building tempo under the bridge of my nose. I handed the hot plastic to K to put in the glove box. We backed out of the driveway and down the road as K shuffled through napkins and bandages and tape cases. Operatic design wrapped its insistent embrace around me.

The too bright early summer sun glared through the windshield. The visor pulled down did nothing to block the light. My torso pulled up tall and straight to adjust my height did no good. Squinting, my eyes pushed down heavy exhausted from having to focus. Damn that tape Edith gave us, Callas was forcing Medea herself down my throat.

Medea. The cunning one. Goddess, divine. Too strong for some people's liking, so she's said to be a jealous woman, a wicked witch. As if she were the only pushy one in the family. Her father Sun's warmth tired me, I wished he would calm down his bossy bright so it wouldn't blind me like it did. The fact that Helios wouldn't back off bothered me, but not as much as it did to know that he had chosen not to melt away his grandbaby Medea's pain. He must have liked girls dainty and full of compromise. Callas drilled her story into me in the heat.

I heard you giggling right then, Weeping. Your laugh sounded like Joey's back in school when she told me, "You're too hot, Leti."

A momentary rush of your ego mine that day, I responded, "You're not too bad yourself, Joe."

"Watch it, girl. I mean you have too much *hot* in you." She gave my shoulder a light shove to get me to behave and listen. "That's why you've got all that damned wiggling energy. I swear it makes me crazy how you never stay on a single subject for more than a second without jumping out of the pan and into another hot pot."

Remember how Joey took me to her family's house for dinner? It was a lovely gesture, wasn't it? I still feel bad at times that I didn't send her carnations on her birthdays like I heard you tell me too faintly somewhere deep in my dreams once she moved away. She was always good to me. Like that time she took me to her family's house for dinner. Serving us chicken adobo, pushing the crispy empanaditas away from my reach, her mother remedied in Tagalog and Joey translated into English that I was not allowed fried foods,   that I would drink chilled coconut milk with no sugar added, avoid papayas, and never wear the color red. I doubt Josefina's mother would approve of you blasting *Medea* in the scorching afternoon.

Young love at my side. K looked for music, her gaze downward and away from me. We made our way to the end of our street. My hands were as tired as my vision. I drove down our street's sloping hill. My body twitched with what felt like immediate sleep. My feet heavy. My hands dropped to my side. Waltz spin blur, I drove the car into the old town lamppost at the street's corner.

Screaming. That was me. Or was it you, Weeping? Screaming. You and I stared at the passenger seat. The body had already returned its course from through the windshield's glass. Melted strawberry-colored crayons coated K's face and throat. In elementary school her nickname was Red for the hue of the one leotard she wore to gymnastics practice each day. When we were fixing up our gingerbread house, she counterbalanced the outdated peach bathroom tile by painting the cabinet and door and heater grate primary red. Our first-month anniversary, I cut a construction paper sheet into a valentine and left it on her truck's windshield for her. Rubies are her birthstones. K was covered in red. Across the street at the corner diner people dropped their forks on steak and egg breakfasts. Orange juice spilled on their morning newspapers as they ran out toward us. Someone inside somewhere picked up a phone to call an ambulance. Callas's wrenching voice played so noisy that I wished to be deaf. Screaming, you and I, we danced closed-eyed silent grim so loud that I barely heard the tapping.

K knocked soft on my closed car window, and Weeping, you took your arms from around me quick and disappeared like you were scared to get caught holding me. I opened my eyes, half expecting to see you. Instead K stood smiling a hesitant smile with a brown bag in her hand. I opened my door and she handed me the bag.

"I threw some snacks together for your drive. Sure I can't drive you down to Orange?"

"Thank you," I put the bag on the passenger seat, "I just needed to rest for a second. This headache is miserable."

"I'll go get you some water and aspirin . . . "

"I just want to start my drive now, K. I'll call you soon."

If I had only known what was waiting for me, I would have begged K to come with me.

24

I stood next to Nana's bed in the hospital's intensive care unit overprocessed air, shivering in the room's constant lukewarm. I had to breathe low and deep to keep from shaking outright. Nana needed me to maintain control. I was demanding answers for us both. The attending doctor, she pulled back her slouched twenty-four-hour-on-call tired shoulders as I growled my response to the concise explanation she had greeted me with upon my arrival.

"Precisely what the hell do you mean, Doctor?"

Nana was completely silent. No proud stubborn words, no "tsk tsk tsk," no nothing except the beeping and wheezing and droning of the machines attached to her veins, connected to the tube entering her nose and mouth, linked to the wires clipped onto her finger to monitor her heartbeat, the pulse itself a product of the machines plugged into the wall.

"On the phone, I wasn't told she was like this. The doctor on the phone said Nana had a stroke. She only had a stroke. Lots of people have strokes. Why can't you fix her? You *are* a doctor, aren't you?"

"Yes, Miss Torrez," the doctor sighed like she had a right to be tired from the situation. "I am a physician, a neurologist. As I said before, I apologize that the severity of the situation was not properly communicated to you over the telephone, but, and I apologize again, I really do, there is nothing medical science allows us to do for your grandmother at this point except to keep her comfortable."

I put a hand on Nana's arm to protect her from the slap of the doctor's insult.

"Comfortable? You call this comfortable? Look at her."

Lips chapped and cracked, eyelids closed swollen thick, skin drained of all its bronze depth, and bruises had started to form where needles tapped into the veins on Nana's hands.

"Tell me, Doctor, you think she looks *comfortable*?"

"Miss Torrez, I can assure you that your grandmother is not uncomfortable. The level of stroke she experienced has left her unable to discern discomfort or pain."

I wanted to take the doctor's rhetoric and knock her upside the head with it. She didn't fucking get any of it—Nana was *not* comfortable playing mannequin in the hospital bed while people talked about her like she wasn't even present. Nana was proud, self-sufficient, fierce. No, I was absolutely certain, Nana was not comfortable resting in a coma so deep that the doctor told me she would never regain consciousness.

"I can't believe there's no medicine you can give her to snap her out of this. You really mean to tell me that there's nothing you can do to fix strokes?"

"The indicated drug, TPA, works to dissolve the clots obstructing the cerebral arteries blocked by a stroke like the one your grandmother experienced. We can hope that the

symptoms will be reversed, that she might regain consciousness and at least partial use of her body, brain, and speech.
But there is no guarantee. We aim to minimize the damage."

"So that medicine can make people normal again?"

"The odds are generally in the patient's favor for milder
strokes. In your grandmother's severe case, there is nothing
to lose, as without TPA she would probably be severely dis-
abled if she were to survive."

"What more do I need to say? Give Nana that medicine."

The doctor picked up the chart hooked to the foot of
Nana's bed, opened the metal folder, and scanned the top
page, "Unfortunately—"

"Look, I don't know what your assumptions are. I
don't care if it's expensive. I know she doesn't have insurance, but I don't care how expensive it is, we'll find the
money . . ."

"What I was going to say is that, unfortunately, too much
time has already elapsed. TPA must be administered within
three hours of onset of stroke symptoms. It has been approx-
imately four hours since the estimated onset of her stroke."

"Then the medicine just won't work as good, but it has
to do some good, right? Give her the medicine."

"Miss Torrez," again with the sigh, "please try to understand what I'm saying—TPA is not safe to administer after
the third hour. Worse than ineffective, it can cause deadly
swelling of the brain. It is absolutely inappropriate to administer the drug to the patient at this point."

"At this point. At this point? So why didn't you give her
the medicine when she first came in? Why? Tell me exactly
why you decided not to give her the drug when the ambulance brought her here. Tell me." I was close to the doctor,
eyes staring hard into hers, my hands chalk white with how
tense they balled up at my sides.

"Standard procedure was followed. Your grandmother was obtunded—"

"I know you don't speak Spanish but you could at least do me the favor of speaking English."

"Obtunded. Your grandmother could not feel even high-level tests of pain. She was completely unresponsive. In addition, her vital signs were not stable when she arrived; she was dangerously hypertensive. Those factors in combination with her age and the severity of the stroke were all taken into consideration. The attending emergency room physicians decided that stabilizing her was the appropriate degree of care for her."

Cared for. Even Mamá Estrella would have been tempted by the undeserved use of that claim to spit on the doctor's shoes.

"But you said that drug was for people who had strokes like hers."

"Yes, but it was decided she wasn't an optimal or appropriate candidate for TPA."

"But it could have helped her maybe, right?"

"It is possible, but it is more likely that it would not have."

"So, basically, even though there was nothing to lose, you decided not to even try."

"It wasn't me who decided. As I explained, the attending emergency room physicians . . ."

The headache was pounding through my bones. Dots swam in my eyes. My knees were rubber, my vision darkened, and I began to sway. The doctor reached her hand out to me, to brace me, but I pushed it away. I leaned up against the wall and slid down until I sat on the cold linoleum floor. The situation flooded me. A force entirely real had stolen Nana from me, from herself for that matter. I cried hot and angry and sad and frustrated and lonely and scared and tired. Crying hard, really fucking serious tears, I wanted to know where the hell Weeping and her miracle sisters had been when Nana had needed their powerful protection most.

25

rudel! Crudel! Ho dato tutto a te!"
Stomping out of directed character, Callas once screamed Medea's lines at a heckling audience. Cruel world, I have given you everything. Screamed. Her anger must have been something to behold.

Me, I can only whisper right now, but you still hear me, don't you, Weeping? Perk your ears up, woman, because, I swear, you better listen something good.

I have spent my entire life wrapped around your fingers, tangled all cat's cradle in your grasp. I kept you close by my side since my earliest little girl days and this is how you return the gesture? So do tell, why didn't you lend your strong when Nana needed you to breathe a gust of wind into her lungs, when she needed your fire to keep the blood flowing lava smooth?

The fix-it drug could be mending Nana this very moment. Medicine could be making its course through her to bring her back to normal. Tell me why you decided Nana would never speak again. Right now she could be waking up from

207

what could have been not much more than a forced nap. You could have chosen for her to recover, you could have been the one to hold her elbow for support so she could walk slow one foot in front of the other, hands out for balance. Real fast she would have been back to her charming bossy, wouldn't she have?

My body entire, my voice, me, I'm shattering from ice cubes on me for too long. But you are not going to silence me. No, mujer, not you, not nobody, you are not taking my voice from me.

26

"an you put her on the phone for a second?"

"She's resting right now, but I'll tell her you say hello."

Air from the vents in the ceiling pushed its way down my collar and built icicles on my spine.

"Please do. How are you doing?"

"Tired and cold, it's really cold in here."

"Get some rest, promise?"

"K, I decided to stay overnight."

"Sounds good, Leti. After you left this morning, Edith called to see if we needed help cleaning up from the party. I told her Nana was in the hospital."

"That was nice of Edie to call."

"Nol insisted that she wants us to come down to visit you and Nana. They should be here soon, we'll leave when they get here."

"But, K, remember I told you, the hospital only lets family visit."

"Nol said it wouldn't be a problem."

"Do you know how to get here?"

"We'll figure it out."

"See you soon then."

"See you soon."

I hung up the phone and sat at the edge of Nana's bed. Thick locks of her bangs kept matting themselves against the sticky sweat on her forehead. Those rebellious dense sprigs of gray infuriated me. Nana would never let them be so disobedient. I was about to brush her hair back into place for the millionth time with my fingertips, but then it occurred to me that I shouldn't. Nana couldn't speak, she couldn't open her eyes or reach, but maybe she was telling me she was alive. I stared at my nana, willing her to move again.

Nolan told me that the security guard was going to get socked, that she wanted to spill his blood all over his uniform in protest. She wanted to, but Nol's got some pretty constant grown-up control. She talked mean and laughed it off. The guard, probably already home for the evening by the point she told me the story, lived another day.

K, Edith, and Nol arrived at the hospital and walked up to the reception area's automatic double doors. That's where they found the sign at the front desk that maps out which color lines painted on the linoleum floor lead to which places in the hospital. They followed the orange line into an elevator, up two floors, down a hall, and to the ICU's closed heavy door with a salamander security guard sitting on a stool in front of it.

"Our grandmother is in intensive care," Nol took the lead with self-assured matter-of-fact in her voice.

"Your grandmother?" The guard stared at my three girls.

"Yes, our grandmother."

He examined the clipboard on his lap. "What's her name?"

"Guadalupe Estrella Torrez."

His fat forefinger scrolled down the list of patients and stopped at Nana's. "And what's your name?"

"Lorelei Arleen Nolan."

"I just needed your last name."

"That's not what you said." Nol's face pulled tight peeved.

Edith touched Nol's shoulder to calm her. Nol said I should have seen how beady fast the security guard darted his eyes at Edie's gesture, like she'd flipped him off at Sunday service or something. He wrote Nol's name down on his papers and told her she could go in to visit, but only for half an hour and, since it was Sunday, not past 4 p.m. Those were the rules, take it or leave it.

"Yes, but, sir, they need to go in, too." Nol pointed to K, her tall getting taller by the second, and Edith, standing royal with expected privilege.

"You the patient's granddaughter?" he asked K even though he knew the answer.

"They are both my cousins," Edith cut in quick, calm and deliberate.

"Cousins," rude disbelief, "right, 'cousins.' Look, *girls*," the word a pejorative bursting from him, "it's not going to happen. Policy is immediate family only. I'm already being flexible here. And 'cousins,' especially your kind of 'cousins,' isn't immediate family."

Before they could argue, he continued, "You," he poked his finger so far toward Nolan that it almost touched her jacket, "you can go in. For half an hour."

"K, you need to go in. This isn't right," Nol said.

"A lot isn't right, Nol. Say hello to Nana for us. Tell her we'd visit if they'd let us. We'll call the room later, all right?"

K stared so fierce down her long nose at the security guard that he suddenly felt the need to harvest lint from his uniform pants.

I always thought that unless you were locked in a crashing

airplane, it was an embarrassing exaggeration to claim that things were spiraling down and out of control. Call me a convert, bit by bit, the spiral was sucking my life into its grip.

Nol walked into the room and tried her best not to crumple up with too much confusion when she saw Nana. It was useless. Nol's attempt at comforting me with a smile hello was outweighed by the perturbed dark in her eyes.

"Give me a hug, princess."

I pushed myself up out of my chair and let Nol wrap her thick arms around me. That sturdy woman, she held me up as I sobbed so hard it made my teeth ache dry and acid worn down.

***

"Nol, put on channel 64, I like channel 64." My voice was extra crackle with overprocessed air.

I stroked Nana's hand warm glow. Nol found channel 64 and turned her attention back to me.

"Didn't you say they were going to call," I asked.

"That's what K said. They just probably had to go to the cafeteria or something. You know how Edie gets, she's so damned skinny that when she needs to eat, she needs to eat."

Nol had spent hours sitting at the foot of Nana's hospital bed. She had watched as nurses came in and checked Nana's machines. She had gone to get me a soda. She had arranged with the nurses to get me some blankets for the night. She had given me her jacket to wear when she saw that I was shivering goose-bumped and clammy. Nol held my hand and got me tissues when I told her that the doctors said I needed to decide how long I wanted to keep Nana on the machines. Second and third opinions were absolutely certain that Nana would never wake up, no matter how long she rested.

Nolan and I sat and watched the muted television.

Channel 64 is strange, very strange. Basically channel 64 was in-house reality TV transmitted from a closed-circuit camera in the hospital chapel. Burgundy and gold stained-glass windows lit cherry wood and velvet-cushioned pews with an eerie warm blood glow.

Another hour passed and Nol and I were still staring at channel 64.

"Where do you think they are, Nol?"

Before she could answer, the television screen dragged us both silent.

There was Edie up on the television, kneeling at a pew, eyes closed, her folded hands to her forehead. I had never imagined Bird on her knees for anyone, especially God. I watched her lips as they moved. Strange become stranger, Edie was praying.

The concentrated ticking of the hospital room fluorescent lights above us was interrupted only when the phone rang a few minutes later. I couldn't move. Nolan answered.

"Hi, K. Yeah, she's right here. Hold on just a second. Leti . . ."

I shook my head and closed my mouth, realizing it had been hanging open for who knows how long.

Weeping, you were crying right then. Those hot tears, they burned powerful strong.

I listened to Nol's side of her conversation with K. "Yes, unfortunately the doctors say they can't really do anything." "Yes, I know." "Leti's holding up, but I'm sure she wants to see you." "Yeah, that sounds like a good idea." Nolan told me K suggested they spend the night at the hospital, that maybe when another guard came on duty, K could try to get in. I wasn't very hopeful.

"Nol, you guys have to go to work tomorrow."

"We'll all call in sick." She stumbled after that because we both knew it was the wrong thing to say given the situation.

213

"Besides, missing work isn't what's important right now. We want to be here."

"Nothing is going to help. It's fucking disgusting how helpless this whole situation is."

"I agree, Leti, I agree . . . K wants to talk with you."

I took the phone from Nol.

"K, I need at least tonight to be here with Nana."

"Leti, I really want to stay and try to get in. Maybe your cousin could arrange an exception?"

"Maybe, but I almost don't even want to see Ernesta right now. The nurses said she'd be by later, but I wish she wouldn't. Having Ernesta here would make me think about being in the store, Nana all young and healthy. I don't think I can deal with many people right now, you know? I think I just want to be alone with Nana tonight."

"But I'd like to see Nana, to be there with you."

"Nana wouldn't want you to see her like this . . . you know how proud she is. They've got her hooked up to so many machines, it's awful, K."

"Let me try to come by the room, all right?"

"I think I need to be with Nana now."

K didn't argue. I was clear about what I wanted. What I needed. That was to be alone with Nana. K gave me her love. I sent Nol off with a hug. I sat back down in my chair at Nana's side, put my head down on her bed, and tried to rest.

214

27

The sun broke through the tinted hospital windows at five in the morning. My neck cramped and piercing stiff, I sat up in my chair and looked at Nana, unmoved in her bed.

That morning after I arrived at the hospital to be with Nana, that morning I touched Nana's hand and she told me. It's not something I can explain, I just know I heard Nana talking to me as clear as when her voice was still hers to use. I kissed her forehead, her skin unfamiliar with a sour scent. "Nana, I love you too." I wiped away the tears my kiss left streaming down her face as if they were her own. Before I rang for the nurse, I smoothed Nana's hair into place and straightened the collar of her hospital nightgown.

The nurse paged for the doctor to join us in Nana's thick-air hospital room.

Outside, tall palm trees lining the hospital road stood completely still. Not a single bit of movement. Weeping was nowhere in sight. There wasn't even a breeze trace of her.

By sheer virtuosity, she carried off the palm.

That was the closing line from a kid's book I'd read years ago sitting in Papá's barber chair. I'd always thought the palm leaf was a strange symbol for a valued prize. I mean, with any kind of wind at all, the damned clumsy heavy leaves fell out of the sky, tangled in phone lines, and came tumbling down in messy piles on the sidewalks. I'd been told that rats live in palm trees. If the wind blew hard enough, vermin came clunking down with the palm leaves. No matter if my childhood book of the girl with the palm leaf was a sanitized, idealized version of reality, I'd loved its illustrations. The story's victorious main character girl with her palm leaf had reminded me of Pippi Longstocking—really tough and likable.

Damn it, Weeping, I couldn't even see what was right before me. The conductor's wand was blurred and all I could make out was the potential for more pain. How was I not to wisp away? Too cold by Nana's side, my hands were as tacky with fear as the limbs of aloe cut open in the rain. I had become a small damp particle in the fluorescent air. Where were you? Where the fuck were you?

I listened to Nana and told the doctors, "Please take her off the machines. My nana, she's ready now."

Snap of a switch, my world lost its familiarity. I left the hospital and went to the pink house and arranged for Nana's body to be picked up by the mortuary where Mamá and Papá had been buried alongside my mother. The pink house was cold and creaked too much when I walked across its floors. I had planned to spend the night, but by the time noon came around, I called K to say I'd be back at the gingerbread house that evening.

A constant powerful wind arrived as I drove home. My car was pushed out of the bounds of its lane by the gusts of Weeping's tantrum come too late. The winds stayed for nearly a week, tangling life up well past the day K filled our gingerbread house with packed cardboard boxes.

28

olan's car was parked in the driveway. K opened the door to greet me.

"We have company."

"Did you invite them?" I whispered at the gingerbread's threshold.

"Edith and I thought dinner would be a good idea."

"Honey, I'm really tired . . ."

K turned and walked away toward the kitchen.

I slapped on some makeshift version of a hostess face to cover the grimace that had glued itself to my bones since I left the hospital. I found Nol and Edith fixing a salad in the kitchen.

"Hi there." Nol gave me a long hug. "These two thought you'd like a homemade dinner, but if you need us to leave so you can have some quiet time, just tell me."

"Thanks, Nol. I'm not good company tonight, but dinner sounds nice."

Edith didn't say hello. I was so drained that I didn't even notice, but I should have, I should have sensed that a hurricane was cooking.

After K served the salmon, Edie served up the storm.

"Amy's father has purchased a grand Craftsman in mid-city for her. She is absolutely thrilled to finally be leaving her trashy trailer park." Edie took a sip of wine and cleared her throat delicate dainty. "About a month ago she told me that when escrow on the house closed, she'd be looking for roommates . . ."

"And what does this have to do with anything, Edie?"

Nol held her water glass in hand. The way she was looking at Edith, I wondered if the water would soon boil.

"I have decided to rent a room in Amy's house. I will be moving out of our cottage this week, Nolan."

Nolan didn't look very shocked. Pissed, yes, but shocked, no.

"Fine, Edith." Nol placed her glass on the table very deliberately, pushed her chair back from the table, turned to face Edith, and crossed her arms across her barrel chest, breathing slow and trying hard to stay calm.

"That's fine, Edith, but why exactly do you feel the need to make a bulletin of your plans tonight? I thought the familia Contreras prized themselves on their etiquette. It's sure inconsiderate to do this now, here. Leti just got back from being with her nana. One of these days maybe you could do the world a favor and learn how to chill on the melodrama." Nol pushed her chair back to the table and picked up her fork. "We'll talk about this later, Edith."

Edith started crying mean and angry like I hadn't seen since I told her I was exorcising my life of her prima donna poison red apples. A fucking telenovela in my dining room, I was speechless. I couldn't even get myself together enough to pretend to have to excuse myself to go to the bathroom. I just stared across the table. Nolan, completely dry-eyed, leaned forward toward Edith and hissed, "Fucking cut the theatrics, Edith, this is *your* decision. Quit crying."

Help me if I hadn't entered a scene scripted by Rod Serling himself, Edith's tears dried into thin air and she looked at my girl.

"K, are you going to tell them or shall I?"

K shifted in her seat like it was on fire.

"What is going on?" Speaking even simple words made my skull throb. I'd been so numb since leaving the hospital that I'd all but ignored the burning headache that suddenly screamed for my immediate attention.

K cleared her throat. "Actually," she looked up at me and put her hand on mine, "I've decided to rent a room at Amy's too."

"Excuse me?" I was convinced I'd heard her wrong.

"What the hell is going on?" Nolan pushed her chair away from the table again and stood up, her fists on the table.

"Leti," K talked to me as if no one else was in the room with us, "I'm sorry, it's just that I don't know if I can do this marriage house thing yet, maybe it's just too soon. I know we can work things out . . ."

"Work things out?" Nice girl had checked out and I was practically screaming at all three people in the room with me. I flung K's hand off mine, "You've got to be joking, right? This is a joke, right? This is not funny, you guys, this really isn't funny."

"I don't think they're joking, Leti. And if they are, they better stop real soon." Nol's jaw was clenched tight and she was so quiet that her words were barely audible.

And Edith, she was quieter than I had ever seen her. Her beautiful face was distorted, ugly. Mascara raked down her cheeks.

"Leti, I know it's bad timing—"

"No, K, this isn't bad timing, this is really fucking perverse horrible timing."

"I agree, but please understand that I'd decided about the room and gave Amy a deposit long before Nana got sick. I wouldn't have made this decision if I'd known at the time that Nana was going to end up—"

"Dead, K, Nana's not 'sick.' Nana is dead. And what do you mean you decided this long before Nana got sick? Jesus, we'd only lived here for a few weeks before that. And Amy knew? Don't you dare tell me that woman knew you were going to leave our home when she came to the housewarming, K. Don't you dare tell me that."

K stayed silent. Nol sat back down and was fuming, alternating between Edie and K with her mean stares.

"We just moved in here a month ago, K. Why the fuck did you even bother?"

"Because I was really hoping I could do it. I really was. You couldn't have stayed at the apartment much longer anyway."

"Don't act like you've done me some sort of favor, K." The headache swelled and I had to close my eyes to keep nausea at bay. "My god, how am I even going to pay rent? Did you bother to think about any of that? I can only afford to pay half the rent. This is selfish mean, K."

"Leti, I know you won't have any trouble finding another roommate. You'll be happy here, you really will be."

"Don't patronize me, K. I have every right to be angry, I'm not letting you off whatever fucking emotional hook you've put yourself up on . . . I'm not going to be polite to spare you feeling creepy like you should."

Edith started crying again. I snapped a look at her.

"Fucking quit it, Edith! I can't stand your fucking crying right now." I looked back at K. "So, are you two seeing each other or something?"

"Nothing is going on between me and Edie. We just both needed a change, that's all."

"Well, you've got what you want then, haven't you, K?" Nol said scary calm, and stood up. "Leti, I'm going to Crystal's, would you like to join me?"

"I don't think so . . . not right now." Breathing, let alone going to Crystal's and bumping into the old gang, was almost beyond me right then.

"We can go someplace else, anywhere. Where do you want to go? I just don't know if it's best for you to stay here right now, Leti."

My body shook uncontrollably. Even clutching the seat of my chair didn't steady my rattling.

"This is my home. I want to be home. I am not leaving my home tonight."

"And you shouldn't have to." Nol refused to give K and Edie another look. "Leti, you know how to get a hold of me. Call me when you want to talk." Nol hugged my trembling shoulders. "Edith, you can call a cab. Or maybe K here can give you a ride home."

The door closed heavy behind Nol. My eyes were blurring with the thunderbolts pushing through my temples. Careful not to black out, I pushed myself up out of my chair, walked to the bedroom, closed the door, curled up in bed, and barricaded the world away.

29

"Your shoes are never dirty, are they, dear?"

K asked me this a few days later as she opened our closet to pack her work boots, the paint-speckled boots I had just polished a couple of weeks before at most, the ones that dust never touched as long as I was around to keep them full of shine. Still in bed, I watched K push my oxfords aside so she could reach her boots in the far corner of the closet. My shoes, my oxfords, their wax polish so often applied that it came off onto the cuff of my ironed slacks.

Polishing shoes was love. Nana's polish kit had been handed to me early every Sunday before church. She'd sit me down on the back porch steps with a sheet of newspaper funnies under my Mary Janes. A sand dollar tin of waxy black in my left hand's grip, the right hand dabbed and buffed and shined. An old toothbrush and a little cup of diluted baby shampoo scrubbed clean the sole through and through.

My shoe polish kit. Love. The shoeshine box that Nana gave me when I moved to Los Angeles sat in the gingerbread house's bedroom closet on the built-in whitewashed bench with drawers. The kit's wooden handle bounced sunshine off the smooth place where decades of hands had reached out to it. Light sparkled from the shoeshine box to the knobs on the bench's drawer. Those simple little knobs were one of the gingerbread's jewels. They dated back to the twenties, they were crystal under all the decades of paint flecked on them. The kumquat oval knobs were probably only glass, really, but crystal is what I liked to think they were. When K and I first moved into the gingerbread house, I had tried to chip the paint off the crystal. It wouldn't budge, not even when scraped with a razor blade. Each day I went back and forth. I either loved the layers or needed them to be gone.

Shallow anxious dizzy breaths, I watched K pack to leave. She was walking out.

Just an hour before, the blue unzipped sleeping bag that K and I use as our comforter had been tucked under my girl's chin as she slept in our bed facing me, her mouth slightly open and her cheeks warm with rest. The morning light never woke her as it came in through the top row of windows on our bedroom's east wall. I couldn't filter out the brightness like she could. K slept late into the morning, the moon still visible in its sky, I shifted up on my right elbow to watch my girl.

My hand had searched for bone at the strong-edged curve of her jaw, her warm exhalation on my fingers. I leaned toward her, careful to keep the bed from whining under my shifting frame, and I tilted my head over hers and kissed the crescent scar above her left eyebrow, such pale little baby soft eyebrows. She adjusted deeper into her pillow and I saw the deep pink of the birthmark on the back of her neck. Her eyes shifted and pressed up under closed lids.

K often sighed when she woke from sleep. And I knew exactly how she propped herself up with pillows to read in bed, her legs stretched out before her on the covers. When she was intent flipping through the thin gloss pages of her low-rider magazines, she'd bite her lower lip serious focus. But that morning as winds threw torn bits of the sky against our bedroom window, K had been asleep tender baby angel in our bed.

That last morning we slept side by side, I kissed the scar above her eye, hoping to wake her. My early morning awareness of her deep sleep frightened me. As much as I dreaded her waking, her parting hour, I needed to know that K would open her eyes.

30

My throat tightened as my heart swelled. Pulse beat faster. Clammy hands. Each moment for two weeks I resisted the urge to summon up Weeping. Two weeks since Nana died, an entire week since K walked out with her boxes. What an accomplishment, my refusing to bow down into Weeping's skirts again. She had left me stranded when I needed her most. But, you know, the frustration swelling inside me built to where I couldn't resist anymore. Fuck if I could be proud about begging to her again, I was hungry to hear her whispering voice acknowledge my presence. I needed to connect with her, to be recognized by her. My voice became that of a doting schoolboy again, crackling and static jumps in the middle of words with hope of being heard by Weeping.

My hands were a mess. Skin rough to touch. Any human would have edged away from my scratching reach, but not Weeping, she could bear my caresses. I promised to tread lightly, to not scratch her with the raw spots and dry strips of skin that decorated my hands. Torn edges around fingernails. Ionized red. Dried blood. Weeping did not come to keep me company, she stayed far away where I had told her to go the day she left me with no choice but to take Nana off the machines.

Alone in the gingerbread's living room. Tarps heavy down against the windows. No lights turned on. I sat on the green couch K had bought for us, the monument she left in her stead. My brow knit into a wrinkled knot. Eyelids heavy. Eyes darting. Looking down. Just where was it that life had taken a turn? Was the exact spot visible if I searched? Didn't see it. Couldn't see it. I didn't see it. Kept looking. Could you see it, Weeping? Could you when you were still with me? Where was it?

My mouth shut firm. Lips pouted. Teeth clenched. Cheek muscles rippled. Chewing. Nothing in mouth. Teeth grinding. Chest determined to soothe with its constant lullaby. Up and down. Up. Down. Tears? Please. Where are the tears? Eyes hot. Nostrils tingling. Mouth turned down at corners. Scratch left ear. Breathe harder. Calmer. Sniffle. Focus. Method acting tricks. I tried my damnedest to wash away the anxiety that began to overflow from the inside out.

No. No tears.

Head tilted forward. Shoulders slouched, pulled centerward by an invisible bind of thorny rope. A hand pushing chest back. Concave. Hands on neck. Noose too tight. Nails picking at flesh of throat. Damn it, stop clawing at yourself. Stop it. I said stop it. Bite the hands that feed you. Nibble at skin toughened at nails' borders. Loose snag. Take it in between teeth. Tug. Gently. Gently. Not too fast. Stop. You're going too far. Switch fingers. Stomach sour. Saliva bitter. Eat. Own. Flesh. Consuming. Angry. Blood. Each finger torn. A complete set. Set. Complete. Alone.

Alone. In the living room of my gingerbread home.

A knock at the door. It was one of two people and since the Penny Saver and phone bill had already arrived, I knew it wasn't the mailman. It was two in the afternoon and I was still in my white undershirt and flannel pajama pants. Considering K was on the other side of the gingerbread's front door, I wished I could transform my melancholy into silver-screen Rock Hudson seduction to bring K to her senses.

"Just a second, I'll be right there," I yelled from the couch as if I had to run across a mansion to get to the front door. Only a couple of inches between me and where K stood, but I needed to buy some time. Frantically I scanned what remained in our closet and threw on the only clean thing I could find, a crappy baby blue polyester cardigan eaten away by stupid moths with severe heartburn. I pushed up the sweater's too big sleeves. More Mr. Rogers drag than hunky, but no matter, K once told me that I looked good in blue and the sweater was the only thing that didn't belong in the hamper. Off came the pajama pants, on went a pair of slacks from near the top of a pile of dirty clothes on the closet floor. On went a black fisherman's wool hat to cover my hair. Good god, I must have looked like a freezing idiot in the middle of the June heat wave. My heart was pounding. Crap, what if she thought I was being nonchalant about getting to the door? What if she thought I didn't care? I pounced out of the bedroom and, in one good leap, landed at the door. Thank god K at least knew she better stop by to apologize for her ridiculous behavior, her fool decision, the bad ending she'd forced on our relationship. I opened the door.

A tall guy sweating in his UPS uniform balanced a clipboard in front of his beefy chest. At his feet was a medium-size box. Bigger than a bread box. Smaller than an icebox.

"You have to sign for this." He handed me his pen to use.

"Oh." I signed my name and tried to smile casually. The signing part worked, the other didn't.

"Here." He handed me the box.

"Thanks."

"Have a good day," said with no smile.

"You too," I said as I closed the door.

There was no return address on the box. The address label was typed. The postal code stamped on it gave no clue other than "Los Angeles." I wished the box were ticking. If it had been ticking, I would have sat on the green couch and used the box as a footstool, the humming steady against my soles. A reflexologist could have told me how to position the ticking box so it would soothe my aching heart and thoughts and the sour stomach that comes with the aching heart, not to mention the hot throbbing behind my eyes. And when the timer caused the dynamite bundle inside to ignite and explode, everything would be calm.

If there was dynamite inside the box, it was the very quiet kind. I walked into the kitchen and put the box on the yellow tile counter next to the sink. I grabbed a butter knife out of the sink, rinsed most of the peanut butter off it, shoved it under the mailing tape that sealed the top edge of the box, and jammed it between all the flaps until they opened. Both the box and I, we were jagged and tired, a mess from my frantic messy job.

I wished I didn't immediately know what the contents of my delivery were upon opening it. But I did.

Inside was a strip of paper and a small handmade book with a porcelain gingerbread house on its cover. The book was really just several pieces of white typing paper folded in half horizontally and cloth taped together. The strip of paper beside it was stiff and about an inch and a half wide and six inches long.

Photos. The ones we took with Nolan and Edith in San Francisco at the Fishermen's Wharf penny arcade photo booth. Black-and-white squares with us in them. The four of us were crammed next to each other on a tiny circular stool, sitting in front of a wickedly ridiculous backdrop with a sunny mountain lake scene airbrushed on it. It had been overcast as hell that day, K and I figured that the Lake Tahoe summer image was the perfect way to immortalize our bizarre double-date tour.

flash

Smiling huge laughing smiles.

flash

Cocking our eyebrows, making fish lips, squinting.

flash

Sitting straight up, trying to look very sophisticated in our faded tee-shirts, stringy hair, and denim jackets.

flash

K kissing my forehead, not looking at me, not seeing the blush she brings to my face, my smile shy.

flash

Nol had stomped out of the booth right before that final flash. I had gone off to find her. The fifth picture had been one of K and Edie in the booth alone. Edie sitting on K's knee. Her right arm around K's neck. Back then the image hadn't been a big deal. Whatever, Edie was a physical kind of girl. Whatever, K and I were head over heels in love. I had been so sure. Whatever.

During the weeks K and I lived together, the long strip of photos she had hung in the gingerbread living room twirled up and down with the changing weather, the humidity at night causing its edges to curl in upon itself. A flower. A living thing.

229

One frame was torn off the strip of photos. The last photo. The one that Edith had been in with K. Talk about adding insult to injury. If K had been planning to mail them back to me, why didn't she just leave the damned photos on the living room wall when she packed up and left? Did she think I'd appreciate it that she'd ripped off the one photo of her and Edie?

Acid tears down my cheeks. Defeated. Completely defeated. The box was so fucking huge.

Bracing myself against the pantry door, I emptied the box's contents onto the counter and broke down the container, ripping it into small pieces. I threw the shredded cardboard in the grocery bag trash can on the floor. Slid down the wall and landed sitting on the floor with the strip of photos in my hand. I didn't feel myself breathing anymore. Every part of my body was motionless. My eyes didn't need to blink. My blood stopped coursing through veins. Only the cold linoleum under my bare feet kept me awake.

The photos, they blurred. In each frame the four heads became a fluid mass. The smiles and winks and hands and necks all turned charcoal. The mountain faded to dust. The lake rippled. I swept my left foot around the trash bag and dragged it to my body. With my left hand, I fished around in the trash. The heads in the photos, they became one. I still didn't blink. My hand in the trash, I felt what I was looking for. The address label from the box. Intact on one single piece of cardboard. I held the cardboard-mounted label to my lips while I cried and looked at the bomb my boy Berenike had sent to me.

That evening there was a knock at the door. Considering the trick prize I got the last time I opened the door, I felt less than inclined to answer again. Solitude seemed the safe choice.

"Leti, I know you're in there. Please open the door. Leti?"

Nolan knocked lightly again.

I was still sitting on the kitchen floor and the walk to the door was too much to ask. I listened through my headache noise and when Nolan's car started up and drove away twenty minutes later, I stood up, got my keys, turned on the porch light, and walked out to my car.

31

I may never know for certain, but I wonder if it was the contents of my basket? Maybe my lack of shower or my boy slacks and cardigan? Or maybe the way my eyes were bloodshot? It wasn't that I'd taken to smoking dope, tears are full of stinging salt, you know.

When we moved into the gingerbread, K and I had been beyond cartwheels that we wouldn't have to drive across town from home to get what we needed anymore. Long drives for daily errands were common when we lived at the apartments. The stores near the Third Street building were always understocked and dirty with discrimination and imposed poverty. Only one cashier was ever on duty at a time, even when thirty people stood in line and there were ten cashier stands available. But the drugstore down the street from our new home, ah, it had glistened in the sun the day we drove past it in our U-Haul.

Why was it that the night I went to buy aspirin for my headache, the apron-clad lady at the drugstore register took one look at me and got so mad? Mad. Back when I was little, learning English at school, Nana heard me throwing a fit, huffing through my breath that I was mad. She stopped me, "No, Leticia, beasts get 'mad.' People get 'angry.' "

Well, the lady at the checkout counter, she was mad, like a dog, not angry like a human could be. Did she remember how K had paid for my things the last time we were in? Was it the way K and I had stood close to each other all the times she had seen us in the store? Was it simply because I was an easy target, alone and tired and looking wrinkled deep past the edges?

The cashier finished her flirting with the "sir" in front of me and then turned to me. She looked me up and down, staring extra long at my blue cardigan, and quickly concluded that I wasn't a woman worthy of respect. She puckered her face in disgust and shook her head.

"Hello, how are you doing today?" I asked, turning up my good girl grace.

K, able to pass as a sir whom the register lady might find herself flirting with before catching on, K would have remained silent in the face of such an immediate nasty vibe. But not me, always trying to pour some sugar in people's bitter cups. Right then I realized that my flight attendant may-I-fluff-your-pillow tendencies were definitely a perverse personal fault.

No answer—the apron didn't tell me my total when she was done ringing my things up. She bagged the stuff and stared at me, her lips pursed and nostrils bloodless white, trying not to inhale. Girls who look like boys stink? Please, lady. Lord, it was like a playground in that drugstore. I looked at the total on the register and slid my ATM card into the machine at my side. The apron hissed.

"You want to use your *ATM*?"

"Yes, please."

She punched buttons on the register.

"I'd like cash back, please."

"How much?"

"What's the maximum amount allowed?"

"Ten dollars."

"Ten dollars?" I knew she was lying.

"Yeah, ten dollars." She smirked.

"OK, that will be fine then, thank you." I smiled as if she couldn't ruin my happy mood if she tried.

"Look, you can get fifty back if you want."

She handed me my fifty and I said thank you and she practically spit on my shoes and I walked out and got in my car and I tried to breathe, really breathe, deep and all, and I decided then that it was little things like what had just happened that had the potential to build up and tear down my wobbling structure.

Not that anyone else could hear me as I sat in my car, I said, "I can't believe what a fucking shit that woman was. I swear, what was wrong with her? I was polite and everything."

I stayed there, staring out the window for a good long minute before driving away. My hands and shoulders started to ache from how hard I gripped the steering wheel.

My small hands matched my small body but I could smile a radiant smile to make nearly anyone laugh. My smile was my fight. Sometimes the punches I threw backfired, turned right around on my face and reached out to strangle me. Even while certain people voted me out of town, I tried to make them smile with my charm.

Driving past the old town diner at the corner on the way home, I told myself that maybe I should do something radical like ask for a malted and demand to sit at the lunch counter. I was angry and I wanted to cry, but I'd be damned if I'd let one stranger at the drugstore tear me down or make me feel like I didn't belong.

Popping bitter aspirin saviors into my mouth, I heard Nana over the years teaching me that it was the small things that count.

Fine, if it's the small things that count, a small gesture just might have the power to bake life into peach pie.

Small things number one. I showered, scrubbed hard, put together the best outfit my hamper allowed, combed my hair into an extra perfect sleek boy style, and went shopping for a small thing. Specifically, I went to the mall to find a small bra. Small thing become huge gesture, the bra would be the first I'd owned since the entirely unnecessary training one Nana had bought for me early in my adolescence. The novelty of her well-intentioned purchase had worn off completely after one short week. "What exactly does this grody thing train me for," I had demanded from her as I threw the stretchy little bra away. It's training you for life, the drugstore cashier would have told me. Girls need to be perky.

Yes, well, the perking underwire of the bra I bought at the mall to complete the peach pie deal dug into my flesh and rubbed my ribs raw. That pain, it wasn't pleasurable. When I drove back the next day to return the cotton contraption to the pink satin store, the lady behind the counter busied herself with straightening tissue paper under the counter after she looked up and saw me. I breathed deep, smiled, and put the store bag that I had carefully saved without wrinkling on the counter.

"Hello, I need to make a return, please."

"We're all out of change. Come back later," she said as she rose and turned her back to me.

Hello, who said I needed change?

I stood as towering as my short frame allowed and asked if she could please help me now. She turned back around, glared at me, and walked away without a word. I wasn't sure if she'd come back, but fifteen minutes later she reappeared and slammed rolls of quarters and a pile of bills on the counter next to her register. I doubt the cash drawer was hungry. She had to continue the show.

"You don't have the receipts, we can't give a refund," she said.

Who said I didn't have receipts? I took my wallet out of my back pocket and reached into it to get the tags and receipt. My wallet disgusted her. For that I hated her. Deliberately I returned the wallet to my back pocket and stared with a blank slate face at her.

I signed the customer refund form she pushed at me. She stared at my tie with a crinkled nose and asked me what was wrong, why *didn't* I want the bra? Sincere concern was nowhere in the room. I looked up in the middle of signing my first name and told her that there was a growth in my left breast, where the bra's wire cupped on the side. I told her it had been physically unbearable to wear the pretty little thing. It was true. I couldn't bear it. Her face melted. I was glad to induce momentary guilt in her. But later I wondered, would she take relief in thinking I would soon be dead? Would she think that my breasts had attacked me for not appreciating pretty little things? The lump, though it didn't hurt and the doctors at the student health center in college had said it was just from stress and my period, that it was no big deal, the lump really did exist. But let's get to the important facts. The pretty little bra. It really did hurt me to wear it, to be encased in such a pretty little thing.

If I could have called Nana to say hello that day, she would have said, "Why don't you grow your hair out like when you were younger? Or maybe even just to how you had it before Mother's Day. And maybe don't dye it or bleach it anymore. Just natural and long like other girls' . . ."

"Nana, other girls I know have hair like mine."

"You know what I mean, Leticia. I just want you to be

236

happy. Besides, you always did have such pretty long hair when you were my little girl."

I walked out of the store to my car, massaging the back of my neck to calm down. Short velvet hairs tickled my fingertips. Tight barbershop fade above the beauty mark at the base of my skull, hair gradually lengthening to the short sprigs I slicked down with pomade at my crown. If I grew my hair out again, I'd buy bobby pins and lots of barrettes. Anchor bobby pins and barrettes in my tangles to keep the hair out of my face. "Looks too severe," the ladies in my neighborhood would say. They would laugh at the seams of my drag showing. "Why don't you do something softer with it?" "Look, like this," Nana would have demonstrated. Braid it pretty and sit like a lady once in a while. Just a little rose lipstick would really bring sunshine to your smile. Maybe tweeze those stray strands of eyebrow, the ones bridging your nose. What do you mean it started to feel like your pearl choker was strangling you?

My girl drag would never please anyone.

I drove toward home under a sky that was neither blue nor gray, not even a predictable acrid yellow brown from the smog. Milky white and heavy air, not fog exactly, but moist pollution at its purest. It was beautiful. Don't laugh, but for the first time in two weeks I felt a charged rush of antici-pation. The polluted air that my car cut through had me looking forward to the arrival of sundown. Smog makes for the most amazing sunsets, intense crayon colors created as ultraviolet rays ricochet off dense layers of thickened air. I needed that bright something bad. And I needed something to sweeten my mood. I stopped at the panadería for sweet breads on the way home.

I have no idea what sassafras is, but that's what it smelled like in the panadería. When I walked in, I gave myself permission to do no more than select my pastries, hand the tray to whoever was working the register, pay, mumble a "Thanks," and walk out the door without ever making eye contact. Instead Mamá's and Nana's manners took charge. When the little girl working at the cash register handed me my small brown paper bag, I couldn't help but face her politely to say thank you.

I looked up. And I saw her. Eyes.

The inside corner of her left eye was white. Hang with me for a minute, give me a chance to explain this. I don't mean just the part that is supposed to be white, beyond that point, past where the white usually curves off and gives domain to the iris, brown in this case. The white had taken over the girl's eye, a pie-shaped section of white invaded the brown, nearly reaching the pupil. An isthmus. A peninsula. Which was the right word? I cheated on all my elementary school geography tests and it had finally caught up with me. I tried not to stare. Nana raised me not to stare. But I was an uncivilized shit, and I stared. Long and hard. Locking the little girl's gaze with mine. Neither of us blinked. I saw a brown speck dot too far out, right near the tear duct, as if it floated away from where it should have been and was the only part of the brown that the white pie slice hadn't melted.

The little girl wasn't upset that I was staring at her. I wondered who was the last person to be stunned by her beauty. Playground friends, teachers, and baby-sitters had avoided her gaze for years, I was sure. If I were her age, she and I would have become great friends.

The sun was going down when the phone rang at home. I turned up the volume on the answering machine to listen, but I wasn't going to move from my spot at the kitchen window. Electric colors magic dense in the air, the sunset was beyond incredible.

"Leti, are you home? Please pick up. It's urgent. I know you're there . . ."

32

The voice drilling out of the answering machine and into my empty house had stopped for the time being. But that sunset, bright red as the blue of the sky in the princess bedtime stories Mamá used to tell me, insistent as the demands in Medea's voice, deliberate strong as Nana's love had always been for me, that sunset haunted me something good.

For three days I lived to watch the sunset. The fourth day it was clear skies, not a trace of smog to be seen. Anemic pastel yellow and clean. The air was depressing. When the phone rang that evening, I was easily distracted away from my kitchen window view. Three rings and my outgoing message started its grating cheery greeting. The machine beeped, I listened and picked up the phone.

"Hi, Nolan. What is it?"

"I've been thinking about you . . ."

"Nol, you said it was urgent."

"It is, I've been worried about you. Didn't you get my messages? Are you doing all right, Leti?"

"As all right as I can be, I guess."

"Why didn't you come to the door the other day?"

"I haven't been feeling very social, you know?"

"Don't you think you should get out of the house for a little bit?"

"I've been out of the house."

"Leti, don't push me away."

"Things are just really hard right now, it's hard to sleep, it's hard to stay awake, it's just hard, Nol."

"That's why I think it'd be good for us to go talk over a bite to eat."

"I don't want to go to dinner, I don't even really want to talk right now."

"All right, how about this—we can go somewhere you don't have to eat, talk, or do anything but just sit around and have a change of scenery."

I didn't respond. Nol continued.

"There's a new club across town that we could go to. It'd be fun. What say?"

"Where's the club?"

"Across town."

"Where across town?"

"Boy Town, where else? But it's a girl club, and since it's on the other side of town, we won't bump into anyone. I might even buy you a drink . . ."

"Lucky me."

". . . with plastic monkeys and maybe even a parasol or two."

Nolan knew me well enough to hear my smile over the phone.

"So we're on?"

"Yeah, sounds good."

"I'll be by in a couple hours, go take a shower and dress to impress."

"You're asking for a lot, Nol."

"I know. But I promise a lot in return."

Nol drove us a traffic-filled forty minutes to get to the lounge starting up on the other side of the world, specifically the West Side—the most extravagant of queer fantasy lands. The West Side was very popular with boys and the men who loved them. After all, the interior of the self-devoted boy bubble lovingly mirrored its handsome gym-bodied Narcissus inhabitants. No matter how boy I myself dressed, no matter how many dykes I had gathered around me, I always felt out of place in Boy Town.

It was simple, remember? Boys born boy own the world. Boys even owned the club we went to. One night of a girl lounge at a boy venue. In Boy Town.

Fully aware that egalitarian things like public parking didn't exist in Boy Town, Nol gave her keys to the fifteen-dollar-plus-tip valet. We walked into the lounge and immediately I realized how stupid we had been to think, even for a second, that just because we were going to the West Side we wouldn't see anyone we knew. The lounge looked like Crystal's had projectile-vomited all her babies for the night. New club, same old faces. A solid handful of dykes cramped in a small space that had no lounging opportunities, let alone chairs for sitting or wall space for leaning. Wall-to-wall with the same women I had seen for years. The ones I had shared beers with and knew nothing about. The ones I had flirted with and slept with and teased and knew nothing about. The ones I had become friends with and knew very little about. Even with each other, we shielded ourselves amidst the boys who owned the world.

241

Nol bummed a couple of cigarettes off this cute nerd girl who looked like she'd ditched Key Club to come to the lounge. Key Club smiled at me so hard that her round cheeks pushed her square-framed reading glasses crooked on her nose. I waved a thank-you and dragged Nol quick to the patio out front. We stood in the walled-off patio with the rest of the girls. Key Club tracked us down and started chatting up Nol. I blinked and they had wandered away. Me, I stayed fixed in my spot. I watched. Thousands of boys walked around. Name your type and he was there. We blinked, all fifty of us dykes did, and we stood on our borrowed patio in the warm summer night and smoked the cigarettes that would make some good old boy of a different type rich.

Blink of the eye and all sorts of strange things occur. Across the crowded patio a sterling silver cigarette holder floated a blinding glint of light high in the air.

The lilacs had arrived.

Wish I hadn't looked in Edith's direction that night. Wish I hadn't strained my neck to see her more clearly. Wish I hadn't ever felt that familiar pull toward her to begin with. But I did. And I did. I did. I looked over to where Edith was. But I wish I hadn't. More than anything, I wish I'd never seen Edith's perfectly brushed lipstick lips land where they did.

33

grabbed Nol and rushed us out the club's side door.

"We're calling it a night?"

"Don't be cute, Nol."

"We're giving them an awful lot of power running away like this."

"Whatever. I want to go home."

"Maybe Edie and K are just out for the night same as we are, as friends."

"Right."

"It is possible."

"Like hell it is. Don't, Nol. Let's go, I don't want to be here."

"If we leave, they win this round."

"What the fuck ever, let's go."

We went. On the way back to the gingerbread house, Nol asked if she could spend the night.

"Are you serious? Fuck, Nol, I wouldn't mind having one thing in my life stay the way it was three weeks ago."

"Not like that, Leti, I mean like a slumber party. A mellow

slumber party. Completely innocent. We'll throw some pillows and blankets in the living room and make popcorn, something comforting lame like that."

"Right, and then we can talk about the boys in this month's *Tiger Beat* and paint each other's nails and giggle until our folks tell us to quiet down."

"Is it exhausting being so completely negative?"

"Nol, give me a break. Life sucks right now, OK?"

"But a slumber party would be fun." She pulled her car into the drive.

"That's what you said about going to the club."

"Leti."

"Fine, you can come in, you can stay and talk, you can even fall asleep on the hardwood floor if you really want to, but we're not calling it a slumber party. Deal?"

Nol walked in behind me, plunked herself down on the living room floor, and smiled stupid cute.

There was no popcorn to pop. In fact, there wasn't much of anything to eat in the house, so Nol grabbed a Tupperware of stale Trader Joe's peanuts from the earthquake emergency kit she kept in her car. We had been on the living room floor for long enough that my pointy bones were starting to hurt, but that didn't matter. I was not going to sit on the couch that had taken to smirking at me. Still sans pillows, still aching bones, I stretched out on the floor close next to Nol.

"Leticia, things are going to get better. You know they will. Just tell me if there's anything I can do." She draped a reassuring hand on my shoulder.

"Thanks, Nol."

My head on my arms, I closed my eyes, breathed out slow, and relaxed just a little. Maybe I started to fall asleep. Maybe I was just waking up. Whatever was happening, the air smarted. Shiver zap, I remembered the diamonds. I sat up, smiling.

"Know what you can do?"

"Name it." Nol edged away, a little freaked at how suddenly sloppy smile I was.

"Let me tell you a story?"

"I think I can manage that," Nol laughed.

"Fab," I clapped my hands together, "do you want to hear one Mamá used to tell or one Nana would tell?"

"Either, it's up to you."

"Mamá's stories are prettier, sweeter."

"Leti, it's up to you."

And it was. It was up to me. Nol was right. It was entirely up to me.

I shut my eyes to remember it right. I bit my lip to keep it from jumping forward before I was ready. The static crackle jangle of my voice hummed warm reliable, and Nana, she began walking deliberate and measured through the pink house backyard.

Clipped birds-of-paradise bundled in Sunday funnies under her arm, Nana watches me fill the third grocery bag with avocados picked from the sturdy shade tree in the center of the yard.

"You've done enough work for now, Leticia."

Nana goes inside the house and returns with two tall metal tumblers and a small plate of Holland butter cookies balanced careful on a television tray. When she moves to sit down on the porch steps, I reach out to brace her and she shoos my hands away like bothersome flies. I sit down at my nana's side. She hands me a glass of tea and reaches her stiff arm up to brush a broken leaf from my messed hair.

"You should move back home. A little work and the store would shape up nice."

"Nana, you know I love you very much, right?"

"Yes, I wasn't asking about that."

"Thank you for the tea, Nana, it's perfect."

Nana cackles her beautiful laugh.

The woman who tells me to move through life with a slow and steady stride. The woman who shows me how to be strong. The woman who lay limp in a hospital bed for the most stabbing day of my life. That woman, my nana, she stomped something stubborn that her mind and body and words come back to her. And they did when she told them to. Like everyone else, they knew it was best not to disobey. The woman I have admired and feared and adored all my life, Nana speaks no-nonsense to me as we sit on the chipped red paint of the back steps.

She tells me cuentitos that she's kept secret or maybe invents on the spot as we drink tall blue tin tumblers of iced amber hue.

The pigeons that stole diamonds, yes, girl, now that's a story you need to know.

Listen.

Mamá Estrella, once she told me about this small pueblo where magnificent diamonds were mined. That pueblo, it was known for miles and miles all around. But believe it or not, what made that pueblo famous wasn't diamonds. It was pigeons.

The pigeons from that pueblo, they weren't anything fancy in their feathers, not even special in how they flew from one spot to another. No, in those ways they were just pigeons, plain and simple. But those birds, those incredible birds, they would come flying into the pueblo and, whoosh, dip their beaks into rough piles of mined rock, swallow sparkling diamond pebbles whole, and fly away proud.

After weeks of this, one of the field bosses was beyond mad as a dog. It was late June and the air was desert hot, just like now. Some say it was too much dry air in his lungs that made the boss act the way he finally did. But, for whatever reason, that man, he caught one of the pigeons he thought he'd seen eating diamonds the day before and he cut its belly open as it cried desperate. There were no diamonds to be found. The man, that horrible person, he threw the slaughtered pigeon's body aside. The bird's blood covered the great piles of diamonds and melted them all red clay mud.

My eyes open wide incredulous.

"You look like a cow with your eyes that way."

"Nana . . ."

"Don't doubt so much, Leticia. What I'm telling you, this really happened." She stamps her foot down on the red porch step to mark the story's validity.

I open my mouth to protest, to say I didn't know of any diamond mines near the pueblo Mamá and Papá came from, to ask her how she could expect that I wouldn't doubt such an outrageous story, to remind her that I'm not a baby anymore. Nana locks my eyes with her own and tells me to hush up, just listen.

"It might not have been what some thought was proper, for those pigeons to have the diamonds, but that was the way it was supposed to be. And no one should have messed with that. The diamonds those birds were taking weren't even stolen. They knew nothing in the world was too great to be theirs. They knew they wanted that mined glisten glow. No matter what, those pigeons, they claimed their diamond birthright."

Orange blossom with a wham of dynamite, Nana takes a drink of tea and watches me.

ACKNOWLEDGMENTS

My sincerest thanks to: John Glusman, for his generous kindness and for honoring my writing with his editorial brilliance; Gloria Sterling, for teaching me magic tricks I use each and every day; Bob Moeller, Lynn Mally, and Nora Mally, familia I thank my lucky stars for having met in this life; Peter Gadol and Jon Wagner, who gave even the earliest drafts of my novel their thoughtful critiques; Howard Junker, for publishing *ZYZZYVA* and for including my short story "Random Tea Parties" among its pages; Aodaoin O'Floinn, for insight and assistance in all things publishing; and Millie Wilson, who told me to keep it fierce and showed me just how lovely and genius fierceness can be. Un millón de gracias to Susan Bergholz for giving a kid audacious enough to once submit work on hot pink paper the most fantastic of second chances. Stuart Bernstein, my agent, is an absolute dream of a person, colleague, and friend. A mi familia, those living and in spirit alike, I am ever grateful to learn from you. And to Heidi Kidon—mi amor, what can I say? Thank you.

ABOUT THE AUTHOR

©MARION ETTLINGER

Felicia Luna Lemus graduated summa cum laude from the University of California, Irvine, and received an MFA from the California Institute of the Arts. She lives in New York City.

SELECTED TITLES FROM SEAL PRESS

Under Her Skin: How Girls Experience Race in America edited by Pooja Makhijani. $15.95, 1-58005-117-0. This diverse collection of personal narratives explores how race shapes, and sometimes shatters, live—as seen through the fragile lens of childhood.

Secrets and Confidences: The Complicated Truth about Women's Friendships edited by Karen Eng. $14.95, 1-58005-112-X. This frank, funny, and poignant collection acknowledges the complex relationships between girlfriends.

Colonize This!: Young Women of Color on Today's Feminism edited by Daisy Hernández and Bushra Rehman. $16.95, 1-58005-067-0. It has been decades since women of color first turned feminism upside down. Now a new generation of brilliant, outspoken women of color is speaking to the concerns of a new feminism and their place in it.

Cunt: A Declaration of Independence by Inga Muscio. $14.95, 1-58005-075-1. An ancient title of respect for women, "cunt" long ago veered off the path of honor and now is considered an expletive. Muscio traces this winding road, giving women both the motivation and the tools to claim "cunt" as a positive and powerful force in the lives of all women.

Chelsea Whistle by Michelle Tea. $14.95, 1-58005-073-5. In this gritty, confessional memoir, Michelle Tea takes the reader back to the city of her childhood: Chelsea, Massachusetts—Boston's ugly, scrappy little sister and a place where time and hope are spent on things not getting any worse.

Atlas of the Human Heart by Ariel Gore. $14.95, 1-58005-088-3. Ariel Gore spins the spirited story of a vulnerable drifter who takes refuge in the fate and the shadowy recesses of a string of glittering, broken relationships.

Shy Girl by Elizabeth Stark. $12.95, 1-58005-047-6. A stunning debut novel that the *Village Voice* called an "inspired, unconventional story . . . about bigotry, courage, and self-actualization."

Seal Press publishes many books of fiction and nonfiction by women writers. Please visit our website at **www.sealpress.com**.

CPSIA information can be obtained at www.ICGtesting.com
Printed in the USA
LVOW06s0549050815

448624LV00006B/25/P